A PATH O

About the Author

R.E. Sanders was born in England and moved to Wales to study archaeology. The novella *Tann's Last Stand*, set in the same fantasy world, was published recently and *A Path of Blades* is his first full-length novel. He lives in Cardiff.

Visit https://resanderswrites.wixsite.com/r-e--sanderswrites for more information about R.E. Sanders.

A PATH OF BLADES

R.E. SANDERS

This novel is entirely a work of fiction. The names, characters and incidents portrayed in it are the work of the author's imagination. Any resemblance to actual persons, living or dead, event or localities is entirely coincidental.

Copyright © 2023 by R.E. Sanders

All rights reserved. No part of this publication may be reproduced, stored in a retrieval system, or transmitted, in any form or by any means, electronic, mechanical, photocopying, recording or otherwise, without the prior permission of the copyright owner.

First edition July 2023

Edited by Claire Cronshaw

ISBN 9798850472948

https://resanderswrites.wixsite.com/r-e--sanderswrites

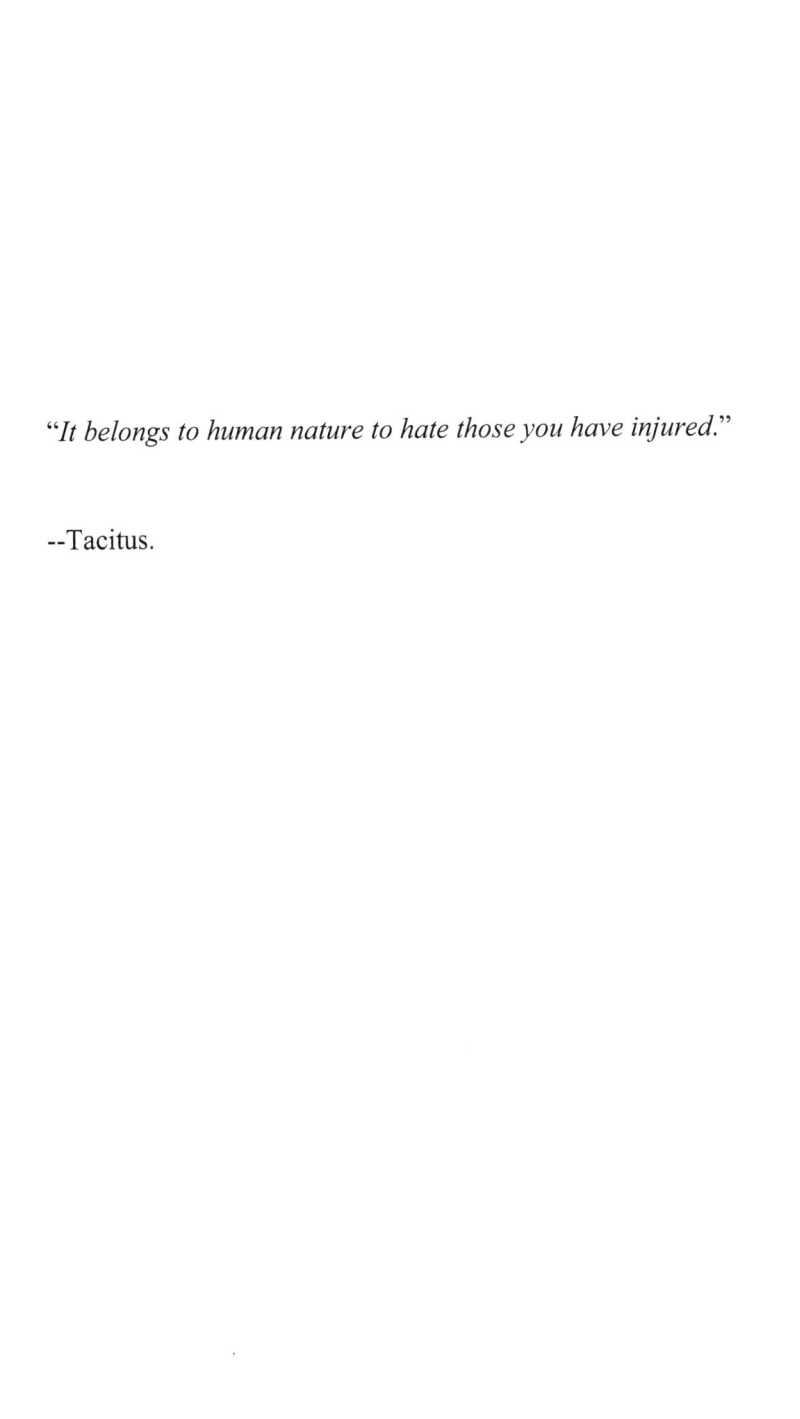

"It belongs to human nature to hate those you have injured."

--Tacitus.

One for fortune, Mordea the mother

Two for fate, Kaled law-maker

Three for unity, Tureank hunter-gatherer

Four for heroes, Conferan favours the bold

Five for death and eternity, Ome ever last

Five gods there were, five gods will always be

Living, sleeping, dead; may they watch over me

- Traditional children's rhyme, Re'Emsser

CHAPTER ONE

Ingvar Darelle tightened his grip on the hilt of his sword. He hated war.

He raised his hands powerfully, freeing his arms. With a step forward, he slashed the longsword diagonally downward, right to left. The impact jarred through his wrists and up his arms, the unyielding sharpened steel cutting through flesh and bone. He stepped back out of range of reprisals and tried to ignore the agonised scream that followed his strike, turning to look for the next threat, his eyes wide.

Survive. Survive and go home.

The sun beat down on the battlefield, a heat haze rising like the spirits of the slain. Ingvar stepped forward again, blade raised, shaking his head at the pointlessness of it all. His soldiers were around him, some bloodied, some panting with fear, all still fighting for their lives.

"Press them!" he bellowed to the troops around him. "Force them back!" He hated war, but it was his duty to fight. And it was his duty to take as many of his soldiers home with him as possible.

Survive and keep them alive.

"We cannot let them breach the wall!" he shouted. If they broke through anywhere, the army of Tayo would sweep through into the occupied lands beyond and all would be chaos. It would be the first step towards an invasion of Buren itself. "Lock shields!"

His soldiers were armed with spears and rectangular shields, and at his command, drew tightly together, shoulder to shoulder. A group of Tayan warriors, clad in the typical bright colours of their peasantry, backed away rather than challenge the locked shields of Ingvar's battle line. Relief surged in his breast.

In the slight lull, Ingvar glanced left and right to assess the battle. Across the field, in a wide area of yellowing grass sloping down towards marshland, Bureno forces were winning the day. There should be no need for any more of his troops to die. They should all get home safe.

Breathe. Stay alive. Do not let your guard down now.

The Tayans were falling back, seemingly disheartened by the Buren troops' staunch resistance. It was not a rout, yet, but knights were pressing the enemy hard across the hillside. Ingvar hoped fervently that if they held their position, all that would remain would be for them to watch the enemy retreat.

The assault on the border defences had begun early that morning. While the initial Tayan charge had been savage, the lines had held and the Bureno forces had been able to clear the gates in the hilltop palisade, allowing the cavalry to gallop forth in counterattack. The Tayans were good fighters, but many were mercenaries, motivated only by coin and silver. They had been the first to fall back when the battle turned.

Hoofbeats sounded and Ingvar looked around to see a group of mounted knights cantering forward. At their head was a majestic figure on a tall, pale horse. Ingvar flinched inwardly at his appearance. Three long eagle feathers in his gilded war helmet displayed his rank. Count Crowmer.

"Sir Darelle," called out the Count. His eyes were intense, shining out from the darkness beneath his helmet. "Lead your soldiers forward. We must drive them back further. Now they have lost the high ground, the field is ours. Make them pay for this revolt."

No! There is no need to risk any more lives!

Ingvar was happy to let the Tayans run back to their marshes and rice fields. Some soldiers had a lust for battle and an urge to fight, and kill, but he was not one of them. He would rather have been at home, on his quiet estate with his family. He wanted to deny the order and lead his troops home. But Crowmer was his Count, so Ingvar had no choice but to obey.

"Yes, my Count."

In the blazing heat, Ingvar led his troops down the hill. Armour made of overlapping metal scales hung heavy on his shoulders, and the thick leather arming jacket beneath added to his discomfort. Sweat trickled down his face and soaked into the jacket. He could already smell himself.

"Shields up, spears level," he called to his soldiers. "Let's keep them a spear's length away." *And hope they are a long gallop away by the end of the day,* he thought.

The Tayans backed away slowly as Ingvar's troops edged forward. Across the hillside, he could see the same scenario playing out: the Bureno forces advancing in a strong position, and the Tayan army, disorganised and retreating.

At that moment, there came again the rhythmic thudding of hoofbeats, and movement flickered in Ingvar's left eye. It was Crowmer's mounted knights, galloping around to harry the Tayan flanks as they retreated. Suddenly, the enemy before them was nervous, uneasy and twitchy. Ingvar could see soldiers glancing around, muttering brief conversations as they tried to watch in all directions at once.

Ingvar cursed under his breath. The threat of a cavalry charge made foot soldiers nervous. A nervous army might do anything. He looked to his soldiers, noting they were still advancing in good order, shields locked together and spears raised.

Then it happened. The flanking cavalry charged and the Tayans downslope of Ingvar panicked, surging forward.

Either they were just trying to escape the cavalry, or one of their commanders had seen a possibility of breaking through the Bureno lines with the element of surprise. Either way, Ingvar's troops found themselves under attack and overwhelmed by numbers.

His vision was filled with bright colours – yellow, orange and vivid green, the traditional garb of the Tayan peasantry. Lines crashed together with a shuddering impact that he felt as much as heard. Screams and groans filled the air as many Tayans died on his soldiers' spear-points. There were more behind them and they pressed hard into his shield-wall, forcing it back.

His arms were trapped by the crush of his soldiers all around him, who stepped backwards while trying to stay upright. Why had Crowmer ordered his cavalry forward when the enemy was already in retreat? Ingvar guessed that he and his knights were just desperate for the glory of crushing their foes. His breathing came in rapid gasps as panic rose in his chest.

To his right, a knot of Tayan warriors forced forward between his soldiers' shields, fracturing the line and knocking several of his troops to the ground. All semblance of organisation disappeared in the maelstrom of clashing shields and slashing blades.

Ingvar's mouth went dry with fear, and he desperately brought his longsword up as a bellowing, frantic Tayan warrior flew at him. He barely had time to raise the point before the long-haired man was on him, but such was his haste to attack that he ran straight onto Ingvar's sword. The point drove deep into his body. His momentum pushed Ingvar backwards, and he tumbled onto the ground. The enemy forces swept around them as Ingvar's soldiers fled.

The Tayan's bulk pinned him to the ground and trapped his arms. The hilt of his longsword was an uncomfortable pressure on his stomach, cushioned only slightly by his armour and gambeson beneath. A harsh, hissing sigh in his ear, accompanied by the stink of bad breath over rotten teeth, told him that the man lying on him was dead. Footsteps sounded all around him, some frighteningly near his head. Were they friend or foe?

Ingvar held his breath against the smell, which was made worse by the cloying, relentless heat. If the enemy noticed him lying defenceless, his death would be swift. He would never see the strike coming. Perhaps that would be the best way to die?

Survive. Get home. Think, Ingvar. Think!

He tried to free his arm to draw his sword from the dead Tayan's body, but froze as voices above were raised in fear and challenge. There was a clash of weapons, the unmistakable metallic sounds of war. People shouted in anger, wailed in fear and screamed in agony, and there were several soft thumps as bodies hit the turf around him.

He gambled. Summoning all his strength, he heaved upwards, lifting the body. As he jammed his sword hilt against its guts, more foul air was pushed from the corpse's mouth. But he managed to push it away, and it toppled to the ground. He was free.

Clambering to his feet, he dragged his sword clear of the body. The hand gripping the hilt was a tight claw, shaking even as he attempted to master his fear. The body at his feet was dressed in a bright green smock, its face twisted in a rictus of agony even in death. Ingvar swallowed his revulsion and looked up, seeing the reason he was still alive.

Olya Ferras, his friend since childhood, had swept forward and driven the enemy back. Household troops in shining scaled armour and peasant levies in baked leather followed, but she led the way. She was several years older than Ingvar, and her blonde hair and youthful face belied her strength and astonishing skill with a blade. Olya Arodbil, they called her sometimes. Olya Quickblade.

Bless you, Olya. Bless you, my friend. I may get home soon after all.

"That cavalry charge was nearly the death of me," he grumbled, sheathing his longsword. "Lost a few good men."

He stood next to Olya, looking down the hillside as the ragged Tayan army backed away again. It was still hot. He was sweating freely from beneath his helmet, the salt stinging his eyes as it ran down his brow and temples. His thick arming jacket was soaked beneath his heavy coat of scale armour in the relentless heat of the day.

Olya turned to him and smiled. Beneath her helmet, her eyes shone out vividly from the stripe of black ash that Bureno knights painted across their faces before every battle. A single eagle feather stood proudly from the crest of her helmet, the fragile plume having somehow survived the chaos of battle unscathed.

She did not appear to be sweating or winded, although her blade was splashed with blood. He knew she must have seen the risk to his position, quickly leading her troops over to help. Caught between Olya's flashing blade and the returning cavalry, the Tayans had no choice but to turn and flee again, this time leaving the field.

The distant pounding of hooves on the hard earth sounded as knights pressed the retreat. The battle was done.

"There is nothing to be feared from a glorious death," Olya said as they turned and began the walk back up the hill.

"The service to Buren will be rewarded when judgement falls."

Ingvar shook his head. Olya was prone to talk this way after a battle. Their troops had fallen into line behind their leaders, trudging wearily along with the wounded being carried at the rear.

"I do not fear death," he replied. "At least, I do not fear that death." He pointed at the body of a fallen Bureno soldier. The only mark he bore was a neat stab wound through the chest. His face was calm and his eyes were shut as if sleeping.

"I fear this death." This time he indicated a moaning, wailing man in Tayan colours. His stomach was open and he was bleeding heavily onto the dry ground. His face was pale and twisted with agony. As they walked past, one of their soldiers ended his suffering with a swift spear thrust. "I fear pain and the terror of suffering."

"The end is the same either way." Olya turned away from the scene. "The only difference is a few moments of pain. If you live with honour, obedience and virtue, then the judgement received will be worth the suffering. It has to be."

They walked in silence for a few moments, both deep in thought.

"Will they ever stop trying?" Ingvar's voice was bitter and regretful.

The region was known in Buren as the Swarthland and it had been taken as reparation from Tayo in a past border war and as a buffer to future Tayan attacks.

"If you'd ever spent time in Tayo, you would know the answer to that!" replied Olya with a grin. "Everything is based on war in Tayo. The only two things to do are growing rice and fighting. They would attack us more often if they didn't spend so much time fighting each other."

Ingvar knew the truth of this, but still begrudged these pointless wars that dragged him from his home and made him risk his life.

"Anyway," she continued, "you would miss this if there were peace. To stand shoulder to shoulder with someone is to know they are a true friend. Sharing the victories, sharing the glory…" She gave him a hard look.

Ingvar grunted in vague agreement. It was not worth arguing with her. Besides, in one way, she was right. Without the call to war, he would spend a lot less time with her, and he would miss that. "I'm just glad we made it through alive again," he said. While he would never say as much aloud, she inspired him, and being able to stand beside her in battle made the risks worthwhile.

They led their troops through the gated archway in the defensive wall as evening began to fall. More knights and their bondsmen went past them in the opposite direction, marching out to watch the passes and bridges into the marshes beyond. But the Tayans were beaten, disappearing deeper into Tayo as the blazing sun dipped towards the horizon.

Ingvar thought of his tent, where a folded blanket was his bed, and then thought of his own bed at home. He closed his eyes and pictured the familiar, comforting surroundings. He yearned to be back there. He exhaled deeply and followed Olya down into the camp.

There should have been no more death that day.

CHAPTER TWO

Olya and Ingvar led their troops into the bustle of the tent village that formed the Bureno army camp. They joined a throng of tired soldiers, all filing through the gateway and shuffling down the slope, eager to eat, and then to rest.

All looked bone-weary, the rush of energy that carried the knights and soldiers through the battle fading away to leave muscles feeling like water and heads yearning to rest on something soft.

Ingvar slumped in his saddle as he and Olya led their ragged column away from the dark earth banks of the palisade and down into the camp. The feet and hooves of the Bureno army had worn the dry, yellow grass thin and bare, and brown trails had appeared, leading through the tent village.

Raising his eyes, he could make out the green, rolling hills of Buren in the distance, and when he glanced north, he fancied he could see the dark smudge of the northern mountains. He yearned to be back at their feet, away from this war and away from these people.

A group of soldiers ahead of him turned aside, shuffling doggedly towards their camp. Ingvar came face to face with Count Crowmer and shuddered.

The Count sat on his fine white horse with an air of studied superiority, and had placed himself where none could go into the camp without passing him. As Count, he commanded the knights of the northern territories in battle, and as the soldiers passed, they saluted or bowed their heads respectfully. They had no choice. He held his vassal knights in an iron grip and demanded absolute loyalty.

Ingvar's father, Omar, had always refused to fall in line, remaining obedient but never subservient. He had never fully explained why, but Ingvar wondered if there was some history between the two men. His father was close-lipped on the subject.

"Soldiers of the north!"

Ingvar glanced around and noticed he was surrounded. His own troops, Olya's, and those of the other northern knights had stopped at Crowmer's voice.

"Gather around! Gather around! I would congratulate you on this great victory!"

The mass of troops surged forward and Ingvar dismounted before following Olya through the crowd, tucking in behind her to avoid standing at the front. Crowmer vaulted from his horse and climbed up onto the flat bed of an empty wagon.

"The Tayans have fled with their tails between their legs once more," he began. The overlapping scales of his armour gleamed warmly in the fiery light of the fading sun. The day remained hot, but a light breeze stirred the hem of his rich blue cloak. He was tall, with a hawklike face and sharp blue eyes that stood out brightly against his coppery skin.

"I am no longer surprised by your valour and strength." His voice carried across the field. "But I am immeasurably proud. You are the sword and shield of Buren, casting our enemies back and defending our honest citizens. You have shown the whole of Tayo the mettle of our swords and spears! They will not be fool enough to attack again this season, so soon we will ride back to our estates. There are loved ones to see and harvests to bring in. I know that when we are needed, we will answer the call once more without hesitation. For Buren!" He unsheathed his sword and raised it skyward to roars and cheers of agreement and appreciation.

"No, you are the fool!"

A new voice came from Ingvar's right and he swung around. A knight strode across the baked ground from the direction of the southern army's camp. A guard of troops was with him, but they struggled to keep up with his long strides. His face twisted into a mask of fury as he pointed up at Crowmer, his other hand clutching at the hilt of a longsword at his hip.

The tall, blocky man raised his voice. "Your reckless charge could have lost us the battle!" He cleared his throat and spoke more slowly. "Your lust for glory cost many lives. Lives of *my* soldiers. I would have your apology before these witnesses."

Crowmer said nothing for a moment, a half-smile on his lips. "And who are you?"

"I am Sir Bardest of the southern county of Mertan," said the man, brushing his long, dark hair away from his face. "War leader of the southern estates. And I know who you are, Count Crowmer." He spat the words. "I would have you make amends for your failure of leadership."

"The battle was won, Sir Bardest." Crowmer looked away, unconcerned. "Soldiers die in battle, and will be judged well as they pass through the veil. If more of your soldiers died than you would have liked, then the question of leadership surely rests with you?"

Bardest stepped forward, his mouth twisting. "How dare you? You insult me, Crowmer." He drew his longsword. "You insult me and now I demand two apologies, or I must defend my honour."

"Defend your honour?" Crowmer looked almost bored as he dropped down off the wagon and approached the tall knight. "Say the words, if you dare."

Sir Bardest looked as though he tried to resist stepping back. He bared his teeth in a grimace before he spoke again. I challenge you," he said, his voice clipped through his clenched teeth. "In a Just War. I will duel you now. You give me no choice."

"No choice indeed." Crowmer touched the hilt of his own longsword. "And I accept. I am in the right, and fate will judge me so when I am granted victory." He turned his back on Sir Bardest and took a couple of steps away into the open area before the wagon. "One thing." He half turned, speaking over his shoulder. "The laws of Just War permit nomination of a champion. I intend to do so."

Any Bureno noble could declare a Just War against another, if they felt that their honour had been offended. A duel was a common resolution and could prevent a conflict spiralling into civil war.

"Very well." Sir Bardest unbuckled his armour, the shimmering sections of layered metal sliding to the ground. The rage still seethed in his face as he strode forwards, clad in his long gambeson. Soldiers from either side surrounded them. A duel between two skilled knights was something that not many common soldiers would want to miss. Standing beside Ingvar, Olya bounced on her toes with excitement.

"Sir Vaikhari!" called Crowmer. "I nominate you." The tall elf strode forward, also now unarmoured, his famous sword held in both hands. His skin was the colour of aged mahogany and his dark, curling hair was cut short, revealing his upswept, pointed ears.

He shunned the gambeson worn by his opponent, stepping into the circle wearing only his shin-length thobe and gauntlets. The northern soldiers stamped their feet and clapped for their Count's champion. Ingvar groaned inwardly. This was foolishness, and Sir Bardest had been baited into giving Crowmer exactly what he wanted.

The two knights faced one another. Bardest was a tall man, but Vaikhari towered over him. Where Vaikhari was lean and long of limb, Bardest was bulky, broad in the shoulder, and had powerful arms. Crowmer vaulted back onto the wagon. He had much to lose if his champion was defeated, but he looked calm, a half-smile on his thin lips.

"The Just War will now be settled by duel," he said, raising his voice so that all in the crowd could hear. "I swear to be bound by the outcome, and may I be judged on it when I pass through the veil. Sir Bardest, do you also swear?"

"I do," Bardest growled in response, his eyes locked on Sir Vaikhari. "May fate grant me victory in reparation for my honour." He stepped forward, his sword held towards his opponent. Vaikhari paused a moment, a smile on his face, then also held his sword out, tapping the blade lightly on Bardest's – the signal to begin.

As soon as the blades clashed for the first time, Ingvar knew what the outcome would be. Bardest was a very good swordsman and had clearly trained hard on his skills. His movements were precise and balanced as he stepped forward and back, taking the centre line and trying to find an opening in Vaikhari's defences.

But, there were none. Ingvar had never seen a swordsman as complete as the tall elf. Each time Bardest attacked or feinted, Vaikhari's reactions were so quick it was as if, for him, time had slowed. He barely needed to move, and yet Bardest could get nowhere near landing a strike.

Ingvar grimaced in sympathy as the tip of Vaikhari's longsword opened a gash up the outside of Bardest's forearm. Bardest shook droplets of blood from his sleeve and returned to his guard, giving no sign of the pain he must have felt. Sweat poured down his brow, his whole face shining in the evening sun. Vaikhari was not sweating.

He attacked, feinting a thrust, then an overhead strike, then in the same movement took a huge step to his opponent's left. His long legs took him almost past his shorter opponent and, before Bardest could turn, the elf slashed his sword across the back of his legs.

Bardest grunted with pain, collapsing to one knee.

Vaikhari backed away, spreading both arms in a gesture at once victorious and questioning. The blow would be enough to count as a winning hit, if Bardest felt he could not continue the duel. Would he yield?

Ingvar felt himself sweating as he willed Sir Bardest to drop his sword and surrender the duel. Enough Bureno blood had been spilled that day. Bardest remained on one knee for several heartbeats, shaking his head.

"He will fight on." Olya turned to Ingvar with a conspiratorial whisper. "If he can stand, he will continue."

He nodded sadly. She was probably right.

Bardest hefted his sword, looking up at his opponent with determination in his eyes. With one motion, he got to his feet and attacked, thrusting, quickly following with a low cut then a high slash. It was fluid and fast, and a lesser opponent might have been caught by surprise.

Vaikhari's face showed nothing as he stepped to the side, then diverted the slash with his own blade. The blades caught together in a bind for a moment, Vaikhari's spiralling around his opponent's, and then the elf stepped back again into an elegant high guard.

Bardest raised his hand to touch another cut on his upper chest, where the elf's blade had pierced the thick, dark fabric of his gambeson. Blood welled through the rent. Once more, men and women turned to their neighbours, muttering over whether Bardest would concede at the wound. Once more, he hefted his blade in both hands and returned to the duel.

Ingvar could see he was tiring, and his weary strikes were evaded with increasing ease. Vaikhari rolled his neck and shrugged his shoulders, eyeing his opponent. The message was clear. The elf was not tired, his skill had not been tested, and perhaps his opponent should reconsider his reluctance to concede.

Bardest glared back with furious, desperate eyes and attacked. He launched a wild thrust, but Vaikhari was far too quick. His hands were raised in a heartbeat, knocking away Bardest's blade and turning the parry into his own thrust.

Time seemed to slow as Bardest followed the path of his lunge, his body moving unstoppably towards the elf. At the same time, Vaikhari extended his parry, both hands holding the grip of his longsword at chest height, the tip of the blade pointing directly towards his opponent.

A less fatigued duellist might have seen the danger and halted his thrust or thrown himself aside, but Bardest was exhausted. He staggered forward and his eyes bulged with horror for half a heartbeat before his own momentum drove the merciless point of Vaikhari's sword into his throat.

The crowd gasped as dark red blood poured out from the wound and from Bardest's gasping mouth. It quickly soaked the front of his gambeson and dripped down over the ornate hilt of Vaikhari's longsword.

The elf turned towards the crowd, and then to Count Crowmer, his head tilted to one side. He had a rueful smile on his face. It seemed the lethal thrust had been an accident. Was that possible? Ingvar chewed his lip.

Bardest writhed, his hands rising to his throat as if to tear away the sword and plug the hole, but it was hopeless. A few more moments passed before the elf shrugged to himself and twisted the blade before withdrawing it quickly. The stream of blood became a torrent, and Bardest collapsed to his knees, before slumping bonelessly to the ground.

He died as the dust settled.

Ingvar felt sick to his stomach at the pointless death. Duels were usually not fatal, although there was always risk of one or both parties being seriously hurt. It was a foolish waste of life.

"Shame," he muttered, turning to Olya. "We waste enough Bureno blood fighting against Tayo, without spilling our own."

"The last strike was an accident," she replied, her eyes fixed on Sir Bardest's body. "Bardest ran onto his sword after the parry. Vaikhari did not intend the killing stroke." Olya's tone was that of someone trying to convince themselves.

"What is this?" A new voice rang out. All heads turned. "What madness has happened here?" Ingvar looked and saw a russet-skinned man with well-cropped silvery hair approaching from across the camp. Beside him was a tall, slender woman with a pale complexion and raven-dark hair.

The man was Earl Maurer, the ranking noble of the northern army, and the woman must be Countess Mertan, his counterpart for the forces of the south. They paused at the edge of the circle, taking in Vaikhari's bloody blade and the slumped corpse of Sir Bardest. Maurer glared up at Crowmer, who had remained on the wagon bed.

"It was a Just War," he replied, brushing a speck of dirt from his sleeve. "Legally prosecuted. I accepted Sir Bardest's challenge and my champion was victorious."

"And your champion slaughtered him?" Countess Mertan's voice was low. Her eyes flitted anxiously between the body and Crowmer.

"Regrettably," acknowledged Crowmer with a slight bow of his head. "Accidents do happen. Sir Bardest's family will be compensated for their loss in accordance with the usual precedents."

"My apologies for his loss," put in Sir Vaikhari in his deep, rumbling voice. "He will be judged with honour as he passes through the veil."

Mertan summoned some of her soldiers to remove Bardest's body to their part of the camp, and Maurer beckoned Crowmer down from the wagon. As the two walked away in heated debate, Ingvar felt weariness hit him anew, and he turned to find his way to his own tent.

Evening was falling, the sun a fiery, swollen orb sinking rapidly towards the earth. Ingvar and Olya walked together, silent in contemplation. The bulk of the camp stretched away down a shallow slope to their right, and the bulk of the border defences rose to their left.

On the timber palisades between the towers, the spear-points of the soldiers left on guard duty reddened in the glow. Towering over them, a stone watchtower above one of the gates cast a long shadow on the yellowing, trampled grass.

In the open space between the rear of the palisade and the camp, soldiers were gathering the bodies of the fallen and laying them out for burial. The battle had been won, but there had nevertheless been a great many Bureno bodies to gather and lay out.

A pair of soldiers were raising a tall *pentang* above the bodies, a five-armed symbol of the gods fashioned from sturdy, stripped branches. The pale heartwood of the branches recalled mourning white and made a symbol of memorial and hope for the souls of the departed. Olya paused before the sombre collection.

"We count the cost of victory," said Olya in a solemn voice as their troops gathered behind, paying their last respects to the fallen. She lifted her head to address the small crowd. "May we remember their sacrifice for our great country, as they pass through the veil to the other side."

"Their judgement will be fair," added Ingvar. "Honour in life, glory in death. May they pass safely through the veil." He spoke because he felt he should, not because he believed it.

Most said that death in service of one's lord, king or country ensured a favourable reckoning after death. Some said the gods themselves judged each soul that passed the veil. Some said the gods were dead, or sleeping, and that all that waited in the afterlife was an eternity of waiting, looking back down at the living. Some fringe cults even said there was no afterlife.

All Ingvar knew was that he did not know – and no one truly could – but, to him, the idea of dying in a foreign country in a war that achieved nothing did not seem honourable or glorious. But he kept those thoughts to himself. Before long, his thoughts turned from the battle to the ride home and the overdue reunion that awaited.

Ammie.

CHAPTER THREE

Ingvar lifted his bruised behind gingerly from the saddle, wincing.

It was the second day in the saddle since striking camp and he was sore and tired. He was still wearing his armour and the smell of his unwashed arming jacket beneath was becoming offensive. He raised his eyes forward to where Count Crowmer led the column into yet another village. After the battle, he had hoped to lead his troops straight home, yet it was not to be.

Crowmer had made them wait nearly a week to ride home after the battle. Each morning, Ingvar had sought permission to leave with his troops. Each morning, he had been told 'Soon' by one of Crowmer's senior knights.

"You should hold your tongue," said a deep voice as Ingvar had stalked away from Crowmer's tent on the fifth morning. "I have heard that knights who ask too much may end up guarding the walls for a whole season." Ingvar turned, then looked up.

"Sir Vaikhari." He nodded respectfully at the towering elf, who looked down at him with a smirk on his lips. He made Ingvar nervous. "No disrespect intended. My troops are just eager to be home."

"As are we all." Vaikhari chuckled again. "As are we all. But we must wait for the order." Ingvar nodded again in reply, before turning on his heel and hurrying away. He could almost feel the elf's glare as a prickle between his shoulder blades as he strode across the camp.

"You need more patience," said Olya when he went to her with his frustrations.

"He is keeping us here as a show of power," grumbled Ingvar. "If Tayo attack again, it will not be when our full army stands on the palisade!"

"True or not," she replied, "we are here in service of our country and the High King. You are doing your duty. Your obligated duty." She gave him a meaningful look, and all he could do was roll his eyes.

The following day, the order to pack up and ride out had finally been given. Ingvar had sighed with relief.

Crowmer had led them out of the Swarthland, this wide land that Buren had annexed from Tayo some years ago as reparation for the last border war. He had marched them hard through this territory, where villages still populated by Tayan peasants huddled in the shadow of square-built Bureno stone fortresses.

"It must be a great honour to be the lord of such a castle," Olya had said, turning to Ingvar. She indicated a knot of serfs in brightly coloured working smocks. "Surrounded by enemies and with the responsibility of keeping the king's peace."

"I heard they were given out as a reward to knights who led the conquest," replied Ingvar. "Doesn't feel like much of a reward to me. If the defences are ever breached, it will be here that the first hammer blow will fall. Fate knows we've given these people enough to be angry about." He watched the locals as they rode past, and they returned his gaze with blank, challenging stares.

They had ridden quickly along the road east and north, sweeping through more villages without stopping. They must have looked a glorious cavalcade, Crowmer at their head in his shining and unstained war gear, his knights riding hard at his tail.

"Progress at last," Ingvar muttered to Olya, riding at his side. "We will be home soon at this rate." Ammie's face came to his mind again, her sharp blue eyes framed by hair so blonde it was almost white. *Soon.*

The road, hard-packed and dusty, passed over several bridges where the low hills dropped down to lazy rivers and green marshes. This was the easternmost extent of the Great

River delta that spread like grasping fingers through southern Tayo. A ridge ahead, darkly purple against the skyline, showed where the higher ground that formed the original border between Buren and Tayo lay. Away to their right, blurred and hazy in the heat of the day, Ingvar could make out the towering peaks of the Crown.

Seen up close, this range of mountains defied belief. Five huge conical and almost identical peaks climbed abruptly from rolling green hills, dominating the landscape for miles. They formed a circle, or perhaps the points of a star, arrayed about a central vale. Within this vale lay the Jewel of the Crown, rising from the bases of the five surrounding mountains. The Jewel was small compared to the peaks of the Crown, but strikingly unlikely, a perfect cylinder of rose-veined granite thrust up into the centre of the vale.

"And they say magic is a myth," said one of his soldiers, gesturing towards the distant peaks. A few nearby chuckled, but more shook their heads, muttering to each other.

"More like a children's story!" A short-haired woman chuckled, leaning around in her saddle to check that others were laughing. "It's just a mountain. Mountains weren't made by wizards!"

"Enough!" Ingvar spoke up, wanting to quell any arguments before they started. He had no strong opinions about whether there had been magic or not, or whether the Diminishing, the fading of the magic, had really happened. "We still have a long way to travel. Ride on!"

The Jewel could not be seen from this distance, and Ingvar turned his face from the distant peaks as they climbed the ridge into Buren. Crowmer now slowed, easing his horse along at a steady walk as they took the left fork at a junction in the road and turned north.

Eastwards, the road continued for many miles to Glithoniel, Buren's capital, but Crowmer's county was the rolling green hills of the north. The estates of both Olya and Ingvar's families lay there, and had for many generations.

The road descended slightly, and a village spread out before them. The main road passed straight through the middle, with the houses clustering unevenly on each side. Despite the warmth, smoke spiralled lazily over the tiled roofs into the clear sky above.

"Whoa! Easy!" Crowmer's voice rang out, his hand raised as a signal to the riders around him to slow still further. "I will lead the column from here."

As if by command, villagers appeared in the streets to welcome Crowmer and his troops. News of their victory had spread quickly and, for these people who lived in the shadow of the uncertain border with Tayo, the relief was tangible.

Crowmer rode at the head of the column, graciously accepting the cheers and applause with a wave.

"Bless you!" a wild-haired man shouted in Ingvar's direction as he rode past slowly. "And bless you eternally, lady!" This was to Olya, and she acknowledged the praise with a nod and rolled her eyes at Ingvar.

It was unusual, but not unknown, for a noble's daughter, rather than son, to take up arms in his name. As the only child of the family, Olya had always felt that answering the call to war on behalf of her family was her duty, and in battle, she was as brave and skilled as any man. She had always accepted that her gender would cause her to be judged differently from other knights, but it could still cause a certain frustration.

"Your ladyship," Ingvar murmured to her, with an elaborate bow from his saddle in mock deference. She leaned over and shoved him upright before riding on ahead.

Ingvar's family had seen things differently, and his elder brother, Edvar, had concentrated on learning how to manage the farm while he had trained as a knight. But then, the Ferras family were wealthy, yet the Darelles were not. Making the family farm a success had always been Ingvar's father's priority. Omar Darelle saw military duty as a necessary and unavoidable burden.

They had ridden on to the next village, where once again the streets thronged with people cheering. The sky was still bright, but the sun was near the horizon, so Crowmer ordered a camp to be made. The knights were found rooms in the inn, but the household soldiers and levies pitched tents on the brittle, dry grass around the outskirts of the village.

"Why so slow?" Ingvar muttered to Olya as they sat in the inn's common room, waiting to eat that evening. "I would have been home by now, riding alone. Time is wasting."

"You know why," she answered, leaning in close and speaking quietly. "The people must know that their borders are protected. You must have noticed the joy?"

Ingvar said nothing. The adulation of these people meant nothing to him. Crowmer was his Count, though, and so he had no choice but to fall in line.

At that moment, a girl appeared at his elbow, carrying plates of food for the table.

"Food at last!" said Ingvar, before tucking in gratefully. He picked up a large chunk of stewed, spiced root and crammed it into his mouth.

"Barbarian." Olya sniffed as Ingvar continued to devour the meal with his hands. She used her knife to cut her food into small chunks, passing it to her mouth piece by piece, skewered on the point.

It was simple but wholesome fare: a leg of goat with a sauce flavoured with curry leaves; spices and peppers, served with a mix of roots and a heap of flat blackened bread. Crowmer held court, almost like a bard, as he recounted the story of the battle. Vaikhari sat at his right, a knowing smirk on his face as always.

"They had paid their savage mercenaries well," he was saying, eyes scanning the room, checking he had everyone's attention. "Their pouches were heavy with coin and they came at us like wild animals. But staunch Bureno hearts beat in our chests, and we met steel with steel. Not one Tayan fighter would reach the palisade while I drew breath and had the strength to hold a sword…"

He told the tale as if he had defeated the Tayans single-handedly. Ingvar glanced across at Olya and was met with a grin and another eye roll. He shook his head slightly and returned to his food. If Crowmer wanted to take all the credit, he could. All Ingvar wanted right now was to get home. Home to Ammie. As Crowmer spoke, her face haunted his thoughts.

"What is your hurry to get home?"

Ingvar started at the sound of Olya's voice near his ear. He had drifted off and had not noticed Crowmer and most of his followers had left the table. Ingvar did not answer.

"This is no hardship, is it? We are out of danger and the food is not so bad…" A broad smile was on her lips as she gently poked fun at him.

Ingvar did not feel like telling the truth. Olya was his oldest friend and he trusted her with his life, but this was one thing he did not want to share with her. He shrugged.

"I have tasks around the estate," he replied gruffly, evasively. "My father will be impatient for my return." Olya eyed him uncertainly. "This delay is unnecessary. And it is caused by one person."

Olya made a scolding sound. "Patience with your superiors is a noble virtue!" she exclaimed, but she was smiling. Her smile faded. "He is difficult," she acknowledged, "but you must realise he is strong. He has ambition and the will to enact it. You must realise that we would be better off as his ally. Better off to follow where he leads."

Ingvar grimaced. There was sense in pledging loyalty to a strong leader. The rewards could be victory, glory, reputation and all the things that brought: wealth, land and increased status. Yet, there was something about Crowmer that he could not trust. Something cold. His father had said much the same on occasions.

"I'll consider it," he said, even though he had already thought about it many times, and rejected the idea. He stood and stomped off towards the back of the inn and his bedroom, the need to lie to his friend an uncomfortable sensation. Doubt hung over him.

Tired from the journey, he lay down to sleep but was kept awake by the roiling of his thoughts.

CHAPTER FOUR

He woke as the first light of the day flashed into his room through the cracks in the shutters. Dawn was a good time to be up and outside, before the heat of the day built and began to cook the air. Olya joined him after a few minutes and made sure her men were getting ready to depart. Her long hair was tied up tightly as if she was riding into battle, and the small, individual plates of the armour to her chest, shoulders and hips gleamed like the scales of a freshly caught fish.

"Home today," she said to Ingvar.

"Aye," he replied, "with luck."

Crowmer had still not appeared, and as they waited on the dry, brittle grass the sun climbed into the crystal blue sky. To escape the mounting heat, Ingvar and Olya ducked back into the inn's common room.

Despite the early hour, a crowd in the corner had gathered around a table where a carved, pale-wood figure had been placed. The figure represented a beloved family ancestor, and the guests were paying tribute. These ceremonies were such an integral part of Bureno life that Ingvar barely registered it. It was uncommon for there not to be some sort of ceremonial observance in every village, every day.

Ingvar watched as an older woman picked up a polished pewter jug. The other observants gathered around, holding out their hands. She carefully, gently, poured a stream of water from the jug over the outstretched hands. Once wetted, they took a white salt cake from a plate on the table. The water represented the journey through the veil from life to death, and the cake was a symbol of the transition of the body after life. It was a ceremony of remembrance as well as signifying their hope for fair judgement beyond the silver veil of death.

Ingvar's thoughts drifted to the recent deaths he had seen: the horror of battle, and the pointless slaying of Sir Bardest. Imagining life beyond death, free of the troubles and pains of life, was some small comfort. He watched the ceremony and found it eerily comforting.

"On your feet!" Crowmer's voice was harsh and loud in the confines of the common room. "We ride now!" He had appeared from the bedrooms, sweeping through the room and to the door.

He strode outside and one of his men scurried away to bring his horse. The scales of his armour rippled and shone as he mounted his horse with athletic ease, the rich blue cloak he always wore draping across his mount's powerful hindquarters. He was an impressive figure, and Ingvar found himself considering once more the worth of an alliance with the man. He bit his lip with doubt.

Like the day before, they trailed in his wake as he led them along the road which wound steadily northwards through rolling hills and open fields. The heat increased as the day wore on, a haze rising before them over the dry, compacted dirt of the well-worn trail.

Occasionally, the path dipped to ford the tiny streams that ran down from the hills into the vales to the west, and as they rode through the narrow belts of trees – oak, maple and carob – the cooling shade was a blessed relief. Down to their left, deep, narrow valleys split the land, which carried more small, tumbling streams. Wild woods clustered menacingly on the valley floors, the road seeming to cower away from the ancient trees as it carved a path along the hillsides high above.

They had paraded slowly through another three villages during that slow morning, gradually heading north. Ingvar's impatience grew and he ground his teeth in frustration.

The final village, Locton, was the first in Crowmer's county and a number of his troops were dismissed to go to their homes. Vaikhari inclined his head deeply and respectfully, despite the slightly mocking smile he wore, before riding away. Crowmer sent off another number to ride straight back to his manor and prepare for his arrival. After issuing this command, Crowmer reined in at the junction and waited for Ingvar and Olya.

The village temple loomed behind him, its ancient timbers dark and shaded in the afternoon light. The temple had been built in centuries past, and was the oldest structure in the village, and for miles around. It was now used as a meeting room for the village council but had been used for worship by previous generations.

The floor of the temple stood around the height of two men above the ground, and was supported at each corner with an upright log. The local ancestors had raised their temples as high above the ground as they could to escape the mundane, and to be closer to the gods. The gods were slowly being forgotten, but the carved faces of Mordea and Kaled, Ome, Tureank and Conferan still stared out from where they had been carved in the wood. Ingvar found their faded, sombre expressions to be a sad reminder of what had been lost.

"Your estate is but an hour's ride from here, is it not?" asked Crowmer, ignoring the ancient building. He sat very upright on his horse, his eyes seemingly focused on a spot six inches above Ingvar's right shoulder.

"Yes, my Count," replied Ingvar quickly. "I will be home before nightfall." There was a long pause as Crowmer tilted his head and waited. After a silence that seemed to last a long time, Ingvar cottoned on. "And you would be very welcome to visit, of course."

"The offer is most kind, Ingvar," said Crowmer, smiling slightly. "I have not seen Sir Omar for some time. Your hospitality will be appreciated."

Ingvar put his heels to his horse's flanks and they rode on. He tried to school his face to blankness. It seemed to be his fate to forever have his choices made by others, especially when those others included Count Rauf Crowmer.

As the afternoon wore on, Ingvar led the way through gentle hills, Olya riding at his side. A rough track wound between shallow slopes and down into a sheltered vale. Crowmer and his remaining troops followed behind, talking quietly among themselves as the road passed green pastures and through orchards of apple and pear trees. Horses grazed in small groups nearby and the soft brown shapes of goats could be seen scattered up the more distant hillsides. Nestled in the middle of the natural bowl formed by the surrounding hillsides was the blocky outline of the Darelle family manor.

Home, at last, thought Ingvar. He exhaled deeply in relief, as the familiar shape of the house grew in his vision. He had always been baffled by those who enjoyed being away from home. Unfamiliar sights and unusual beds were not something that he ever looked forward to. He would much rather be here, where he knew every tree, every soft green curve of the hillside, and where his family were nearby.

He turned to Olya and smiled broadly. She returned it with a chuckle.

"Back where you belong, hey?" she said. He ignored the mocking tone in her voice.

"Where I belong," he replied. "Indeed. Where I belong."

The manor house sat on a slight rise in the middle of the vale. Olive trees lined the track approaching the house, and tall cypress trees stood to the west. The house itself was framed with huge, squared timber columns and beams, infilled with pale blocks of quarried stone. It was square-built and defensible, with thick timber doors and small window openings on the ground floor. The windows were bigger on the upper floor, covered with timber shutters that were painted a light shade of blue.

A red-tiled roof sat solidly over the house like a war helmet, eaves hanging low on each side. Ingvar shook his head, surprised at his own thought. He had left war behind, hopefully for a long time. His own helmet hung from his saddle, its shining cheek-guards engraved with the boar's-head insignia of House Darelle. Soon it would be hung up on a hook in the house, where it would stay for a long time, if fate willed it.

One of the family servants appeared from the side of the house, a tall half-elf girl with white-blonde hair and tawny skin. Ammie. Her cheekbones were tinted with a hint of purple. Ingvar dismounted, holding his own reins while she waited for the other soldiers to dismount. Their eyes met for the briefest moment and Ingvar felt a shock, sparking like a hammer striking an anvil. He smiled.

"I will help Ammie with the horses," he called to the group as they dismounted. She turned away, leading the horses towards the rear of the house, where the stables lay. He grabbed a handful of reins and followed.

The stable building was a large square structure attached to the rear corner of the house. Dark, aged timber walls were topped with bright new tiles that matched the roof of the house. Ingvar's father had repaired the roof last winter. It had been the last repair on the estate that he had been able to afford.

A wide timber archway led into a square courtyard, floored with packed earth and littered with straw. Ingvar's attention was immediately drawn to Ammie, and he watched her for a moment as she moved between stalls, finding space for all the horses. He copied, putting his own horse in its usual stall and quickly tying up the others.

Glancing around to make sure there was nobody else near, he strode quickly across the courtyard, approaching Ammie from behind. He reached out to tap her shoulder, but she spun on her heel to face him even as his hand began to move.

"Ammie," he said softly. Her face had been hard as she turned, but it warmed quickly. "It is good to see you again. I'm so happy to be home." He reached out for her then, putting his hands on her slender hips and looking up into her eyes. She sighed, a small frown crossing her face.

"I feared you would not return this time," she stated. "Your death weighed on me every day." He moved closer, and she lowered her head to gently touch his. "But you know this cannot be. Especially not here, now, when others might see."

"I know, I know," said Ingvar, shaking his head. "I just needed this moment with you. I have to spend more time with Crowmer, and it will be more bearable after this." She returned a slight smile and he leaned forward and embraced her. If the touch of the hundreds of metallic plates that made up his armour was cold against her skin, she gave no sign. She wrapped her arms around him tightly, but just for a moment.

A soft cough sounded behind them. It was subtle but deliberate.

They sprang apart, Ingvar spinning around to face back into the courtyard. A tall, slender elf woman stood there, her dark eyes fixing them with an intense stare. It was Lamaina Cowl, Ammie's mother and one of the Darelle family's longest-serving household servants. Her dark skin gleamed in the sunshine still streaming into the open courtyard and she towered over Ingvar as she took a step closer.

"Come, Ammie," she said briskly. "There are house guests. You are needed." As she spoke, her eyes did not leave Ingvar's. Ammie brushed past him and out into the courtyard, taking her mother's hand as they hurried away towards the house. Like most servants, they were provided a house on the estate and treated with respect. As a family, the Cowls took their service seriously.

"Yes, Mother," she said. As they disappeared from view, Ingvar overheard her final words. "I am sorry, Mother." He paused, biting his lip with worry. His parents would be outraged and furious with him if they found out about him and Ammie.

Relationships between nobles and their servants were strongly discouraged. He knew he was risking much. Ammie could be sent away, her parents with her. He cursed himself, as he had so many times before, swearing to be more careful, swearing to stay away from her.

Yet he always found he could not. He turned towards the front entrance to the stables and headed for the house. As he turned, he tried to shake off a strange and sudden sensation. The sensation of being watched.

CHAPTER FIVE

As Crowmer's soldiers had made their way around to the back of the stables, the Count had waited at the front door. The troops would make a camp in the lee of the walls while the nobles stayed in the house. Ingvar acknowledged his presence with a perfunctory nod of his head, before leading the way inside.

The interior of the house was blessedly cool after the heat outside, and it seemed extremely dark at first. Ingvar stepped forward, waiting for his eyes to adjust to the gloom, but could soon make out the familiar interior, the long hall stretching back into the house and a double row of thick timber columns supporting the ceiling. This main hall was the full width of the house, and through narrow window slits in the side walls, bright shafts of light pierced the interior.

A long, dark wooden table ran down the centre of the hall, and as Ingvar moved forward, he heard chair legs being scraped back on the stone floor as the occupants of the room rose to greet the guests.

Closest to the door, and hurrying forward with arms outstretched towards his son, was Omar Darelle. Short and stocky, with a barrel chest and a slight hunch to his back, Ingvar's father had been a useful soldier in his time but had always preferred to be working on his farm. He embraced his son and took a step back, running a hand over his balding scalp.

"Welcome home, my son!" he boomed in his deep, loud voice. "I hear your victory was resounding!" He turned now to the other visitors. "Olya! They are saying great things about your skills and bravery, my girl!" Olya bowed her head, accepting the praise graciously.

Not many could get away with calling her 'my girl', but Omar had known her since she was a baby. Last, he turned to the third guest, bowing low and sweeping his hands out in welcome. "Count Crowmer," he said, lifting his head again. "You honour my humble house with your presence."

"Rise, rise, Omar," replied Crowmer graciously, reaching forward to grasp Omar's shoulders. He looked slightly tense as he straightened. "The honour is mine." Crowmer was some years younger than Ingvar's father, and his ascendancy had coincided with Omar's retirement from fighting. They nevertheless knew each other well from years of living in the same region.

"And it seems we have quite the gathering of honourable men this evening," he continued, turning to the other man who had been sat at the table when they arrived. "Sir Frankess, it's a pleasure to see you again." Frankess stepped forward and bowed before the Count. Like Omar, his age meant he wore a beard, but where Ingvar's father was broad, Frankess was whip-lean. As tall as Crowmer, he had long, white hair, which was bound at the nape of his neck.

"My Count," he said, simply, as he straightened. Crowmer brushed past him and moved over to the room's last occupant, Ingvar's mother, Etsel.

"My lady," he said, taking her olive-skinned hand and inclining his head. "The jewel in the Darelle crown!"

As Etsel ducked her head in return, lowering her dark eyes to the ground, Ingvar noticed the pure, white strands that ran through her dark hair. Were there more since he had left for war?

"You flatter us, Count," she said, with a smile that did not quite reach her eyes. "Please, come. Sit." She motioned to the table. The three soldiers and the two older men moved to take chairs. "You have travelled far and must be hungry. I will get a meal prepared for you all." She moved off to the back of the hall, disappearing through a curtained archway that led to the kitchens.

As the curtain rippled and swayed back into place, a pair of women came from the other direction, both holding a burning candle. It was Ammie, followed closely by her mother. Lamaina's short dark hair was brushed behind her upswept elven ears, making them impossible to miss. It could have been his imagination but Ingvar was sure she fixed him with a fleeting, knowing stare as she moved past.

Ingvar concentrated on not looking in Ammie's direction as she carried her candle around the room. Perhaps it was obvious anyway? What if Lamaina chose to tell everyone, now, before the Count?

Ammie and her mother moved around the room lighting candles and lanterns, and the conversation at the table paused as they worked. The sun was sinking behind the hills to the west, the room darkening as evening approached, but soon enough, candles were lit to bathe the room in soft orange light. Ingvar kept his eyes fixed on the aged boards of the table until they finished their work and left the room once more.

※

"We hear it was your leadership that secured the victory, Count Crowmer," Omar was saying. The small talk flowed easily between the people sitting around the table as they waited for the food to be ready. Ingvar tried to catch Olya's eye at his father's praise of the Count, but she pointedly looked away. Frankess stayed silent. Crowmer smiled broadly.

"A leader is only as good as the troops he commands, Omar," Crowmer replied, "and Sir Ferras and your son are some of the best. Their loyalty and valour aided me greatly in gaining victory."

"But, do you think it will give us peace?" asked Ingvar's father. "The Tayans never know when they are beaten. I begrudge the waste of Bureno lives to protect the border."

"Come, Omar," said Crowmer, a hint of a sneer in his voice. "War is part of life when we border Tayo. It's where the steel of our blades is tempered. Soldiers have always happily paid in blood to defend their borders."

"But it's not just the soldiers, is it?" Omar leaned forward, a deep frown on his lined face. "This war has been a bad business for everyone. You must have heard about that Tayan warlord up north? Led his band behind the lines and attacked the camps. Women, children…it was horrific. There was a Bureno general that way, called Tann, I think. They took his wife. Raped, killed. I heard he was a solid man before that, but it ruined him. That's not what you march for." Ingvar started at hearing that name mentioned. He had served under a man called Tann the previous year.

"That tale reached my ears too." Crowmer nodded. "The Tayan nobles would wash their hands of the crimes committed in the name of their ambition. Remaining part of

Re'Emsser is worth much, and yet in private they plot and scheme against us." Re'Emsser was the name for the alliance between the four neighbouring nations of Tayo, Anish and Kotev, with Buren as the lynchpin.

"Aye, true," replied Omar. "They want our trade so the nobles must denounce the wars. I'm certain it's the same nobles who are raising the armies, though. They would celebrate if the Swarthland was won back. How long would we hold it if the Tayans there rose up in revolt?"

Whatever Crowmer might have said in response was lost as the curtain to the kitchen rippled and Ammie and her mother emerged carrying plates and trays. At the same time, as if the food was a signal, the front door opened and another man stepped inside. He was dressed in rider's leathers and made a tall and imposing figure silhouetted against the dusky evening light. He pulled the door shut and moved inside.

"Perfect timing for food, as usual," said Etsel from the kitchen archway where she was overseeing the laying of the table. "My eldest son has an amazing sense of smell." Ingvar's elder brother, Edvar, strolled around to a vacant seat, casually slapping him on the shoulder as he passed. He ducked his head and made the usual formal greetings to Count Crowmer, who nodded in acknowledgement. Edvar pulled out a chair.

"Little brother," he said as he eased his tall frame into the seat, "it's good to see you return safe. I hear you fought bravely." Ingvar shrugged off the compliment. Edvar turned his gaze to Olya, who seemed to be sitting up straighter, an unreadable expression on her face. "And the same goes for you, Sir Ferras," he said, formally. "But I would never doubt that you could take care of yourself." Olya laughed and Ingvar grunted at the joke.

Etsel picked up the water jug and poured a splash onto the flagstones, before taking her place at the table. This traditional observance was the signal to eat. There were cured meats, dripping with spicy sauces, and roasted vegetables from the farm, with heaps of flatbread from the morning, slightly stale and stiff, but still delicious to a hungry traveller. There was companionable silence for a time as everyone ate, but soon the talk turned again to the wars, the hope for a time of peace and the political situation in Buren.

"Earl Maurer loses support, I hear," said Edvar. "He ages and ails. He doesn't have the strength of will he once had. It wouldn't surprise me to see someone rise up to replace him." He looked pointedly at Crowmer as he spoke. Crowmer kept his face blank, making no reply. Instead, he changed the subject.

"How are fortunes with your land?" the Count asked. Ingvar's family all shifted uncomfortably. It was an open secret that their land was poor and did not sustain the same level of wealth as their neighbours' farms. "I know young Edvar is working wonders with your stock of horseflesh. The mount I bought from you is the best I've ever had!"

"Yes, that's true," replied Omar wearily. "I just wish the rest of the farm could do so well. But we mustn't complain, we get by." Crowmer was listening intently, chewing a mouthful of bread as his eyes flicked from face to face.

"You needn't struggle, old friend," he said, swallowing and looking now at Omar. "Even if times are tight. You don't stand alone." He paused, and there was an attentive silence. It seemed everyone could tell that Crowmer was leading to something. "Noble families should support each other, through good times and bad, thick and thin. And traditionally, the way families like yours do that is by bonding with each other. Through marriage."

There was a longer silence as this statement was digested. Ingvar noticed Olya and Edvar looking instantly at each other, before both looked quickly away. Omar stared at Crowmer, then glanced down the table at Edvar and Olya, a thoughtful expression on his face.

"Well, yes," he conceded. "There can be a lot of benefits to a considered marriage. But this is not the old days. We cannot force young people into a marriage against their will."

"It would not be!" Olya looked down, blushing. "I mean, I can see that a marriage between the Ferras and Darelle families would have benefits for both families." She looked up at Edvar and smiled. "And for my part, it would certainly not be against my will." She leaned back on her chair, tucking a loose strand of blonde hair behind her ear.

"Nor mine," stated Edvar, a smile spreading across his face.

"So!" Crowmer clapped his hands. There was a look of triumph on his face. "It is decided! I'm sure this will bring joy to all of you, as well as security and prosperity for both families."

Ingvar's parents stood at Crowmer's words, with mixed emotions on their faces. He remained sitting, shocked, while Olya and Edvar shared glances and smiles.

"We must celebrate!" Etsel, flustered, bustled off to the kitchen. She returned moments later with a wax-sealed clay bottle of local wine. She moved around the table and poured everyone a generous measure. "It's the right time of year for the asters, Edvar," she said as she poured wine into his cup.

It was traditional in Buren for a proposal to be offered with a bunch of fresh asters. They flowered all over the countryside in late summer, which was generally considered an appropriate time of year for a wedding.

"To the future!" toasted Count Crowmer and they all drank deeply.

"Olya?" asked Ingvar, sometime later. "I never knew."

The two brothers had been turfed out of their own bedrooms upstairs to make room for Olya, who had taken Ingvar's room, and for their parents, who were in Edvar's. Despite his initial protests, Count Crowmer had of course been given the biggest bedroom, which Omar and Etsel usually shared. Ingvar and Edvar had grabbed handfuls of blankets and were making themselves comfortable in front of the hearth in the main hall.

"I didn't know either," said Edvar wistfully, lying back and putting his hands behind his head. "I mean, I knew. How I felt. But I was never sure she felt the same."

"She's kept it very quiet," replied Ingvar. "But that's not surprising."

"Shut up, idiot," retorted his brother, reaching out with a fist to thump Ingvar's arm. "It will be good for us all.

Bonding the families and giving us security. You should be happy for me."

"I'm happy for you. That good enough?" Ingvar replied, gruffly. He stared at the darkened wood of the ceiling beams for a moment, thinking, before turning to his brother. "Don't hurt her. Don't let her down."

Edvar's eyes were dark but lit with dancing flecks of light from the fire, burning low. He nodded slowly. "Goodnight, little brother."

Edvar's breathing deepened as he drifted off to sleep but it took Ingvar a long time to settle. The thought of his great friend Olya and his brother being married was a strange one. He had no reason to object, but the suddenness of it had taken him off guard. Thinking about their marriage made Ingvar consider his own prospects, and as he did so the image of a face with violet-tinted skin and white-blonde hair swam before his eyes.

He shook his head, eyes blinking in the darkness. However much it was what he wanted, it would never be allowed; their status and class were just too far apart.

He sighed, rolled over, and tried unsuccessfully to put thoughts of her from his mind.

Wood clacked on wood as the practice blades locked together. Ingvar was already sweating freely despite the early hour, the morning sun inching over the hilltops and bathing the yellowing grass at the front of the house in warmth.

Olya stepped back, then quickly forward. She swung her wooden longsword two-handed, a high cut towards Ingvar's throat. As he moved his balance and raised his blade to parry, she raised her rear hand, dropping the point. It thumped into his ribs. He was wearing his leather arming jacket, but the practice sword was a solid length of ash, and the impact was painful. He grunted as the air left his lungs and he staggered back, winded.

Olya's blade spun back the other way and came to rest above her head as she leaned back into a high guard. Ingvar shook his head in frustration.

Compared to most, he was a good swordsman. He was fast, had quick reactions, and had strong shoulders and wrists to make his cuts and strikes accurate and powerful. Despite that, he rarely landed a hit on Olya, and she seemed to be able to get past his guard whenever she chose. Over the years, he had studied her, hoping to discover what made her so good, hoping he could learn and improve. He had so far completely failed to get anywhere near matching her speed or balance.

He sucked in a deep breath and moved forward again, his longsword held low. He would try attacking quickly and more directly. He feinted left then took a long step forward and thrust at Olya's right. There was a sharp clack as her blade moved around quickly as if to parry, but this time she swivelled and used it to guide his sword away, pushing it hard with her own. Caught off balance, he took another step forward, and, at the same time, Olya stepped to her right and Ingvar felt her blade tap him in the small of the back.

"Never turn your back on an enemy," she said, letting the point of her sword drop to the ground. She put a hand on her hip and grinned. "That's in the first lesson, isn't it?"

Ingvar could not think of a clever response, deciding instead that their sparring session was over. He shouldered his wooden sword and turned to head back to the house.

"Is that it?" She hurried to catch him up. "I was just starting to enjoy that. Did I leave any obvious openings in my guards?" Ingvar knew she revelled in training, always wanting to do more, always wanting to improve.

"I'm done for today," he replied. "You have made me feel like a novice, again. I will just hope I don't meet anyone as good as you in battle." He would force himself to train through winter, knowing it might keep him alive next summer.

Before she could reply, movement in the grove of olive trees to the left caught their attention. Ingvar's father and Count Crowmer were walking through the olive grove together. They appeared deep in conversation. Crowmer was gesturing all around them, and Omar was shaking his head repeatedly, his face grim.

Ingvar wondered what was being discussed but had no polite way of finding out. He would have to wait. Besides, the heat of the day was rising and he felt like he was being stifled by his arming jacket. He rushed on into the cool of the house to take it off and to find some clean water to wash. Olya followed him, a concerned expression on her face.

Before either of them had a chance to get further into the house than the main hall, Crowmer stormed in. His mouth was set in a tight line, his displeasure evident.

"It is time I left," he stated, directing his words at Etsel, who was standing beside the kitchen archway.

"But, my Count," she replied quickly, "we hoped you would stay for another meal."

"I have important business to attend to," he said, "and I must return to my estates promptly." At that moment, Ammie appeared from the kitchen holding a tall ewer of cool water. Crowmer looked at her, then swung around to look at Omar, who had followed him into the hall but had not spoken.

"One more thing, Omar," continued Crowmer, "this half-elf girl is of age to marry. There is a suitable elf for such a match working on Olya's estate. It will be one less mouth for you to feed and will be another bond for the families. You will arrange it." He finished, glancing between Omar and Olya to see that they understood, then turned and left again through the front door where his horse was already saddled and waiting.

Ingvar felt like he had been dealt a crushing blow to the stomach. He glanced over at Ammie, who was still standing in obvious surprise near the table. Her wide blue eyes met his, and he opened his mouth as if to speak, but could not think of anything to say. She slammed the water jug down on the table and turned on her heel, her long white-blonde hair flashing around her shoulders as she disappeared back into the kitchen.

Rauf Crowmer closed his eyes and turned his face towards the sun, basking as the midday heat hit his skin. His country was glorious in summer, when dawn came early; evenings were long and warm and everywhere was lush and green.

"You're sure this is true?" he asked. "You are certain?"

His bondsmen had ridden after him when they had seen him leaving the house, catching up a way down the track.

One of his captains, a sturdy woman with a striking combination of bronze skin and pale eyes, had reined in her horse alongside his, eager to share her news.

"Yes, my Count," she confirmed, nodding vigorously. "Although 'tis still a secret. Not even Sir Omar's family know."

Crowmer rubbed a hand across his chin, a small smile spreading as he considered the implications of this new information. "Thank you, Captain Tinos," he said, dismissing her.

The old fool Darelle had refused his offer that morning. Even though it was what Crowmer had expected, Omar's refusal was still a disappointment, and would make certain things more difficult to achieve.

However, the news he had just received from Tinos was unexpected but useful, and interesting. Very interesting. This was a lever Crowmer could use to push some pieces into the right places.

The first wedding, between the elder Darelle boy and Sir Ferras, was the first step of his plan. Strengthening the Ferras family and weakening Omar at the same time was too good an opportunity to miss.

This country had been founded on strength and prowess. Individuals with the will to exert their influence – and the determination to hold on to what they could take – had prospered. They still did, with the strongest knights taking land, wealth, and as a result, power, from their weaker neighbours. The most resolute of all would rise to the very top. This was the backbone of the great country of Buren.

However, history remembered those who conquered and ruled with blood and fire, and judged them harshly. A knight could make himself the lord of a vast swathe of land with a campaign of violence, but an unpopular leader would always struggle to hold on to what he had gained.

Therefore, a new way had arisen. Alliances were formed, debts were earned, and now conquests were often quiet and bloodless. Crowmer considered himself a master of this path, carefully considering each subtle move and steadily gaining power. It was a path that would leave his hands clean and his reputation untarnished. Other people would not even see the strings being pulled.

Omar Darelle had refused to cooperate, but he had always been stubborn. Crowmer had other dice to roll yet, though. Other dice that could be loaded, by favour or by fear, to fall more favourably. Darelle would discover that some decisions were not truly his to make.

Crowmer smiled to himself. The second wedding, taking the *helf* girl away from the moon-eyed Ingvar, was an afterthought. It served no particular political purpose, but it should show him that actions had consequences. Tinos had seen him embracing the servant girl in the stables, and had told Crowmer immediately. A foolish deed, punished.

Where the track into the Darelle estate joined the main road, Crowmer spurred forward and turned left, away from his own estates. What he had just learned from Tinos would allow him to strengthen his interests further still, in the fullness of time.

"We ride north," he announced, half-turning in the saddle, "to the Ferras estate."

If his bondsmen were surprised, they gave no sign. They were utterly loyal to him, or did not remain part of his retinue for long. They trusted him. Their trust was well rewarded. It was time to see if the Ferras family still retained the same trust and could earn their own reward.

A flash of movement above caught his eye, and he glanced up to see a banded hawk arcing overhead like an arrow. He decided it must be a good sign. A favourable omen.

When he had been appointed as Count, they had joked that he was Duke Caralas's hunting hawk. Once the Duke had aimed him at a target, he would never miss. They had laughed behind their hands at this back-handed compliment and it was this petty scorn that drove Crowmer on. The nobles he was forced to bow to were weak and narrow-minded. Buren required strong leadership and his rise would provide the country with just that.

The world was going to discover that he was more than a mere hawk. He was an eagle, his wingspan wide and his talons sharp, and he would fly higher than anyone had yet guessed.

CHAPTER SIX

Olya Ferras was no stranger to fear.

She was used to the dull anxiety that filled her whole being before a battle. She was familiar with the growing dread that built as the battle lines closed, and she knew too well the frantic terror that raced through her veins as she was forced to use her sword to fight for her life.

The sense of unease that she felt from the moment she had pulled back her bedcovers that morning was new and completely unfamiliar. She strolled over to the window, pushing open the shutters and looking down into the perfectly manicured garden. She bit her lip as she noticed the strings of coloured flags fluttering in the morning breeze, and the servants moving around to decorate the garden with bunches of flowers, purple asters and pale-blue *pervinca*, and sheaves of myrtle branches. She imagined the house and garden full of guests, and thought about them watching the moment when she—

She struggled to finish the thought. Taking a deep breath, she set her jaw and steeled herself. She was getting married. That did not feel too scary. She would be a wife. That thought made her stomach give a slight lurch. She would be Edvar Darelle's wife. At that, she exhaled loudly and smiled.

Brushing her blonde hair back behind her ears, she turned from the window to dress for breakfast. Edvar Darelle had always held a special place in her heart, but she had not often considered marriage to him or anyone else. Her devotion was to the sword, and using it to protect the country of Buren.

She had considered it a lot more since Crowmer had first suggested the idea those months ago. Edvar was perfect for her, and while the thought of being a wife was strange – and imagining herself as the centre of attention during the wedding was terrifying – knowing that Edvar was coming to live with her gave her a warm, comforting feeling inside. She concentrated on that thought, instead of the prospect of the wedding itself, as she left her room and went down the stairs to greet her parents for breakfast.

Ingvar held the gleaming blade tightly in his fist, gripping his brother's shoulder firmly and bringing the sharp steel to rest on the skin of his neck. He took a deep breath to steady his hand and to calm the nerves fluttering in his stomach. With a smooth motion, he drew the blade slowly upward and inward.

He breathed an audible sigh of relief as it passed easily over the curve of his brother's chin, leaving it hairless.

"Have you made me bleed yet?" Edvar asked, his face creasing into a smile.

"I will," Ingvar replied, "if you don't stop talking." He lowered the blade for another pass.

Ingvar was Edvar's groomsman for the wedding, and as well as having various responsibilities during the day, the first was this: trimming the bride's-man's hair and shaving his face.

The day was already warm, and Ingvar felt the heavy fabric of his robes pressing uncomfortably on his shoulders. He hooked a finger into the high, formal collar, trying to ease the heavy silk slightly away from his neck.

They both wore traditional formal dress robes embroidered with the Darelle family crest. Ingvar's was deep blue, but Edvar had been made a new one in rich red, especially for the wedding. Ingvar always felt awkward and self-conscious in formal dress.

"These robes are stifling," he said, pulling out a cloth and wiping the sheen of sweat from his brow. "I'd much rather be in armour." He finished the shave and put the razor away, bringing a basin of water and a towel to his brother.

"Nervous?" He waited while Edvar towelled his face, then passed him a glass of wine.

"No," replied Edvar, drinking deeply. "Do you think I should be?"

"I would be." Ingvar shrugged, pouring himself a glass. "Standing up in front of everyone in these stupid dresses." He plucked up the robe in mock frustration. "I'd be terrified. I think I'd rather march to battle."

Edvar paused, looking up at his younger brother over the top of his wine glass. "It is everything I want, brother," he said seriously.

Ingvar stood, nodding, and rested a hand on his brother's shoulder.

"It will be worth all the sacrifice."

"I'm happy for you," Ingvar said, and meant it. "Now," he went on, putting down his glass and clapping his hands together, "I have to leave you. I have a job to do." Edvar nodded wearily as Ingvar swept purposefully from the room. Focused on the task ahead, Ingvar did not stop to wonder what sacrifice Edvar was talking about.

※

The bride's maid pulled the broad, white silken belt tight around Olya's waist and folded the ends into an elaborate knot in the small of her back. Traditionally, the bride's closest friend would act as her handmaid for the day, but Olya's friends were mostly knights or warriors and nearly all of them were men. The obvious solution had been to give her usual maid and family servant, Cahola, the privilege. Cahola's family had served the Ferras household for generations and the two, of similar age, had always been close.

Satisfied with the knot, Cahola moved around to check Olya's wedding dress from the front. Olya forced herself to stand still and to be patient with the pulling and fussing, aware of her mother, Jerane, looking on from a seat in the corner.

"You are beautiful, and elegant, my dear," she said. She was elderly, white-haired, and somewhat frail, but was radiating delight. "I always feared I would never see the day my precious daughter was wed. We are so proud!" She had said repeatedly that she approved of the match with Edvar Darelle, especially on the conditions that had been arranged.

Olya turned this way and that, showing the dress to her mother but feeling awkward in the stiff and elaborate silk. She tried to force a placid smile onto her face as her mother tilted her head to admire the dress.

"I would rather be wearing mail," she said, aware as the words left her lips that they sounded ungrateful and childish. The dress had cost a small fortune. It was made of several layers of thin silk, which were all elaborately embroidered. These were wrapped in a traditional way and tied in place, leaving a series of visible diagonal overlaps, forming a wide triangle at the chest and at the hem.

The final layer was thicker and made from bright red fabric embroidered with gold thread. It was wide at the shoulders and open in a wide 'V' at the throat to expose the pale layers of white silk underneath. It tapered to a narrow waist which was bound symbolically with a wide strip of white to represent the purity of the new marriage. Olya felt like she was wearing a tapestry.

The door flew open. All three women's heads snapped around, and Olya dropped into a fighting crouch. The dress felt awkwardly snug across her hips.

"This is a kidnap!"

Ingvar had burst into the room with five other men, a mix of household warriors and servants. He approached Olya. "Prepare to be abducted, lady!"

One of Ingvar's household warriors, Taril, a tall gangling man with curly black hair, lunged at Olya. He reached out quickly and grabbed her by the wrist. She reacted without thinking, rolling her own wrist around to escape his grasp. She grabbed his thumb and twisted, locking his arm and using it to force him backwards. Off balance, he tripped and fell heavily into the hearth. He howled with pain, sitting in the cinders and ashes, clutching his hand.

"She broke my thumb!" he wailed indignantly. His eyes bulged in pain, the bright white contrasting against the dark skin of his face. Ingvar stepped forward, anxious that no one else got hurt.

"Olya, Olya!" He held his hands out placatingly. "It's just a tradition!"

Olya glared at him uncertainly, then after a moment relaxed and nodded.

"Thank you," he said, sighing with relief. "Follow me. We won't take you far!"

The wedding-day kidnap had been a local tradition for generations. The bride would be abducted by a group of men led by the groomsman and would be hidden somewhere. The bride's-man would have to hunt her down, ritualistically 'defeat' the kidnappers, and escort the bride to the family shrine for the wedding ceremony.

"Time for my brother to prove his devotion," muttered Ingvar as he strode across the grounds, Olya dragging her feet behind. "You know I did not invent this tradition?" he added, in response to her muttering and eye-rolling. "It's as old as the hills, from when families used to be at each other's throats all the time!"

The wedding-day kidnap dated from a time of turbulence and inter-family warfare in Buren, when weddings were often political tools and took place before they were approved completely by both sides. The tradition had come to show that love conquers all barriers, but like many traditions, the true origin had been largely forgotten.

So, as Edvar dashed around the grounds in an exaggerated show of searching for Olya, the gathering guests cheered him on and thrust flagons of local wine into his hand, which he was obliged to drink. He was hot, perspiring and looked slightly dizzy by the time he found Olya behind a stand of young cypress trees, with one of Ingvar's hands resting gingerly on her arm. She failed to stifle a laugh at his bedraggled appearance, and he took her hand and led her briskly to the family shrine.

Smiles faltered on faces and laughter died away as the couple stood before the shrine and the guests assembled around them in a rough circle. This part of the wedding day was no less steeped in tradition, but the saying of words before the family ancestors was serious, sombre, and a crucial part of the legal process of a Bureno marriage.

They stood in silence, facing one another and surrounded by the memorials of the family's dead, the tall, pale stones carefully inscribed with names and dates. In the background, the family shrine-house loomed: a model of the family manor in pure white polished stone, standing higher than a man. The wedding vows would therefore be witnessed not only by the living but also by the noble dead.

In his next duty as groomsman, Ingvar stepped forward to stand at one side of the couple, his naked longsword held point downward in his sweaty hands. He was to protect the couple from anyone who would disrupt the ceremony. However, there had been plenty of times in history when the couple had required coercion from a blade at their ribs to say the words. Ingvar was grateful this was not the case today. He looked up at Edvar and Olya and could see the warmth and affection they had for each other as they gazed into each other's eyes.

The couple held bundles of green rushes laced with myrtle flowers, to signify prosperity and fortune. The pungent, sweet fragrance of myrtle filled Ingvar's nostrils. In later days, that smell would fill him with dread and anger, a reminder of how the tide of fortune could turn. Today, though, it filled him with calm and contentment.

Next, Count Rauf Crowmer stepped forward. It was the duty of the highest ranked noble in attendance to be the First Witness, to listen to the couple as they said the words that would bind them in marriage. He stood directly opposite

Ingvar, forming a small square with Edvar and Omar as the other corners.

As Crowmer took his place, Ingvar glanced across the circle to where his father, Omar, stood. As their eyes met, he found an unreadable expression on his father's face, and Ingvar thought back to Crowmer's last visit to the Darelle estate.

Crowmer and Omar had been seen arguing, but out of earshot of everyone else, leading the Count to leave in a hurry. His frustration and annoyance had been plain. Omar had stood on the threshold of the house, his hands on his hips. Ingvar and Olya had moved to stand beside him.

"That man…" muttered Omar, then he glanced at Olya, biting off the rest of his sentence.

"By your leave," said Olya, looking awkwardly between Ingvar and his father, "I should also take to the road. I have news to share with my parents." Her face broke into a smile at the words, a contrast to Omar's scowl, and she hurried off towards the stables. A moment later, Edvar brushed past Ingvar and followed.

They watched uncomfortably as Edvar bade his new betrothed farewell. He bowed low before her, touching his hand to his heart, as her face coloured. Though, he was unable to keep his face solemn as he straightened, and they both laughed nervously before Olya mounted and rode away. She let her soldiers ride on ahead so she could turn and look back at Edvar as she rode slowly down the track.

Edvar turned away only once Olya had vanished from view around a corner, walking slowly back to the house. The three of them had filed into the house in silence, Edvar grinning, Omar brooding and Ingvar unsure how to feel. Edvar fetched a flask of wine and poured them each a glass. Omar grunted his thanks before taking a deep drink. The brothers stayed quiet, knowing that their father would talk when he was ready.

"Crowmer," he said, after a long silence, "offered to buy my estate."

Ingvar and Edvar opened their mouths in surprise.

"It has been coming for a while. I am not surprised," continued Omar. "The man's ambition is limitless."

"Ever since he fought under my command, years ago, he has always been looking upwards. Becoming a knight was not enough. He needed more. He needed to command, to have power. The previous Count was considered weak. He had suffered defeats and his vassal knights muttered about his lack of leadership. Crowmer saw the opportunity, gained the Duke's ear, and managed to take credit for a string of victories. Our victories. But when the old Count was deposed, it was Crowmer who took his place.

"Now he covets the Earldom. He would never admit to it, but I know him. Maurer weakens, and Crowmer works tirelessly to undermine him and increase his own influence and power. Edvar has seen it, have you not?" Omar glanced across at his eldest son, who nodded.

"I suspected it was so," Edvar confirmed. "I mentioned it last night to judge his reaction. I fear you are correct, Father."

"I know I am," continued Omar, "and I worry about what he will do next. To obtain the power he needs to oust Earl Maurer, he must have more land, more warriors, and more wealth, all under his direct control. That is why he wants to buy us out. It would increase his standing. He will have made the same offer to others too. I am certain of it. Most will refuse, as I did. What else do I have? But that will not stop him. He will already be plotting, mark my words." He paused, leaning forward to take a deep draught of wine.

"Is it not worth considering what we could stand to gain?" suggested Edvar tentatively. His face fell as Omar glared at him.

"Any gain will be granted on his terms, Edvar." Omar shook his head. "No, he is not to be trusted. I just worry about what he will do next."

Now, Ingvar stood before Crowmer again. His face was unreadable as Edvar and Olya spoke the words of the marriage contract. Speaking these solemn words before witnesses bound them by law.

These laws were enshrined in the customs of Buren and set out how all property, wealth and titles would be shared between husband and wife. Breaking any of the laws of marriage was a serious crime in Bureno law, and the court would usually grant nearly everything to the wronged party in a dispute, leaving the other penniless or even imprisoned. Marriage was taken very seriously in Buren.

It was clear none of this was a current worry for Olya and Edvar, though. Both were beaming with happiness as the formal ceremony concluded, and the circle of friends and family closed in to congratulate the newly married couple. Plaited crowns of green fronds and myrtle, like the bouquets, were placed on their heads. Then they were lifted, shoulder-high, and carried back to the manor house as the crowd sang to them, clapping hands and stamping feet vigorously.

Ingvar was able to return his sword to its scabbard, but had to hurry ahead of the crowd to open up the doors to the house, and to welcome the guests. Olya's parents came to stand beside him, both smiling broadly, so Ingvar positioned himself between them and the crowd streaming inside.

"It's wonderful!" Jerane Ferras exclaimed as Ingvar gently shepherded her and her husband, Tasivus, away from the flow of guests into the hall. They were both elderly and he did not want them to be knocked over in the rush.

Taril hobbled past at the end of the line, cradling his injured hand. "Do you think wine is good medicine for a broken thumb?" he asked Ingvar, his face serious. Ingvar could not help but laugh. The mood of the other guests was already raucous and gleeful.

The formal part of the wedding was complete and now the celebration could begin.

CHAPTER SEVEN

"This is an outrage!"

Omar Darelle was on his feet, his wine glass upset on the table in his haste to stand. The ensuing silence around the room was such that the soft sound of the wine dripping onto the flagstone floor could be heard clearly.

The wedding feast had been extravagant. The Ferras family were known for their wealth and had provided a range of delicacies. Empty flasks of locally made wine littered the surfaces, as well as the floor, and the army of serving staff moved around the tables with a seemingly endless supply of full ones. Many of the guests were red-faced by the time Count Crowmer had risen and asked for order for the speeches.

First spoke the bride. Olya was gracious and confident, thanking all the guests for coming, paying tribute to her parents and lastly complimenting her new husband.

Next, Edvar stood. He was witty and charming as he complimented his beautiful new wife and toasted their future together. The guests laughed merrily and cheered Edvar as he sat, knowing what awaited next. The last of the traditional speeches was made by the father of the bride.

Tasivus Ferras stood, somewhat unsteadily, and made a long rambling speech in his reedy, quavering voice. Everyone's attention wandered back to their wine cups as he told yet another story about Olya's scrapes as a little girl. Eventually, after what seemed like an age, he wound to a close and toasted the new husband and wife.

As he sat, the guests had assumed the speeches were over at last, and that they could return to making merry. However, before they could do much more than lift a glass, Count Crowmer had risen from his seat.

"I just wanted to say a few words," he said, his powerful voice silencing the hall. "As the Count of this region, seeing these two noble families united as one gives me great joy." He paused, hawkish eyes scanning the room. Ingvar thought that there was a strange expression on his face, part victorious, part trepidation.

"Edvar and Olya have an important announcement," he continued, briskly, "and they have asked me to make it on their behalf." He paused, then cleared his throat. His next words tumbled out in a rush. "The Ferras family have invited Edvar to join them living here, and they will make the Ferras manor house their married home."

Muttering rose instantly from around the room and all Ingvar could do was gape in surprise. Edvar was leaving them?

"Furthermore," Crowmer went on, raising his voice above the sudden noise, "Edvar has been invited to take on the name of Ferras with the marriage. An honour which he has chosen to accept."

This was the point at which Omar had risen from his seat in fury. Edvar was crucial in the profitable running of the Darelle estate. Everyone knew that. With him gone, it would be almost impossible to keep the farm running. The name change, although not without precedent in noble marriages, was a deliberate political move orchestrated by Crowmer. It had robbed Omar of an heir and given one to the Ferras family, who only had one female child.

"This is an absolute outrage!" repeated Omar into the uncomfortable silence. "You cannot do this without the permission of both families!"

"The permission was given by Edvar Darelle." Crowmer motioned towards Ingvar's brother, who looked down at the table. "Now Edvar Ferras, of course. None of this is against his will."

"It is against my will!" responded Omar. "And I am the head of this family. I wish to make a formal objection!"

Crowmer smiled in satisfaction. It was an unnerving sight.

"Objections can be made," he replied, his voice smooth as silk, "and settled by a duel. As the objecting party, you may duel either of the parties to the marriage contract."

There was silence as Crowmer paused. Omar clenched his fists in frustration.

"So, who would you choose to duel? Your son or your daughter-in-law?"

Ingvar looked up at his father. The expression of shock and rage was fading to one of hopeless resignation. He glanced up at the top table where Edvar and Olya were clutching each other's hands, faces downcast.

"Of course"—Crowmer had not finished talking, self-satisfaction now evident in his voice—"if you would not duel either of the parties to the contract, you could request to duel the ranking noble of the region instead." He smiled grimly. "Which would, of course, be me."

Ingvar could almost hear his father's teeth grinding in frustration from several feet away. Of course, Omar would not duel his own son or daughter-in-law. Even if he were younger, he would stand no chance against Olya in any case, and as for duelling against Crowmer…

The Count had been his and Olya's sword teacher when they were young. He had been a hard and merciless taskmaster but had taught them everything they knew about the art of the sword. He was a good swordsman and had cultivated a reputation for skill-at-arms and valour in battle, although Ingvar had never seen him fight on the front line.

However, if it came to a duel, he had an irresistible weapon. The laws allowed for the nomination of a representative, and Crowmer would always nominate Sir Sighra Vaikhari. The tall, dark elf was the best duellist in the land. He had never lost.

"You two"—Omar nodded to Edvar and Olya—"should have a long and happy marriage. I wish you well." He turned to glare at Crowmer. "However, I consider my family insulted and I must leave. Come, Ingvar."

Ingvar followed his mother and father out of the hall. He tried to aim a conciliatory look at Olya but failed to catch her eye. Once outside, Omar sent servants off to fetch their horses. Ingvar's guts were churning with a mix of emotions. He felt the same frustration and rage as his father at the insult to their family, but was also worried for Edvar and Olya. He could well imagine their hurt and confusion. He hoped it had not ruined their day.

They waited for their horses to be fetched from the stables, then mounted quickly, eager to be gone. As Ingvar kicked his heels against his gelding's flanks, he turned his head for one last look back at the Ferras manor house.

Ammie. Ammie was there.

It felt like a long time ago that she had ridden with them out to the Ferras estate. When Crowmer had decided she should be married to one of the Ferras servants, Ingvar's parents had not been able to defy his wishes. And with all the drama of the day, Ingvar had almost forgotten she was there.

But as Ingvar followed his parents away from the house, still upset and angry, he saw Ammie at her own wedding ceremony. The formal ceremony was taking place at the Ferras family shrine, as it had for Edvar and Olya.

There were no guests for this wedding, though, and the family steward was holding the sword as groomsman. Ingvar did not recognise the hard-faced woman standing as First Witness, but she was probably an elder from a local village, someone with high standing in the community. All he could see of Ammie's husband-to-be was the back of his head, his long dark hair tied up at the back of his skull. From his height and stature, he was clearly an elf.

What must it be like to be married as a servant, with no choice in the matter? Servants who resisted their employer's wishes were judged harshly, and often ended up as outcasts from society. His heart lurched at the thought.

At that moment, Ammie glanced over in his direction. Their eyes met. Even at this distance, Ingvar could feel the force of her gaze and thought he could read sadness in her sharp blue eyes. Perhaps he imagined it, and as she turned back to her new husband and the ongoing ceremony, he knew he was powerless, anyway. He flicked the reins and turned to ride away without a backward glance.

The ride back south to their estate was sullen and mostly silent. It was late evening, but the sun still burned down, bright in Ingvar's right eye as it slowly descended towards the horizon.

All about them was land owned by the Ferras family. Rich land, with good grazing in the valleys, the shallow-sloped hillsides above cut into sun-baked terraces laden with crops. Ingvar's horse's hooves resounded in the still evening air as they crossed a small wooden bridge, spanning one of the many streams that kept this land green and fertile.

He glanced back, the manor house barely visible where it nestled between two low hills, and thought of Ammie. His imagination painted a detailed and vivid picture. He rode homewards, slowly and uncomfortably, but his mind's eye could see her being led across the grounds by her new husband.

The sun dropped still further, a golden crown on the peaks of the distant mountains. As soft golden light slanted across the hillsides, Ingvar imagined the same light filling the house that Ammie now shared with the dark-haired elf. Their two bodies would be bathed in it as they embraced.

Ingvar could see their own estate in the distance now, lights flickering in the windows of the house as the sky darkened and stars emerged overhead. The candlelight would gleam on Ammie's violet-tinted skin, her eyes closed as her lips pressed against her husband's. Ingvar closed his own eyes and shook his head, trying to clear the image from his mind. When he opened them again, his face was bathed in soft light from within his house. The door was open, and Ammie's parents were there to take their horses and welcome them home.

He trudged up the stairs in a daze, eyes open but thoughts turned inward. He cast his formal robe off and dropped it unceremoniously on the aged wooden floorboards. As the soft cloth crumpled into a heap, he thought about Ammie's wedding dress – simple but elegant. It, too, would be cast to the floor as husband and wife lay down in their bed. The last thought he had before drifting off into a restless sleep was to wonder whether she was thinking of him at all.

CHAPTER EIGHT

The news, when it came, had shocked them all.

It was harvest time, the temperatures dropping as autumn rolled towards winter. Darker clouds could be seen gathering around the summits of the distant mountains to the north, and the Darelle estate was bustling.

As he did annually, Omar had hired as many extra hands as he could afford to round up the animals and to cut and gather the crops. As always, however many hands he hired, there were never quite enough.

Ingvar's hands were sore and blistered from the handles of scythes and reaping hooks, rather than from gripping a sword hilt. He had swapped sparring and drilling for lifting sacks and hefting bales. What with the family being forced into a more frugal diet in addition to Ingvar's labouring around the farm, his excess flesh had melted away to be replaced with muscles that were not there previously.

"Farming must agree with you," commented his mother as she watched him work. It was true that he had never been so fit, but he would have enjoyed it more if he was not also constantly exhausted and regularly hungry.

It was a wagon driver delivering supplies from the south that had brought the news. The Darelle lands were mostly given over to grazing for horses and the growing of wheat, so Omar traded for barrels of salted meat and other essentials to add to their winter stores.

Edvar had taken most of the horse stock with him when he had moved permanently to the Ferras estate, and Omar had not yet been able to buy in a new herd of sheep to put on the land.

The day Edvar had returned had been difficult for everyone. He had travelled from the Ferras estate to collect his things and to round up his horses for the move north. His father had pressed him repeatedly about the move and the name change. Edvar was clearly upset about it too but would not say a word against his new wife, whom he clearly already loved deeply.

"I thought you already knew," he had said again and again. "I thought it had all been agreed." It seemed that Crowmer had surprised everyone.

The loss of the horses had been another unwelcome surprise, although really it made a lot of sense. Edvar truly owned the herd, and even though the land belonged to his father, it was only Edvar that really had the skill and knowledge of their upkeep. It was another benefit to the Ferras family, a valuable one, and another loss of income for the Darelles.

That was not the worst news of the season, though. That surprise had come from the mouth of the wagoner, while Ingvar was helping unload the barrels from his flat-bedded cart.

"You hear about Frankess?" he had asked them, wiping sweat from his brow and leaning against the tall rear wheel of the wagon. Autumn was coming in, despite the lingering warmth, and the leaves of the surrounding maples and oaks were already edged with golds and reds.

"Frankess?" Omar was nearby and hurried over at the mention of his old friend's name. "What has happened? Is he well?"

"You've not heard?" The trader sucked a breath through his teeth. "He's started something, all right. Going to be some big trouble between him and Crowmer!"

"What? No!" Omar gasped. "I saw him but two weeks ago. He spoke no word of this!"

"Here's what happened." The trader leaned forward and told the tale with considerable glee. After his first few words, Omar staggered slightly and sat down heavily on an upturned barrel.

According to the story, Count Crowmer had visited Sir Frankess at his estate. Frankess had no children and was not young, and so the two had talked around the issue of who would take the land when he had gone. Crowmer had offered to buy the land, letting Frankess live there as tenant. The way the trader told it, this was a generous gesture by Crowmer, but Frankess took the offer as an insult and had reacted furiously.

He had ordered Crowmer off his land, forbidding him to return. Worse was to come, as the trader went on to describe with relish. Frankess sent his small household garrison, along with a larger number of mercenary soldiers, to guard the border between his land and Crowmer's. The situation was tense. Tempers flared.

"Some are saying it was Crowmer's lot that attacked first," said the trader casually, "trying to provoke Frankess, you know? Might have been the other way around, though. Either way, there was fighting and a few dead."

Each side blamed the other, of course, and Frankess asserted that Crowmer had offended his honour and had been the one to attack first. He declared a Just War, to settle the matter. Some whispered that Frankess still harboured a lust for power and hoped to supplant Crowmer.

"A Just War…" muttered Omar. "Crowmer isn't likely to apologise or negotiate. And he won't bother trying to pay Frankess off. Honour can make men idiots!"

"Would Crowmer offer a duel?" asked Ingvar.

"Frankess would be a fool to accept!" Omar shook his head. "It could be war."

"I am not sure I believe it…" continued Omar, after several moments of silence. "I can believe that snake Crowmer would make a grab for Frankess's land, but as for Frankess marching? No. It cannot be."

Ingvar knew his father must have been deeply dismayed by the news, despite his disbelief. However much Crowmer's ambition and political manoeuvring irked him, he was always careful to rarely voice his criticisms of the Count openly.

"Bloke who told me it swore blind, he did!" replied the trader, starting to load up his wagon with the barrels of olives and sacks of unthreshed grain that were his payment. "The news is all over the lowlands, all the way south to the Crown."

"What should we do?" asked Ingvar, as the trader lashed down the last of the barrels and made ready to leave. "Who would we stand with?"

"We do nothing," said Omar, standing and grasping the barrel, "because none of this is true. Crowmer is playing games, so we wait for the truth to come out." He turned and carried the barrel into the house.

Ingvar got to work, moving the rest of the delivery, taking it through the main hall and into the kitchens. A small cellar had been dug beneath the kitchen and it was blessedly cool down there. The heat of the day hit Ingvar like a hammer each time he went back out through the main door.

He considered his father's words. 'None of this is true.' Ingvar struggled to believe it. He could very much believe that Crowmer would be trying to turn the situation to his advantage, but it was rare for a story to spread so widely without a grain of truth.

So, what was the truth in this case? That Crowmer had tried to buy Frankess out? That was certainly plausible. That Frankess had refused and had taken offence? Also very believable. That Frankess had declared war and had marched on Crowmer? That was where Ingvar struggled to accept the story.

Nevertheless, it seemed inevitable that there would be conflict. They might be called upon to choose a side. He would expect that his father's allegiance would be to his old friend Frankess. If so, it would set them against Crowmer. The Count would naturally be able to call on a great number of local nobles to join his side and fight for his cause.

There would be sense in pledging loyalty to the man. His banner was on the rise, and knights would follow a strong lord with the promise of glory, gold and land. Ingvar recalled

Olya's words, that she could see the worth in following where he led. It left a sour taste, but he had to admit the wisdom.

Ingvar's stomach gave a sudden lurch as he realised that Olya would almost certainly answer if Crowmer called. Olya had no greater affection for Crowmer than he did, but she had always been extremely loyal. Ingvar considered what it would be like to line up against Olya in battle, and he had to stop to rub a hand across his face. It would not come to that. There would be no war, and even if there was, the Darelles could – hopefully – stay neutral.

But Crowmer came to their estate the next morning.

Ingvar and his father had stayed up late into the night talking. Omar had fetched a large flask of wine from the cellar, poured them each a generous glass, and kept topping each up until the flask was empty. The candles burned low, casting flickering shadows of the two men against the square-cut stones of the walls.

They had discussed the harvest, with some optimism for the winter, although they both agreed there would be times when they would need to tighten their belts. After they had drunk half of the wine flask, though, Ingvar could hold his worries in no longer and asked his father again what they would do about the situation with Frankess.

"We need do nothing," said Omar once more, gesturing angrily with his glass. "The story is a falsehood. This is just Crowmer selling a workhorse as a warhorse, you mark my words."

"But," insisted Ingvar, "what if the stories are based on some truth? If there is to be war, we would have to choose a side. Who do we support?"

Omar was silent as he considered his son's words.

"Do we abandon Frankess, your oldest friend?" Ingvar continued. "Or do we stand against Crowmer? In either case, we stand to gain little and could lose much."

There was silence. Omar took a long draught of wine.

In truth, Ingvar hoped that his father would decide to ally with Crowmer. He despised the thought, but could see that it was the path of wisdom. The path of safety. The silence stretched.

"Then we stand aside," he said decisively, and would say no more on the subject.

Ingvar hoped his father was right, but was still worrying when he collapsed into his bed, as the whole room seemed to spin.

The next thing he knew, a sharp voice was calling out urgently from somewhere nearby. He opened one eye. Morning light was streaming into his room through a crack in the shutters. He opened both eyes, blinking as though they were full of grit, trying to scrape the fur off his tongue with his teeth.

The voice rang out again, loud and insistent. "Omar! Ingvar!" It was his mother's voice, filled with worry. "Come down, quickly!"

Ingvar pulled on a robe and hurried down the stairs to the hall. He met his father on the way, who looked as haggard as Ingvar felt. Etsel was standing by the front door, anxiety clear in her bearing as she shaded her eyes against the morning sun with one hand. Omar squeezed past and Ingvar followed close behind, blinking owlishly in the bright daylight. They both stopped sharply.

Before them was a company of mounted soldiers, armed and clad in scale coats. At their head was Count Crowmer, his armour gleaming like burnished silver in the bright sunshine, his white cloak draping grandly over his fine stallion's powerful flanks. The wind had changed, coming from the north. Cool air borne from the distant mountains hit Ingvar's skin like a slap from an armoured glove.

"My Count," said Omar, quickest to recover from the surprise and having the presence of mind to bow his head. "It is our pleasure to welcome you."

"Thank you, Sir Darelle." Crowmer's cold voice cut in. "I fear that I must be the bearer of unhappy news." He dismounted, handing his riding gloves up to his nearest mounted knight. He strode up to Omar and placed a hand on his shoulder, leaning down to look at him closely. "Rebellion is mounted against me. Order is threatened. I must know who I can count on to stand beside me."

"I have ever been loyal," replied Omar.

"Indeed." Crowmer took a step backwards. "So it has seemed. And yet, now is the time where that loyalty will be tested."

There was a pause, and Ingvar looked from one man to the other. One, tall, proud and lordly, and the other, short, broad and earthy.

Crowmer broke the silence abruptly. "The leader of the rebellion is Sir Frankess." There was another pause as the Count glared down at Ingvar's father. "I see this news comes as no surprise to you, Sir Darelle. Are you in league with the rebel Sir Frankess?"

Omar's head snapped up.

"My Count," he replied with urgency, "of course I am not. I would not dream of such treachery!"

"So, will you send Ingvar and your household garrison to aid me in crushing this rebellion?"

There was a much longer pause, the silence stretching out awkwardly as the wind sighed. Omar straightened, his hands at his sides and his thumbs hooked into his belt. He blinked slowly, setting his jaw, then spoke.

"My Count, I cannot in good honour draw blade against Sir Frankess. He is my oldest friend and my comrade of many battles. House Darelle must stand aside in this conflict."

Ingvar sighed inwardly, although he was not surprised.

Count Crowmer took one step closer to Omar. He was a tall man and Omar was not. As Omar stooped so Crowmer seemed to grow in stature, a tall, stern figure looming over the dark shape of Ingvar's father.

"You must choose, Omar," he said. "You can remain my friend and ally, or you can become my enemy. Remember that as Count I act with the authority of the High King. With me or against me? Which will it be?"

The silence grew. Ingvar forced himself to press his hands to his sides and away from where his sword hilt would have hung. Omar grimaced, looking up towards the sun, then back towards the Count.

"I remain loyal to you and the crown," he said, "but I will not set my house against Frankess. I cannot. House Darelle stands aside."

Crowmer shook his head slowly. "Very well," he said. "In a way, I admire your stubbornness. Nevertheless, I consider this an act of treachery, but it must wait while open rebellion is dealt with. This matter is not concluded, Sir Darelle." He mounted and led his troops away from the house, without a backward glance.

Ingvar glanced at his father, standing at the threshold of his own home but already diminished, shrunken and frail, like a man of straw. It would occur to Ingvar later, much later, that even at that moment his father knew the gravity of the decision he had just made.

CHAPTER NINE

It felt like autumn's last gasp. The daytime sky was crystalline blue, and sunshine streamed down with a warming touch. There was a cold bite to the north-easterly wind, though, and in the distance, dark clouds were gathering ominously. They spurred Ingvar to work faster, trying to get the house and estate ready for winter.

As dusk neared, and the sun was tinted orange as it hovered over the high and distant peaks of northern Timmers, Ingvar was in the saddle. He rode along next to his father, searching for something to say. Nothing occurred. His father was in a foul mood and Ingvar did not want to give him any reason to snap.

Ingvar had been standing at the water trough, scrubbing the worst of the day's dirt from his hands, when his father's head appeared out of the back door of the house.

"Get dressed!" he had snapped. "We're riding into the village. I need news, and a drink wouldn't hurt, either." Ingvar hurried to change out of his work clothes and quickly saddled their horses. Soon, they were riding towards the nearest village as dusk crept over the land around them.

It was less than an hour's easy ride south, but the journey stretched out uncomfortably in the brooding silence.

The Darelle household had been tense since Count Crowmer's last visit. Omar had initially waved the issue away, refusing to discuss it and instead throwing himself into working around the farm. In the evenings, however, he would be taciturn and withdrawn, and Ingvar noticed that he was rarely without a flask of wine. In the mornings, he rose late with bloodshot eyes and a short temper.

"Please talk to me, husband!"

Ingvar had taken one step through the front door but froze when he had heard his mother's raised voice coming from the kitchen.

"What is there to talk about?" His father's voice was thick with wine. "We can and should do nothing."

"I can't just wait!" Etsel sobbed. "Your Count declared you a traitor! Whether or not it is true, there will be consequences, unless you take action."

"Action?"

"Swallow your pride." Etsel's voice was quieter. Ingvar strained to hear. "Go to Crowmer and apologise. Swear your loyalty—"

"I will not!" Omar erupted. "What I have done was right and I will not kneel to that man!"

Footsteps sounded; his father was returning to the main hall. Ingvar slipped out of the door quietly, not wanting his parents to know they had been overheard.

From then on, Ingvar and Etsel had tiptoed around Omar, not wanting to add to his worries or risk his wrath if they said the wrong thing. It seemed his father had aged several years in the last few weeks.

Their horses' hooves crunched crisply on the hard-packed dirt of the road as the first flickering lights of the village appeared up ahead.

Locton had sprung up where the road crossed a small, fast-flowing river. It had quickly become a local centre for craft and small industry. Potters, dyers, tanners and various other traders worked out of Locton, their shopfronts on the main road to catch passing trade.

Many of the Darelle family soldiers made their homes here, warfare being only a part-time trade while the land was mostly at peace. It was also the location of the nearest inn to the Darelle estate.

Omar led Ingvar off the main street and into the forecourt before the inn. Hitching rails beneath long porches to either side of the forecourt provided space for many horses. They tied up the horses and strolled into the inn. It was timber built, like most of the village houses, in a single storey roofed with red clay tiles.

They stepped up a short flight of wooden stairs onto a veranda the width of the building, then through double doors, which were thrown wide open. To either side, wide windows opened into the inn's well-lit interior, the shutters folded away against the walls.

As they entered, the warmth from the central hearth hit them instantly, a stark contrast to the growing chill outside. There was a gentle hum of conversation, the inn busy but not full. Most sat around tables, with flagons of dark full-wine on those occupied by the richer customers, while pale, watered half-wine slaked the thirst of the less wealthy.

Omar took a seat, Ingvar sitting next to him with his back to the hearth, and he waved to the innkeeper. The woman caught Omar's eye and broke off from her conversation with a group standing at the bar. Moments later, she appeared at Omar's elbow with two clay cups and a flask of wine.

"Good evening to you, Sir Darelle." She deftly placed the two cups on the table between them, and poured both a generous measure. "It's a pleasure to have your custom once more." She set the flask down but remained hovering near the table, seeming to sense that Omar would have questions.

She was a tall, sturdy woman with auburn hair drawn into a bun on the top of her head. There were stories of misbehaving customers in her inn being given extremely short shrift, to the extent that her reputation meant there was rarely trouble in her establishment.

"And to you, Gwenhild," Omar replied. He took a sip of wine. "Any news?" he asked. "News of Frankess? Are the stories true?"

"Well," she said, leaning forward and lowering her voice. "You may know better than me, but the talk is all of Frankess's rebellion. Some say he's been itching to raise trouble with Crowmer, thinks he'll profit from it. Others say that it was Crowmer's doing. He put Frankess in a position where a Just War was his only option. It was that or be dishonoured."

"And what say you?" Omar leaned towards Gwenhild. "Who speaks the truth?"

Gwenhild pursed her lips, eyes flicking towards the ceiling momentarily as she thought. "It would be unlike Frankess to start something," she replied. "I can't see that. But it would be very like Frankess to refuse to let something go. I am also sure that our glorious Count Crowmer was beyond reproach, even if Frankess felt needled into a reaction." She smirked slightly at this and Omar rolled his eyes.

"And House Darelle?" she asked. "You stayed loyal to Frankess and stood aside?"

"Of course," Omar replied gruffly. "What are we without loyalty to our allies?"

"Quite right, sir," said Gwenhild, nodding. "Quite right. Your loyalty to Frankess does you credit."

"Have they met on the field yet?" asked Ingvar, who had been listening intently. "I heard there was a skirmish."

"That's right," Gwenhild replied. "Folk said that they were both sides of the border, eyeballing each other, but a few hotheads charged at each other and there was blood. Last I heard, they were forming lines. A bunch came through here a few days ago on their way to join up with Crowmer."

They talked with Gwenhild for a while longer, but there was no more news and no firm conclusions to be drawn. Omar was fretting over whether there would be a battle, or whether Frankess would withdraw his Just War. Both he and Ingvar agreed that was the only way fighting would be avoided. Frankess was stubborn and slow to calm once offended. But would he really risk his and his soldiers' lives for his hurt honour?

"There is more to this than we know," said Omar, sipping his wine. "I feel that the truth is being hidden. I wish I could know what is really happening."

At that moment, there was a flurry of activity outside. Ingvar turned to see a host of riders in the inn's open courtyard hurriedly dismounting.

"He is here?" came a female voice from outside. "You saw him coming in?"

Boots sounded on the wooden steps and then Olya was framed by the wide doorway. She was armed and armoured, her longsword at her waist and her face flushed as if she had been riding hard. Her eyes were blackened as if for battle. She strode over, pulling off her riding gloves and tucking them into her belt.

"I come with tidings for Sir Darelle," said Olya, her face grave. "I was told I could find you here."

Omar stood as she approached the table. He had his head held high, both hands tucked behind his back. His chin was raised proudly, defiantly, but Ingvar could sense his tension.

"The rebellion against Count Crowmer has been put down," she continued. There was a pause, as Olya bit her lip as she tried to frame the words. "And Sir Frankess has been killed."

Ingvar closed his eyes as Omar's chin dropped towards his chest.

"I'm sorry."

After a long, silent moment, Ingvar recovered his composure and gestured for Olya to join them at the table. Omar silently slumped back into his seat, eyes down. Ingvar pushed a cup across the table and Olya took a drink before telling them how Frankess's men had marched towards Crowmer's borders, but were opposed by a much larger force. Crowmer had roused many other local knights, and Frankess's soldiers and mercenaries had been badly outnumbered.

"At the end," she said, her voice quiet, "he charged his men into our lines. It was madness. His own mercenaries turned and fled after the first clash of blades. And Frankess…" She cast her eyes down. "Frankess died on Count Crowmer's own blade. I am sorry."

Ingvar could not be sure, but it seemed as if Olya was trying to avoid his gaze as she recounted the story. He had noticed no injuries among her soldiers, no signs of damage to their armour.

She went on to say that Crowmer had immediately confiscated Frankess's land as reparation for the rebellion, pardoning those of his men who had surrendered, adding them to his own garrison.

"We have ridden far and fast this afternoon," said Olya, "to bring this news to you. We first went to your manor but

Lady Darelle told me you were here, so we turned around and rode back swiftly. I thought you needed to know."

Omar gave no reply. Glancing around, Ingvar noticed that all eyes in the inn seemed to be on them, either subtly or openly. Many went to the inn purely to get news or hear gossip. This evening was turning out to be of great value, in that regard.

"We should go." Ingvar leaned forward and hissed into his father's ear. "Many are listening, and all know you were an ally of Frankess."

Omar nodded, his eyes blank.

Ingvar looked up at Olya. "It's far from your estate, Sir Ferras. We can accommodate you and your soldiers for the night, if you would be minded to stay."

"Of course," said Olya, appearing slightly surprised. "Thank you."

It was a slightly awkward ride back. Ingvar and Omar rode in front, the brooding silence even deeper and more forbidding than on the outward journey. Olya was slightly behind, leading her troops.

Ingvar kept glancing over his shoulder to Olya and then back to his father, the weight of his father's unspoken words hanging over all of them. He knew that Omar was still furious about what had happened at the wedding, and even if he knew Olya was not to blame, seeing her again was a reminder of what he had lost.

"Welcome, my dear." Etsel greeted Olya warmly, gathering her into an embrace, heedless of the cold metal scales pressing against her skin. "Welcome to our house once more."

She clapped her hands to have food brought into the main hall, sending Olya's soldiers off to bed down in the stables. Omar continued to glower in worried, churning silence.

He rose and went off to bed before Olya had finished eating, the candle flames wavering drunkenly in time with his heavy footfalls on the stairs and floor above. Olya made her apologies and followed soon after, making her way to Edvar's old bedroom, leaving Ingvar alone with his mother.

"I worry, Mother," said Ingvar. "The news from Olya is bad for us. All know that House Darelle and House Frankess were great allies. We should have marched with Crowmer."

Etsel looked sad, reaching out to lay one of her hands on her son's.

"Your father is stubborn," she said, "but there are other words to describe him. Loyal. Principled. Steadfast. He is all these things too. To ask him to betray his friendship with

Frankess would ask him to cast aside all that makes him." She paused and rose.

"I worry too," she continued, "but I would worry more if your father ceased to be himself, stopped being true to the man he is. Be brave, Ingvar. We will see this through together."

Ingvar's mother's words came back to him the following morning. He had risen early, eager to escape the house and the awkward atmosphere that would inevitably pervade until Olya left. He had dressed quickly and strolled out into the chill early morning air, heading north towards one of the higher fields.

The farm labourers had been set to work stone picking, pulling large chunks of rock from the dark soil to make the lower fields ready for the plough in spring. The stones had been carted up the hillside and thrown into a large pile, and it was to this that Ingvar headed. Omar had hoped to stock the higher fields with sheep next season, so Ingvar planned to use the stones to build walls across the tops to keep them from wandering too far. He also felt the urge to do something mindless and physical to distract him from the tense situation at home.

He worked for a while, silently. The solitude was refreshing, a cool breeze whispering against his exposed face as feathery grey-white clouds trailed across the sky. He had walked out in a long woollen coat, but warmed up as he worked, so he unbuttoned it and laid it carefully atop the wall.

Stopping to rest, he leaned back against the wall and looked out across the countryside. The land sloped away before him, green grass dotted with the occasional stunted birch or dwarf oak. Directly south, he overlooked the manor house, the roof a red-tiled square against the surrounding green, with the larger open square of the stables just beyond.

The track wound away from the front of the house, chalky and pale, fading away in the distance where it met one of the other roads. To his right, the ground fell and rose in soft green hills beyond the borders of their estate, and far away on the eastern horizon the mountains of Timmers could just be seen as an undulating dark mass.

Movement to the south caught his eye, and he looked back towards the house. Someone had come out of the front door and was making their way up the hill towards him. Once again, he could see that familiar head of blonde hair. He leaned back against the wall and waited for Olya to reach him.

"We're just packing up to leave," she said. Ingvar had watched her from his seat in the lee of the wall as she approached. She was not wearing her usual scale armour coat or even an arming jacket, just a simple linen tunic. Ingvar was struck by how small and slight she looked. He felt torn. He was happy to see her again, as his oldest friend, and wanted to talk to her about her last battle as well as her marriage to Edvar. However, he felt that she represented part of the wedge that Crowmer was using to drive between the Darelle family and their allies. First Edvar, now Frankess. Ingvar felt that they were more and more alone, and Olya was part of all of it.

Also, he couldn't help the feeling that she was not being honest. There was something about how she had talked and behaved during this visit that made him unusually suspicious.

"I hope your journey onwards is safe," he replied, somewhat stiffly. She gave a long sigh then stepped closer, turning and sitting next to him.

"We are not enemies, Ingvar," she said softly. "I have not forgotten our friendship. Your brother is my husband. We are bonded more closely than ever."

"Yes, I know," Ingvar acknowledged. "I don't blame you for any of it. I suppose I should blame Frankess."

Olya shook her head. "Your father should have marched with Crowmer," she said. "You must know that and so must he. It would not have changed Frankess's fate, but it would have shown loyalty. Duty and loyalty must come before friendship."

"My father does not see it like that," said Ingvar, "and he has never wanted to be allied with Crowmer."

"That is not his choice to make," said Olya unsympathetically. Ingvar raised an eyebrow, and Olya tried to explain. "Crowmer is the Count. The knights owe loyalty to his rank, just like we are all loyal to the High King. We cannot choose who is worthy of fealty and who is not. It is our duty."

Ingvar was silent. Of course, she was right. As a noble family they had a great deal of status and privilege, but that was earned with service to the higher ranks.

"Besides," continued Olya, "I think you both judge Rauf Crowmer too harshly. He is not a monster. Loyalty to him is rewarded, and well."

Olya shut her mouth abruptly, as if she had said too much. Ingvar had always thought that they felt the same about Crowmer. They had often joked about the Count's pomposity and self-absorption. But, when he thought about it, Olya had always been careful to never be openly critical.

"What do you mean?" he asked, studying her face, usually so open. She pressed her lips together, and he continued. "I can see you have been well rewarded. The marriage, the possibility of an heir to your family name. All from Crowmer." Ingvar's mind worked. He knew how Crowmer plotted, always pulling strings and manipulating political currents to gain an advantage. An old family like the Ferrases – an elderly couple with no male heir, no way of continuing their family line – they must have been ripe for picking.

"He has bought you, hasn't he?" Ingvar came to a sudden conclusion. "You have indeed been richly rewarded, so the price must have been high. Gold? No, you have no need of gold. Service? Loyalty?" That was it. Olya's uncomfortable reaction showed him to be correct, and it made her comments about lack of choice stand to reason.

"We had no choice!" Olya blurted out. "My parents were getting older and soon it would be just me, alone, with all that land. How long do you think I'd keep it? Our neighbours have been looking over the borders for years, knowing I could be the last of the line and wondering when they could swoop in and grab what they wanted. Well, no more. We are protected, our land is secure, and what's more, our family name will endure." She stood up, hands on hips, glaring out at the landscape.

"I'm not ashamed," she said quietly, glancing back at Ingvar over her shoulder. "I did what needed to be done. I made sure that my allies were more powerful than my enemies. You would have done the same." She swept away.

Ingvar considered Olya's words throughout the rest of the day. He watched while she mounted up with her soldiers and rode away. As the column of riders dwindled and vanished into the distance, he told himself that he would not have made such an alliance.

His father had always impressed on him that trust and respect were crucial in any relationship, be that with friends, in a marriage or between nobles. Try as he might, he could not trust Crowmer and therefore he could not respect him. He appreciated that Olya's situation was difficult, but she had put her faith in a man who would use anyone and anything to gain an advantage for himself. Ingvar worried about how it would end.

That night, he dreamed. He was standing on a high green hill under a bright sun. He could feel the comforting patterns of the leather wrappings around his longsword's grip under his palm as he looked out across the landscape.

A figure appeared, standing across from him on another patch of high ground. He struggled to identify them but felt that they were female. Could it be Olya? Or Ammie…?

As he squinted across the hazy distance, the light faded as black clouds scudded across the blue sky, covering it as quickly as if shutters had been slammed closed. As the darkness fell, he felt an urgency to rush across to the other hill, knowing that there was danger nearby.

But, as he took a step forward to descend the hillside where the grass was now colourless, grey and lifeless, darkness swelled in the valley below. It was as if a great dam had burst, unleashing a sudden flood of dark water across the land. This was no river flow; the valley was filled with blackness as if it were a clouded sky in the deepest night.

He looked around in desperation as the landscape around him was covered by the dark void. The figure on the opposite hillside was likewise looking this way and that, recoiling in terror. Ingvar knew they were waiting for him to help. He hefted his sword. It felt flimsy in his hand, useless.

The darkness rose still further, touching the soles of his bare feet where they pressed down on the grey grass. He felt helpless. Utterly helpless.

The other figure was vanishing in the darkness. Horror and guilt filled his being as he tried to cry out, but no words came.

He took a deep breath before the wave of lightless fear rose and engulfed him.

He woke, breathing hard and staring about him into the darkness.

The next morning, they came and took his father away.

CHAPTER TEN

Ingvar did not recognise any of the soldiers.

Later, it occurred to him that it had been a strange thing to notice. At that time, though, it was all he could think of as he stood on the doorstep, looking out at the line of soldiers arrayed before the house.

He had woken early, unusually so. Autumn was turning slowly to winter and the morning light came later. Ingvar opened his eyes. His room was dimly lit by the grey light of dawn creeping through the shutters. He shut his eyes again, seeking some extra sleep, but moments later they snapped open once more.

Something was tickling the back of his mind, forcing him quickly to full awakening. He stared up at the ceiling and cursed. It was a frustrating sensation, but it seemed futile to fight it. Ingvar rolled out of his blankets reluctantly and began to dress.

He closed his bedroom door softly, mindful of his parents still asleep and his father's constant bad temper. Padding down the stairs, he stopped as he caught a flicker of movement in the main hall below. With his foot raised, halfway down the staircase, he peered into the gloom to where an indistinct figure was hunched over the hearth.

The figure straightened and Ingvar relaxed. It was Ammie's father, Hekyn. Hekyn Cowl was a solidly built, blond-haired man of average height, and tended to keep himself busy out in the grounds. Ingvar saw him infrequently and could not remember the last time he had heard the man speak.

"Morning, sir," Hekyn said, bowing his head slightly. "Just getting the fire started for you." He stepped backwards, towards the kitchen archway. His hands gripped the hem of his work smock uncomfortably.

"Thank you, Hekyn." Ingvar stepped off the staircase and down into the room. He pulled out a chair and sat, still wondering what it was that had woken him so early.

"Honour's mine, sir," said Hekyn, still hovering at the edge of the room. "Honour's mine." Ingvar reached for the jug of water, splashing a drop onto the floor for good fortune before filling a cup. He drank a deep draught, the cool water refreshing on his dry throat. As he lowered the cup, he noticed that Hekyn was still there, mouth twitching and a look of indecision on his face.

"Sir," he began, but paused as if uncertain how to continue.

"Yes? What is it, Hekyn?"

"It's just—" Hekyn licked his lips. "Have you heard from our Ammie?" he asked nervously, words tumbling out in a rush. "We never even met the elf she married, and it all happened so fast, didn't it? And we've had no word since." His voice was thick with the accent of Buren's northeast. "We worry, we do, sir." He tailed off.

Ingvar realised with a jolt that with the worry about Frankess's rebellion and his father's black mood, he had not spared a thought for Ammie recently. Thinking of her as a married woman, and all that entailed, brought on a sick feeling in his stomach, and he wondered if he had blocked those thoughts from his mind deliberately.

He felt himself blush. He knew that he should not be thinking of her at all. What he wanted could never be. She was married now and so that should be the end of it.

He knew he had been silent for too long. "I know," he stammered as Hekyn watched him expectantly. "I worry too." That felt like the wrong thing to say. He grimaced. "I am sure she is fine and happy," he continued hastily, "and I will ask after her next time I am with Edvar or Sir Ferras."

"Thank you, sir." Hekyn bobbed his head and left the room. Ingvar felt as though his words had been to reassure himself as much as Ammie's father.

Hekyn had barely left the room before a soft sound from outside caught Ingvar's attention. His head snapped around. It was no more than half heard, a stamp of a hoof or perhaps a soft footfall, but this time he was sure there had been a noise. He pushed back his chair and moved over to the door, throwing it open to the early morning light.

He froze. He felt as though he had stepped into a memory, standing on his own doorstep before a force of soldiers. Last time it had been Crowmer and his bodyguard, demanding Omar's assistance against Frankess. Ingvar found himself looking in the crowd for Crowmer's blue cloak and hawkish face. He was not there, and as he cast his eyes across the soldiers again, he saw the colours and emblems on their surcoats and shields were wrong. These were not Crowmer's troops. The Count was not here at all.

"Boy." A mounted man stepped forward and spoke down to Ingvar from his horse. "I am Sir Creenan. I have been sent on behalf of Earl Maurer to seek Sir Omar Darelle." Ingvar looked up nervously at the impressive figure, his scale-armour shirt brightly polished and decorated with gilding at the neck and cuffs. His bright blue tabard bore the emblem of a hound.

The ornate hilt of an arming sword glittered near his waist and Ingvar could see from the marks of wear on the tight leather wrappings of the grip that it was well-used. His hair was cropped close to his skull and his eyes were hard and flinty. This was a man with strength in his hands and authority in his bearing.

"Is he here?" he finished.

"Sir Omar is my father," replied Ingvar. "What do you want with him?" The mere fact that it was Maurer's troops instead of Crowmer's this time was a bad sign, Ingvar was sure.

"I need," said Sir Creenan in a flat, slow tone, as if addressing a simpleton, "to speak with Sir Darelle."

An uncomfortable silence stretched while Ingvar bridled at being addressed so rudely; he considered answering back. Before he could say anything, though, the knight spoke again.

"Fetch him."

His tone gave Ingvar no leeway to argue, so he turned without a word and stepped back into the house.

Omar was already coming down the stairs when Ingvar called up, Etsel hovering nervously behind. He looked drawn and tired, his eyes dark pits of worry.

"What is it, son?" he asked.

"Soldiers, outside. They say they are from Maurer."

"Maurer?" Omar's face went pale. "Really?"

Ingvar nodded and Omar stumbled past him, clumsily patting his son on the chest.

"Stay here," he said. "Do nothing." He walked to the door and stepped outside into the cool of the morning.

Omar had been arrested by Sir Creenan. He did not resist, and had not seemed surprised. It was like he had been expecting it from the moment he defied Crowmer, refusing to march against Frankess. It had weighed on his mind, driving him to drink too much wine and had kept him awake long into the night. When Sir Creenan had summoned him to face the charges of treason against his Count, he had almost looked relieved.

The worry was over. The worst had happened.

Etsel had wailed and Ingvar had argued, but Omar had simply gone where Creenan had told him, head bowed.

"No, no, no," his mother had repeated. "They can't, can they? Stop them, Ingvar. Make them stop!" Ingvar had reached out and wrapped a firm arm around his mother's shoulders and they had stood on the doorstep together as Omar was marched away.

The house had felt empty and achingly quiet. Ammie's mother warmed water and brought out a pot of rosemary tea, laying it carefully on the long table in the main hall. The pot steamed visibly, ghostly vapour spreading out into the room along with the familiar savoury scent. Etsel sobbed softly. The words 'It will be all right' kept rising towards Ingvar's lips, but he could not make himself say them aloud.

They had drunk. Etsel had wiped her tears away, risen and left the room.

That is how their days passed from that point. Each day was tense, and often silent, neither of them wanting to dwell on Omar's fate.

Ingvar looked up from his work. Nothing had changed for a couple of weeks, but now, something was different. A lone rider was approaching.

The time had dragged heavily since Omar's arrest, each day a grinding copy of the previous, with Ingvar labouring to make ends meet and Etsel made remote by her worry and sorrow. No news came through, and no one visited. Ingvar felt like he was living on a remote island.

A week ago, he had found a few hours of spare time to ride to the Ferras estate, desperate for some different company, eager for any rumours about his father. It was Wassen-day, the third day of the week and traditionally a half-day rest from work. He had arrived there after a long ride, only to find that Olya and Edvar were not at home.

"They rode south," Jerane had told him after Ingvar dismounted and strode to the grand entrance of their house. "Edvar had a couple of colts to sell, and the Wassen-day stock market in Seyntlowe does a good trade." Olya's father joined his wife in the doorway, and they stood there side by side.

"We were terribly sorry to hear about all that business with Omar and Frankess," said Tasivus in a quivery voice.

Ingvar asked whether they'd heard any news.

"No, no. We have heard nothing more," Tasivus replied. "Terrible for you. Terrible for your poor mother."

They did not invite him inside.

"Send our warmest regards to Etsel," said Jerane.

Ingvar turned to leave.

"She must be finding this very difficult."

He turned to respond, but could not think of any words to say.

"It's oft said," Jerane continued, her voice soft, "'Darker than midnight cannot be.' Have heart."

"My thanks," murmured Ingvar, before striding away.

'Darker than midnight cannot be.' It was a typically glum local saying, used when things were so bad they could not get any worse. He shook his head at the thought, hoping he was indeed at the darkest part of the night.

Then Ammie walked past. He barely recognised her at first, in a long dress, with her face downcast. She looked up as she passed, gave him a quick, weak smile, and was gone through the narrow door of a small shack nearby before he could think of anything to say.

He had cursed himself for a fool, staring at the blank door that had shut between them, and berated himself all the way back to his own estate. Things just kept getting worse.

Now, a lone rider approached, mounted on a fine horse. Ingvar could see they were wearing a bright blue cloak.

He downed tools and went over to the house, watching the approaching rider like a hawk. It had to be Crowmer, but Ingvar could not remember ever seeing him alone before.

"If you have come to gloat, or to threaten me," began Ingvar angrily as the Count reined in, "then you are wasting your time—"

"Sir Darelle," Crowmer cut in. "Please. Your upset is understandable but does you no favours. I have come here, peacefully, as there are matters we must discuss."

Ingvar's mother must have heard the raised voices. She appeared at the doorway, her face lined with worry.

"My lady." Crowmer inclined his head. "This situation is truly regrettable. I hope you do not suffer too much. May we talk inside?"

Etsel moved aside and Crowmer followed her into the house. Ingvar shut the door behind them, his mouth twitching over words but holding them back. Crowmer sat and Etsel brought a jug of watered wine to the table. She did not say a word, and Ingvar could see her hands shaking slightly. Ingvar stood opposite the Count, the age-darkened wood of the table between them, and folded his arms aggressively across his chest.

"Well?" he asked impatiently. "What is your purpose here? Do you bring news of my father, as it was your doing that he was arrested?"

Crowmer hesitated before replying, his heavy-lidded eyes sharp and calculating as he stared down his hawklike nose.

"Sit," he said. "Please, sit. Let us be civilised." Ingvar exhaled heavily, still glaring at the Count, but he pulled out a chair and sat.

"As well you know," said Crowmer, "it was not in my name that the arrest was made. The order came directly from Earl Maurer and he will be tried by the Duke, and soon. It is not in my gift to affect the outcome of the trial and so I can tell you no more of it." He sipped his drink. "But that is not what I came here to discuss." He paused once more, looking carefully between Ingvar and his mother.

"You may not be aware of this," he continued, his voice ominous in the quiet of the room, "but Sir Frankess held quite substantial wealth. Not in land, his estates being modest, but during his life he amassed quite a store of gold. It was enough for him to live out his days in some comfort. He spent little, but he was sometimes prepared to use his wealth to help friends in need." Another long pause filled the space between them with a weighty, solemn silence.

"Your father," he said, and Etsel stiffened, "owed Frankess a large debt. He had been borrowing gold for several years so that he could keep paying for…this." With a gesture, he indicated the house around them.

"When I put down his rebellion," he said, investing the last word with heavy scorn, "I gained possession of all his lands, wealth and estate. This included all debts owed to him."

Ingvar and Etsel stared. Neither of them had any idea that Omar had borrowed from Frankess, and the idea of owing Crowmer filled Ingvar with dread.

"So, you are here just to claim what you are owed?" asked Etsel heatedly. "This is all about money?"

Crowmer smiled, and it made Ingvar think of a hungry wolf.

"You truly think so little of me?" he went on, but did not wait for a reply. "No, no. I am not so heartless. A faithful hound has teeth as sharp as any wolf, but I am not the dangerous beast that some believe." He looked pointedly at Ingvar. "The debt must be paid, in time, but I am not here as bailiff. I am here because I know now of your struggle and I do not like to see a noble family like yours in such difficulty. And, I come with an invitation." He turned to Etsel.

"I have the authority to arrange a visit with Omar," he said, and Etsel sat up straighter, "and I have a house in Seyntlowe where the Earl has his jail. You can stay as my guest while he awaits his trial. You would be able to see him often, to see that he is well."

"My Count"—Etsel's eagerness was clear—"that would be most kind, and most appreciated."

Ingvar thought his mother's reaction was understated. She had been beside herself with worry, waiting for any news, so an offer to visit him could not be refused. Ingvar was waiting to hear the catch in Crowmer's offer. Something was not given for nothing.

"When?" asked Etsel.

"Now. Today," replied Crowmer. "If we begin riding soon, we can reach my estate tonight and go on to Seyntlowe in the morning."

"We must go," said Etsel, rising. "I will pack some things."

She left the room, briskly climbing the stairs. Ingvar sat motionless until he was certain that his mother was out of earshot, then leaned forward.

"I don't know what you think you are planning—" he began in a low whisper, but Crowmer cut him off.

"No, you listen," he said, reaching across the table and grabbing Ingvar's wrist. His grip was like iron. "You still carry a heavy debt, owed to me. That will not be forgotten. I know you cannot pay in gold, yet pay you must."

Crowmer usually seemed remote and aloof, but there was an urgency in his voice and a fire in his eyes now that Ingvar had never seen before. His intensity was frightening.

"You will remember that I am your Count"—Crowmer relaxed his grip and leaned back—"and that I am due obedience and respect. Your family's stubborn insubordination will no longer be tolerated. I have already taken steps to ensure that you fall into line."

CHAPTER ELEVEN

They rode south later that afternoon.

The rain had mostly cleared, but the sky remained a sullen grey blanket, with a chill wind that blew fitfully and snatched at their cloaks. They travelled as a foursome: Crowmer, Ingvar, Etsel and the Darelle's bondsman Taril. The silence between them was only broken by the whistling of the wind, and Ingvar's mood, dark and heavy as the low clouds, made him disinclined to talk.

In any case, he was still brooding on Crowmer's last words from the morning. The Count had demanded silence and unwavering attention as he described to Ingvar the steps he had taken.

"Your garrison," he had begun, speaking slowly and carefully, "have all sworn a new oath."

Ingvar opened his mouth, questions forming, but Crowmer cut him off.

"To me. Your father betrayed me, Ingvar," Crowmer continued quickly, "and we cannot tolerate the risk of his son doing the same as Frankess. You are also in my debt."

Ingvar wanted to object, to show his outrage, but he knew it was futile. Crowmer noticed his agitation.

"You retain your title, your land and your home, Ingvar," he went on, "and for that, you should be grateful. Your soldiers will remain on your estate and you will be their acting general. But, from now on they will be bound to me, and will march when I call and at my direction."

Ingvar slumped over the table, defeated. He was still a knight but only in name. Without a garrison of his own, he was toothless. Crowmer could supplant him at any time, by having one of his vassal knights march on his estate, then ordering Ingvar's soldiers to stand aside. Perhaps that was his plan? In any case, Ingvar could do nothing.

Crowmer glared at him dispassionately, then his expression softened. His next words were gently spoken, his tone that of a father giving advice to a wayward son.

"Ingvar," he said, "you will learn from this and become stronger. I am sure of it. This life is a path of blades, Ingvar, and you must be sure you are holding the hilt, not facing the point."

A path of blades was an apt description, Ingvar thought as the wind tugged petulantly at the corner of his hood. Everywhere he turned, there were daggers, and they all seemed to be pointing towards him.

He pulled his cloak around himself more tightly, following closely behind his mother and Crowmer as they rode slowly through Locton. The rode split just past the southern outskirts of the village, and they followed the left-hand fork that led towards Crowmer's extensive estate.

Ingvar had heard talk of the richness of the Count's land, but he had never visited before. To either side of the track, extensive orchards stretched away, the boughs heavy with apples and pears. Figures moved quietly between the trees, gathering the windfall.

The light was fading as the autumnal evening drew in, and they passed handfuls of people making their way back towards the manor house, each laden with filled baskets.

They emerged from the trees, and the manor house stood grandly before them. The grounds around the house had been cleared, apart from a neat row of cypress trees on either side of the path leading to the main entrance. The house itself was built in the same style as the Darelle's, the walls framed with huge square timber beams and infilled with pale stone.

Ingvar could see it had been extended over the years, though, and was now much larger than his family house. Two wings extended forward into the grounds, flanking the main entrance. Between them lay a white-gravelled drive before a wide and decorated doorway, and it was towards this that

Crowmer led them. They dismounted, and grooms scurried out of the gathering gloom to lead the horses away to the stables behind the house.

"Welcome to my home," said Crowmer as he led them to the open doors. "Please be at ease and treat the house like it is your own, while you remain my guests."

Etsel entered first and Ingvar followed closely behind, while Taril was led away to the servants' quarters. Within was a scene of comfort and understated wealth. The main hall, stretching out before them, was well-lit by a multitude of candles, and their glow reflected warmly in the dark, polished wood of the furniture.

Ingvar was surprised to see a small shrine to Kaled, the god of order and fate, set in an alcove in the thick stone wall to his left. A finely made crystal goblet stood on a golden footing. It was half filled with clear, pure water and golden oil had been poured on top of the water, up to the brim of the glass. As Ingvar stopped, eyes drawn to the shrine, Crowmer noticed and came to stand beside him.

"Dead, sleeping or otherwise," he said, "the god of order and fate is revered in this house, Ingvar. The power of fate must never be underestimated."

Ingvar could think of no reply, so nodded respectfully.

"To honour Kaled," Crowmer continued, "we make this offering of purest water and hallowed golden oil. See they mix not? It shows both how truth and law must be perfectly balanced to bring justice. And do you see how the finest oil remains above the mundane water, Ingvar? So must our society be maintained."

"Yes, my Count," murmured Ingvar in agreement, although he was slightly taken aback by Crowmer being so open about this belief.

The table was already laid when they sat down. To Ingvar, his stomach already rumbling, it looked like a feast. Whole legs of mutton, smothered with oil and spices, then roasted, sizzled on platters next to plump peppers stuffed with herb cheese. Crowmer was already sitting and was chewing on a round of blackened flatbread, so Ingvar also reached for the food.

"We can visit Omar tomorrow?" asked Etsel, a small plate of food before her.

Crowmer chewed for a moment before answering.

"Of course," he said. "If we set off in the morning, we can arrive by midday. He is being held in good conditions, Etsel, and the Earl is amenable to family visits."

"It would be good to see him." Etsel tailed off, an expression of worry on her face. "What will happen at the trial?"

"I cannot say," said Crowmer, leaning forward and resting his elbows on the table. "You need not doubt that he will be tried fairly. Maurer is a reasonable man. Omar has been a faithful servant of Buren for many years, and his crime was one of inaction, not intention. He refused to act, rather than acted in treachery. That, at least, should count in his favour."

There was an uncomfortable silence. The talk of the trial had reminded them of the seriousness of the situation. Crowmer looked between their faces, then straightened.

"What news of Edvar and Olya?" he asked, changing the subject and breaking the silence. "I hear their partnership flourishes."

Etsel brightened, looking grateful for the opportunity to talk about something else. Discussing his brother's good fortunes did nothing, however, to lift Ingvar's mood.

Maybe being able to see his father in person and speak with him would ease his worry. Maybe the reality of seeing his father in a cell, or in chains, would just make it worse. Either way, he had to go. Once more, Ingvar felt as though his ability to choose his own path had been taken away. He rose.

"My Count," he said formally," I thank you for the meal and your hospitality. It was a long road here and I feel I must sleep."

As he made his way to the guests' quarters, he dwelled on his father's fate. His mind was so occupied that he did not think to wonder about the change in Crowmer, from enemy to apparent friend.

Ingvar left the town behind. He rode northwards again. Alone, towards home. The rain teemed down, crackling insistently on the oiled skin of his cloak. His eyes were down, and he watched the water running along the chalky road beneath him, gathering in milky pools each time his horse's hooves trod down and lifted. As he rode, he carried a heavy feeling of dread deep in his gut.

The town of Seyntlowe had felt bleak, dirty and oppressive. A sculpture of Earl Loowe, the town's founder, stood beside the town gate, and the white stone shone starkly through the damp gloom. The muddy streets beyond snaked between a mix of buildings, some ramshackle in timber and thatch, some with smooth cob walls and tiled roofs. As they rode slowly along the crowded streets, they passed a few buildings constructed of well-dressed stone, like the manor houses of the northern hills.

It was to one of these that Crowmer led. The tall, straight-sided building of pale stone loomed over the dirty streets below like an armoured guard. As they drew closer, they saw the building itself was guarded and fortified.

Soldiers in mail hauberks stood sentinel at either side of an arched doorway, spears in hands and arming swords at their hips. The door itself was tall and made of ancient black oak, protected with a mesh of iron bars.

As Ingvar glanced up towards the overhanging tiled roof, he saw each of the narrow windows was likewise screened, the bars hammered securely into the masonry.

"He is here?" asked Etsel, trailing slightly behind Crowmer as he approached the guards. "Omar is truly in here?" She could not keep the worry and hint of disgust from her voice. The Count appeared to ignore her question, but at his word the guards stood aside, and the forbidding door swung open.

"Be warned," he said, turning to them at the threshold, "not all of those held here are of a civilised nature. You may see and hear things that you find...distressing. But, I will guide you to your husband as swiftly as I can."

Within, the building was gloomy, the small barred windows in the external walls doing little to shed light on the interior. A few guttering rushlights crackled and spat in the damp, cool air as Ingvar and Etsel followed Crowmer into the main hall. Taril stayed outside with the horses.

The Count flung out a hand and they stepped back as two more guards bustled past them towards the door. Between them, they half carried, half dragged a limp prisoner. His head was lolling as his bare feet scraped painfully along the rough stone floor. An unkempt beard suggested he had spent a long time confined, and his clothing, which appeared to have been cut from fine cloth, was now torn and dirty. He was a pitiful sight.

"I've done nothing wrong!" he moaned. "I've done nothing. I've done nothing wrong."

Ingvar reached out and laid a hand on his mother's arm. She smiled back weakly, but bravely.

They moved on. They went along the corridor and up the stairs, passing dark, aged timber and cold iron furniture. Solid doors were set into the walls of the corridor at regular intervals, suggesting that the building was divided up into many small rooms. Cells.

They stopped before another anonymous door, pausing while the guard fumbled with the lock. After what felt like an age, the door opened, and there was his father.

Etsel rushed into her husband's arms, smiling and crying at the same time.

"I'm sorry," said Omar, himself trying to hold back tears. "My dear Etsel, I'm so sorry."

"Hush now," she replied. "We all know that there is nothing to apologise for." Her face was proud and determined, her eyes dry. "We will face this as a family. A strong family."

Omar smiled and the three of them talked awhile. They spoke of the past, of good times. Yet, in his father's eyes, Ingvar saw sorrow, and worse. He saw fear.

"He came alone," said Ingvar, speaking of Crowmer's visit. "And, it was he that arranged this visit. He has treated Mother with kindness and respect."

"Oh, did he?" Omar replied quickly, eyes sharp, but then turned his head away and coughed harshly into his hands. He wiped his mouth on his sleeve and went on. "And is our estate still our own? Our garrison?"

Ingvar said nothing, but could not help his shoulders slumping slightly.

"Everything he does, Ingvar," Omar continued, "is only for the benefit of Rauf Crowmer."

The guard reappeared at that moment, rattling his key along the bars of the cell door to indicate that their visit was over. They bid Omar a strained and hasty goodbye and moments later they found themselves out in the dirty street before the jail once more, Crowmer standing over them.

"As you have seen," he said, leaning in and raising his voice over the bustle of the street, "he is well. When I spoke with Maurer previously, he was agreeable to daily visits up to the date of the trial."

"Daily!" Etsel was clearly surprised. She bit her lip. "I could not travel so far each day, though." She looked up at Ingvar, a question in her eyes.

"As I have said, there would be no need," Crowmer cut in. "I have a house here, on the edge of town. You would be welcome to stay, for as long as you needed."

"I could not stay," said Ingvar. "I have work to do and must return to the estate."

"Then it is settled," said Crowmer, smiling. "I will look after your mother at my residence here while we await the trial."

Ingvar clenched his teeth. He did not like the idea of trusting his mother into Crowmer's protection, but he could neither ask her to leave her husband nor could he stay here himself.

"You are, of course, welcome to visit yourself at any time," Crowmer said, turning to Ingvar.

"Do you think that is for the best?" Etsel asked Ingvar. "It feels a lot to ask of everyone…"

"You should stay here, Mother," replied Ingvar, feeling like he needed to act decisively. "As long as Count Crowmer is able and willing to accommodate you, I think it would be better for you to be close to Father. I can manage the estate by myself, for now."

The moment when Ingvar had seen his father huddled on the rough bench in a cell haunted him as he rode homewards. He tugged gently on the reins. He had bidden farewell to his mother and had watched Crowmer lead her and Taril off through the town. He had given the brutal, blocky jail one final look before riding off in the opposite direction.

He rode all day, going over the conversation he had with his father in the cell again and again. As his house came into view and he contemplated his arrival, alone, he thought back to the final words his father had said before his cell door was locked once more.

"Whatever happens now," he had said, fixing his son with an intense stare. "However this ends, remember this and remember it well." He had paused, leaning in close and lowering his voice to a rasping whisper.

"Never trust Crowmer."

CHAPTER TWELVE

The front door slammed shut. The noise jolted Ingvar from deep sleep, and from the complete darkness of his room, he guessed it was the middle of the night. The low rumble of voices drifted up from downstairs, which could only mean that his father had finally arrived home.

He swung his legs out of the bed and went to the doorway, in time to see his big brother Edvar creeping down the upstairs corridor just ahead. He moved to follow. If Edvar was up, then it must be fine for him to be up too.

The two boys crept to the top of the stairs and looked down. Omar's familiar saddlebags lay where they had been dropped just inside the doorway of the main hall, and he was locked in an embrace with their mother. Ingvar could see his father's face, and was surprised to see his cheeks glistening with tears.

"What's the matter, Father?" Edvar had walked silently down the stairs and stopped halfway. Omar looked up and smiled, though his eyes were still red-rimmed and glistened with tears in the candlelight.

"My boys," he said softly, stepping towards them with his arms outstretched. They rushed down and into his strong embrace. Ingvar could see many cuts to his wrists and hands, and one long graze along his cheek. "My friend Sir Jarren fell in battle yesterday." His voice was thick and quavered with emotion.

"Fell?" asked Ingvar. "Fell over?"

"He means he died, dummy," cut in Edvar. He was a few years older, almost twelve, and liked to show off his maturity. He turned to his father. "I'm sorry to hear that, Father. You must be very sad."

"Thank you, son," replied Omar, hugging them again. "And yes, I am sad. He was a good friend, brave and honest. We had known each other since we were boys." He pointed at Ingvar. "We were your age when we met. I shall miss him. But death comes for us all, in time."

"I don't want to die!" exclaimed Ingvar, his face crumpling. Omar laughed.

"For you," he said, crouching so he could be eye to eye with his younger son, "death is far away, in the distance. So far away that you cannot see it and do not even need to think of it. But in the end, it comes, like a long sleep when our work in life is done. You should not fear death, my sons. It will come for me, one day, but I do not live in fear."

Now it was Edvar's turn to look troubled.

"I don't want you to die, Father," he said. "I don't want you to be gone."

Omar looked at him seriously, his brows furrowed in thought. He let them go and he walked over to the doorway between the main hall and the kitchens.

A long curtain hung over the doorway, floor to ceiling, in place of a door. He stopped beside it and thrust an arm through a gap in the doorway. Etsel moved behind the boys, wrapping a comforting arm around each of their shoulders.

"Now"—Omar spoke to the boys, his voice soft—"my arm is gone, isn't it? Through the curtain so you can't see it. Has my arm come off?"

"Of course not, Father!" replied Edvar scornfully. "Your arm is just the other side of the curtain."

"Quite so!" he said with a smile. He pulled back his arm and wiggled his fingers in a comical wave at his sons. They giggled. "Now, watch me carefully." He walked through the curtain, pulling it shut behind him. "How about now? Have I gone? Have I vanished?"

"No! You're behind the curtain!" Ingvar shouted quickly. He wanted to be the one to give the right answer this time. They waited for him to reply, but there was no sound. Edvar tilted his head on one side, listening, then dashed across the room and threw back the curtain. His father was there. He reached out and ruffled his son's dark, curly hair.

"There's no fooling you, is there?" he said to his eldest son. "So, when you couldn't see me, you knew I was still there. And even when you could not hear my voice?"

"I knew you were still there, Father," said Edvar. "You were just standing quietly behind the curtain."

"Yes, my son." He moved over to his sons, kneeling before them. "One day, death will come for me, as it comes for us all. I will pass through the curtain from this life into the next world. They say it's like walking through a shining veil of water. But, just like when I was behind the curtain, even if you cannot see me, even if you cannot hear my voice, I will always be nearby. I will never leave you."

The hoofbeats of the messenger faded away into silence and Ingvar felt himself fading too. The familiar surroundings of the room swam, the details blurring as his eyes filled with tears.

At that moment, Omar's words came back to him, his voice repeating in his head in ghostly echoes. As a child, imagining a lost loved one simply moving to the next room had calmed his fear of death, but it was no comfort now. He could not make himself believe it.

It did not feel as if his father was nearby. It felt like he had gone. The messenger had left no room for doubt.

Omar Darelle had been found dead in his cell that very morning.

As much as Ingvar knew it to be true, he was struggling to accept it. His father was too strong, too stubborn, too vibrant to die. The message did not say how, but Ingvar recalled how drawn and tired his father had looked on his last visit, and remembered the harsh sound of his hacking cough.

He thought about his mother, away from home as she received that awful news. How hard must it be to lose one's husband like this? His stomach clenched and fresh tears sprang into his eyes. He had not seen her since leaving her with Crowmer in Seyntlowe several weeks ago. He wished once more that he had not.

Ingvar clenched a fist and pressed it hard into the knotted wood of the tabletop. Hard enough to hurt. Abandoning his mother was just another of his failures to add to a long list. So much of this felt like it was his fault.

He should have been more insistent. His father should have marched against Frankess during the rebellion. His father would not have been arrested and would still be alive. He could have even raised the household troops himself and marched against his father's wishes. Yes, there would have been hard words afterwards, and yes, friends of Frankess might mutter about the betrayal, but it would have been worth it to avert this tragedy.

That is what he should have done, were he a better, bolder man. His stomach heaved and he nearly lost his last meal as bile rose in his throat. He was such a coward. Such a failure.

He was not the only one to blame, though. Even through his self-loathing at that moment, he knew this. One man was behind everything that had happened, and had profited directly from the consequences. Count Rauf Crowmer.

Every time Ingvar and his family had suffered, it was Crowmer's doing. And it was Crowmer who reaped the benefit. Ingvar sat upright, blinking away the tears as a new thought occurred. Did Crowmer kill his father?

Omar Darelle being removed from the picture was very convenient for the Count. It removed a long-time opponent, one who had ever defied him and withheld loyalty. It left Ingvar as the landowner and head of the household, but totally beholden to the Count.

Surely not. Could it be? Ingvar rubbed a hand across his face, and it came away wet. Crowmer schemed and played different factions against each other to gain an advantage, but would even he stoop to outright murder? Ingvar could not imagine it. He did not want to believe it could be true. He would not be able to be held responsible for his actions if he found out it was so.

Crowmer was easy to blame and revile, but Ingvar had to admit that the main responsibility truly lay on his shoulders. His father lived and died with the courage of his convictions. If only Ingvar himself was man enough to have done the same. If only his father had been more open about the debt he owed to Frankess.

He sighed and rose. The next task was his alone. He must organise a funeral.

CHAPTER THIRTEEN

White. Despite all the physical and emotional demands of the day, Ingvar's overwhelming memory of the day was the colour white.

White clothing was uncommon in Buren, and was mostly used as the colour of mourning. Like the other local nobles who attended the funeral, Ingvar was clad in traditional long white robes, while the commoners tied strips of thin white cloth around their brows, waists and upper arms.

The chill, gusting mid-winter wind tugged insistently at the mourners' clothing, white or otherwise, as the funeral procession reached the high lake amid the northern peaks. Local funerals had used this route for many generations, and the lake and the surrounding mountains were held sacred.

Between them, Ingvar, Edvar and Ammie's parents carried the litter bearing Omar's body. Toiling up the steep slopes, they carried it from the farmlands up to this high place, where the mourners would pay their last respects. The bearers had not finished their work, though, and soon they would bear the litter aloft once more, taking it to the final lonely location high above.

Ingvar flexed his hands, tired and blistered from the rough timber handles of the litter, before taking his place beside his father's remains. He reached out and wrapped an arm around his mother's narrow shoulders, feeling her slight body heaving with silent sobs. Edvar took his place on her other side.

"It is not too much further to the top from here," Edvar murmured knowledgeably.

Ingvar turned. "I'm sure you'd like to get this over and done with as soon as possible." He could not shake the feeling that somehow this chain of events had started with Edvar's marriage. He knew he was being unreasonable, but he could not help blaming his brother, could not suppress his feelings of resentment.

"Ingvar, please." Edvar sighed, but tailed off as mourners began to file across before them.

"I am sorry for your loss," they said. "May his spirit be judged kindly."

"Thank you," replied the brothers, again and again. "Your presence honours his memory." Ingvar's voice remained even and calm, but inside his thoughts were roiling like a bubbling cauldron.

He must take some of the blame, and in fact holding his brother even partially responsible just made him feel his own guilt more keenly. He could also not help worrying about the days beyond the funeral. He was alone now: the knight of the estate, responsible for its upkeep and defence. Was he strong enough? He must try, for the sake of his mother and for his family name, but how long, in reality, could he manage alone?

Tears came then, trickling slowly down his cheeks, and they were only partially from grief.

"I am so sorry."

Ingvar looked up. It was Crowmer.

"Lady Etsel. Boys." He bowed to each of them in turn. "He was a great man and lived a life of courage and integrity. I am certain that as he passes that shining veil he will be received with much honour."

Edvar bowed. "Thank you, my Count."

This is your doing, thought Ingvar. *You put my father in an impossible bind only for the sake of your ambitions! You care not one jot for what happened to him. You are probably glad he's dead!*

He forced his rage down and swallowed it. Today was not the day. "Thank you, my Count."

He had known he would encounter the Count today and had been worried about how he would react. At least that was one worry dealt with, but it already felt like it had been a long day.

His mother had arrived that morning, riding ahead of the wagon that bore Omar's body. Crowmer had sent an escort of mounted soldiers, and beside them, Etsel looked frail and tiny.

Ingvar had met her in the village, thinking it best that the funeral ceremony was kept away from the family home. She had dismounted wearily and rushed into his arms.

"I cannot believe he is gone," said Ingvar, after a time. She sniffed and looked up. Her eyes were dry although grief had carved deep lines into her face.

"How I wish it was not so," she replied, "but no one can fight against fate."

The villagers had gathered, garbed in white or bearing white cloths, and as Ingvar climbed to the back of the wagon, a few men stepped forward to help. Hekyn and Lamaina were there too, and together they lifted Omar's body down to the litter that had been prepared.

It was made of long, straight branches, cut from poplar trees and tied together with leather twine. Omar's body was wrapped tightly in fine linen and bound securely, and they quickly tied him to the litter. The final journey would not be smooth. Lastly, Ingvar laid his father's longsword on Omar's breast and tied that in place too.

This type of funeral had been traditional for longer than anyone could remember, and was still practised by noble families across the north of Buren, including the Darelles. Most Southlanders now looked on the ritual as archaic and unnecessary, and so burial had become more common. Today, though, in the foothills of the Derufin Mountains, the old ways would be proudly preserved.

As the wrapped body lay on the litter, the people of the village filed past in turn, many bearing a jug or cup in stoneware or turned wood. These were filled with water, and as they passed the litter, villagers poured a measure over the body.

"May you pass safely through the veil," they murmured as the cool water splashed down. "May you pass safely through the veil."

Ingvar tried to imagine his father's soul travelling beyond life, passing through the shimmering curtain said to be the final portal, but all he could see was the void in his own life where his father used to be.

A procession formed as the litter was lifted back onto the wagon to begin the drive north. Ingvar walked ahead while his mother rode, with the villagers following behind in a slow column. Soon, they reached the junction where the track to their own estate branched off left, but they continued north and before long the Ferras estate hove into view.

The mountains already looked closer, the green slopes of the foothills rising towards the clouds and the craggy, dark peaks looming beyond. The fields of the Ferras estate were busy with workers, even this late in the winter, and they stretched away on either side of the well-tended track that led to the manor house itself.

Crowmer stood waiting at the junction, with Edvar and Olya. With a bow in the direction of Etsel, he and Olya joined the procession behind the wagon while Edvar strode over to join Ingvar at the front. He did not speak. What was there to say? Olya's parents were too old and frail to climb the mountain, but they came to the wagon and also poured water over the body.

Jerane Ferras embraced Ingvar briefly as they made their way to the side of the track and Tasivus gripped his shoulder with one bony hand.

"If you ever have need of anything," he said, his voice thin and reedy, "we are always here. Please, come to us and ask."

Ingvar nodded thanks, and the procession moved on.

He concentrated on putting one foot in front of the other, his legs leaden. Edvar's presence beside him was something he would rather not acknowledge but could not ignore.

The landscape trudged past slowly, the track ahead curling around the flanks of the rolling green hills and gradually climbing higher. Directly before them, craggy mountains rose up menacingly, their distant grey-black flanks a stark contrast to the soft green colours nearby. Their peaks loomed over Ingvar, a vertiginous reminder of the ritual to come.

Before long, an aged timber structure came into view to their left. It was an old herders' hut, high in the hills and huddled on a scrap of flat, grassy ground. It was here that the rough track petered out into a narrow, rocky path. The cart could go no further.

"This is where our labour begins, little brother," said Edvar as they moved to the rear of the wagon. Ingvar grunted a reply as he climbed up onto the wagon bed and bent to the litter's handles.

The rest of the procession formed up in a ragged line behind the litter as Edvar and Ingvar lifted it shoulder-high. Hekyn and Lamaina Cowl stepped forward to support the corners, serving Omar in death as they had in life.

Clouds gathered on the jagged peaks and then were blown onwards by the gusting wind as the mourners climbed slowly higher. The path followed the bank of a deep-cut and swift-flowing stream at first, before curving to the right to follow the easiest gradients.

They were following the same route used by their early ancestors a thousand years ago or more, carrying the body high to be taken by the clouds.

Halfway up the path, they laid the litter down carefully, reverentially, and stopped to rest. The path ahead passed through a high-sided gap between two ridges and was forced to the very brink of the ravine by the steep slopes above. The stream below gushed and gurgled, filling the still afternoon air with its incessant music.

"Condolences, my friend."

The voice startled Ingvar. He had been staring south, off into the distance where the green hills rolled away down to the flatter Southlands. It was Olya. She was dressed in a plain, white robe and her golden hair was tied up in an intricate braid.

"I cannot imagine how hard this is for you. I am sorry."

Ingvar remained silent for a moment, gazing out again over the wide landscape, before turning back to Olya. "Thank you," he said, finally. "I still cannot quite believe it. I cannot accept that he is gone, and that bundle there is what is left." He indicated the litter with a nod of his head.

"It did not feel like it was his time." Olya looked thoughtful for a moment, before laying a consoling hand on

Ingvar's arm. "But if anyone will be judged fairly and well, it will be your father."

Ingvar nodded. "That is some comfort."

The comfort was slight and fleeting, but he appreciated Olya's words. He was glad she was there. They had been through so much together, sharing experiences from when they were very young, that the wedge that Crowmer had driven between them seemed irrelevant now.

He climbed wearily to his feet and the procession continued, step by step as the path wound higher. Before too much longer it flattened out before them and they arrived at the mountain lake.

Caltonge Lake was a placid but dark stretch of water, huddling in the base of a natural bowl in the mountains. A cluster of peaks loomed above – Rednicht, Hiting Pike and Witesides – and it was towards a high saddle between Hiting Pike and Rednicht that they were heading.

The mourners gathered near the lake shore, where a patch of flat ground had formed a lush green lawn that was a bright and vivid contrast to the dark and forbidding mountainsides above.

This was where the mourners gathered to file past the litter for the last time. They would go no further up the mountain.

The last stretch of the journey would be made by the family and the household alone. They began.

Ingvar turned his back on the lake, eyes gazing upwards at the narrow, rocky path that led to the high saddle. The other three corners of the litter were once again borne by Edvar, Lamaina and Hekyn, and they climbed higher with slow, careful steps. Etsel followed behind. All was silent.

There was no place to rest on this path, no chance to set the burden down for even a moment. The path was too narrow, the loose slopes of jagged rock and scree above and below too steep. The only choice was to keep climbing.

The light had begun to fade as the winter's afternoon faded to evening and the path crossed a difficult rocky band, arriving at an open flat saddle at the base of Hiting Pike's summit. The taller, darker bulk of Rednicht rose on the opposite side. A sharp, chill wind hit them then, whistling over the jagged teeth of the mountain ridge as it blew down from the north.

"By the veil..." exclaimed Edvar, his voice breathy with astonishment. Ingvar himself could find no words. Spreading before him was a mountain vista that filled his entire vision. Although it felt as though they had climbed high, the peaks nearest were mere foothills of the mighty Derufin Mountains. The range stretched from the northwest of Buren all along the northern fences of Anish and Kotev to the east; a thousand miles from end to end, Ingvar had heard. The highest peaks seemed to pierce the very sky, sheer-sided and tipped with white ice.

Yet, it was not the grandeur of the scenery that caught Ingvar's attention. His eye was drawn to the isolated plateau at his feet, and what it contained.

All across the rocky ground were wooden litters like the one they carried, or at least what remained of them. Some had clearly been in this high place for a very long time, and most were rotting away. On top of the litters – or lying mingling with the dry, broken timbers of the oldest – were bones. Ingvar could not tear his eyes from them. They were the remains of his ancestral dead, the aged skeletons of those brought to this isolated place over many generations for their final, long sleep.

This is where their father would rest, beside the bones of his forefathers, until his flesh was swallowed by the hungry sky and his bones were left as a monument. Everywhere they looked, grinning skulls stared back with empty eye sockets. Rusted swords stood upright here and there, the pitted metal of their hilts gleaming dully in the flat light.

"There's a space over there," said Edvar as he attempted to indicate the direction with a twitch of his head. "Follow.

Follow. Over here. Careful where you tread." His voice was tight, his words terse and clipped. They moved slowly, stepping over and around the slumped litters, until at last they found a space. It was a bare six feet long and a few feet wide, but enough for them to finally lay down their solemn, sorrowful cargo.

"I've never seen anything like this." Ingvar looked around in bewilderment. "I knew this place had been used for a long time, but still…this is beyond anything I imagined." He felt like an intruder, an unwelcome invader from the world of the living – the land of flesh and blood – to this hidden, secret world of the dead.

Ingvar watched as Hekyn and Lamaina backed away respectfully, taking themselves to the edge of the plateau where the path had arrived. Their last service to Omar Darelle was complete. The final part of the ritual was for the family alone.

There was a pause. Ingvar knew what needed to be done next, as did his family, but they were all hesitant, nervous.

"Brother," said Ingvar. "It is to you, as eldest, that the task must fall."

Edvar's eyes moved quickly although his body seemed frozen.

"No." He shook his head. "I am no longer a Darelle. My birthright to the name has passed. You are the head of the family now. It must be you."

Ingvar glanced at his mother, who nodded. He sighed heavily, steeling himself. His breath misted in the chill air. He had been dreading this part.

He reached down and grasped the hilt of his father's longsword, drawing the long slender blade slowly from the scabbard. Methodically, he cut each of the ties that had secured the body to the litter and had held the wrappings in place. When this was done, he moved to the head end and gripped the sword firmly, two-handed. With a sudden thrust, he drove the point deep into the hard, gravelly ground. It now stood over his father's final resting place, never to be touched by a human hand again.

"Mother, you need not be part of what comes next," said Edvar as he crouched by the still-wrapped body.

"No," she replied, "I must. I must be strong. He would have wanted it."

"Are you certain?" Ingvar himself crouched near the head.

"Yes."

Etsel put her hand to one edge of the linen wrapping and began to peel it away. Ingvar had been fearing what they would see beneath and almost sighed with relief when it was done. The wrappings came away, draping down to the ground. It was just his father. His face was slightly sunken but, apart from the thick strip of white cloth binding his eyes and the fact he was almost naked, it was as if he was just sleeping.

"Oh, Omar." His mother softly sobbed. "How we wish you were still with us. How we wish it had not ended this way."

Ingvar moved to stand next to her, his arm around her shoulders to support and comfort. Edvar did likewise on the other side.

"How we shall miss you."

"May you pass safely through the veil," intoned Edvar and Ingvar quickly joined in. "May you be judged fair and true."

May the Skyfather take you for his own, thought Ingvar, recalling the words of an earlier pagan invocation. *May his eagle-eyes help you follow the path.* He glanced upwards to see if any eagles soared overhead. It would be a sign of good omen, but the sky was cloudy.

The landscape before them darkened, shadows deepening among the mighty mountains as the three Darelles paid their final respects. The last farewell was heartbreaking, and they hesitated, putting off the moment when they would need to turn their backs on him forever. Tears flowed freely.

Then, abruptly and almost hastily, Etsel turned away to begin the long walk down, and Ingvar and Edvar followed. Hekyn led the way, but Lamaina hung back, and as Ingvar passed, she reached out and grabbed his arm. Her grip was strong. She was a few inches taller and as she leaned down towards him her dark eyes blazed.

"The ones who caused this"—she gestured towards where his father lay—"will pay." Ingvar opened his mouth to respond, but she went on fiercely. "Vengeance will be yours. I know it. Have patience."

He nodded dumbly, taken aback. She gave his arm a final firm squeeze, then grasped one of his hands in hers as they set off again, picking their way carefully down the darkening mountain.

※

Ingvar should have seen it coming. So much that he held dear had been stolen away. His brother, his father, the easy relationship he had with his best friend. Even his sworn soldiers were no longer his own.

After the funeral, winter had swept across the land. First came the cold driving rains, drenching the ground along with anyone who was forced to venture outside. Then, the temperatures dropped as the nights drew in. Each day was reduced to a few fleeting hours of grey half-light. Or so it seemed to Ingvar, as he whiled away the time.

"I cannot just sit and do nothing!" he complained to his mother. He paced the main hall, warmed by the fire roaring in the hearth, but ill at ease.

"Sit. Rest," his mother urged. "You will need all your strength come spring."

He wrapped himself up in thick furs and went out muttering into the cold. He fed the animals, repaired fences and walls, and did what he could with a hoe and rake to tend the fields. Etsel stayed inside, but did her own share of chores. She cleaned, cooked and mended clothing. Anything to keep her hands busy.

"Have you got that end?" asked Ingvar, the rough grain of a stripped pine plank in one hand and a hammer in the other.

"Yes, sir," replied Hekyn from three paces away at the other end of the plank. "Held tight here, sir!"

Ingvar pressed a nail into position and made ready to drive it in with the hammer.

It was only partway through the afternoon but dusk was already falling. This was the last section of the fence to be mended before they both went back inside to warm up. He gripped the sturdy ash handle, worn to polish by years of use, and knocked the nail in until the head was lost in the grain of the pinewood.

"Hear the news?"

Hekyn had become more chatty as he and Ingvar had spent more time working together. Ingvar looked over, shaking his head.

"Crowmer's done it." Hekyn paused before seeming to realise that further explanation was required. "He marched on Maurer. Finally got enough of the other nobles behind him and raised enough swords and spears that Maurer just stood down. It's Earl Crowmer now."

"What?" Ingvar stopped, realisation hitting.

"Earl Crowmer," repeated Hekyn, speaking more slowly. "Maurer lives, though. Crowmer let him take his family and servants and go into exile. Are you well, sir?"

Ingvar had slumped against the fence. This is what it had all been about. All of his plotting and manipulation had been for this. He felt no real surprise, just numbness and a sickness deep in his gut. To that man, other people were nothing, just tools to be used and discarded once they had served their purpose.

He left Hekyn to clear away the tools and dragged himself back to the house. He had been working in the eastern fields, so he approached it from the rear and had to walk around to the front door. As the sun dropped towards the horizon, it briefly appeared below the base of the heavy grey clouds that blanketed the sky. Rays of warm orange light bathed the landscape. The green hills, the brown stubbly fields and the pale square stones of the house were all cast into sharp relief for a moment, before the sun fell further and all was cast into gloom once more.

Ingvar stomped up the steps, the stones cold beneath the leather soles of his boots. Opening the door, he was immediately hit by the warmth inside. The fire in the hearth was well-fed and blazed vigorously. He turned after closing the door, about to call to his mother to share the news, but the scene before him made him stop dead.

His mother was sitting at the table, wearing an expression that combined surprise and worry. On the opposite side, leaning forward with self-satisfaction writ bold across his face, was Crowmer.

In his hands, which were stretched out towards Ingvar's mother, he held a large bunch of asters.

CHAPTER FOURTEEN

It was a joyless wedding. Crowmer's house was strung all about with flags of different colours. Huge garlands of flowers and myrtle adorned every ledge and wall, and the guests numbered in their hundreds.

As befitted his new rank, Earl Crowmer had invited nobility from near and far, and most had come. No expense was spared. Barrels of the finest wine, several years old, flowed freely. Tables were piled high with meats smothered with expensive and exotic herbs and spices.

Ingvar smiled broadly as his mother came to him after the ceremony. Her red silk dress must have been worth a princely sum. She smiled back, but it did not reach her eyes. As Ingvar embraced her, he could feel her tension, and her sorrow.

They had both been stunned when Crowmer had made his proposal. Crowmer was the sort of man who Ingvar never imagined being married. He seemed wedded to his status, his duty, and his ambition.

"My sorrow at Omar's passing was profound, Etsel," he had said, his hand reaching for hers. "The thought of you alone did my heart great injury. I can offer you security, comfort and my devotion."

He paused. He very pointedly avoided looking at Ingvar at all.

"If you would have me."

Etsel's mouth gaped. She was astonished and taken aback by the proposal. She clutched her hands at her breast in a gesture of excitement and surprise. Ingvar could see, though, that her knuckles were whitening as she clenched her fists.

"And, Ingvar," continued Crowmer, turning to him with a broad smile that did not touch his hard eyes. "I come with an offer for you, as well."

Ingvar schooled his face to blankness, although his heart fell. He already had a feeling about what was coming.

"I would hold you accountable for your father's crimes no longer," said Crowmer. "I believe the time has come for the Darelle garrison to be returned to you. Would you not agree? A strong Darelle estate is key to a strong north."

Ingvar nodded dumbly. He did not trust himself to speak.

Crowmer went on. "All I ask is that you prove your loyalty, with a new oath to me. I do not doubt you, so I am sure you will see the sense in swearing. It would benefit us all."

"I will consider it," answered Ingvar after a pause.

"I hope you will." Crowmer's smile was now absent. "And Etsel, I will leave you to consider my proposal to you. I hope that after these difficult times, we can tie our families together in happiness."

"I need no further time."

Ingvar spun to face his mother in alarm.

"I will accept your proposal, my Earl. You honour me and I would be a fool not to accept."

Ingvar wanted to argue with his mother, and he opened his mouth, but she silenced him with a stern look.

Crowmer beamed, and they shared a chaste embrace on the doorstep as he was on his way back to his horse. When he had gone, though, she collapsed, weeping into Ingvar's arms. He knew why. Once again, Crowmer had taken their choices away. He should have accepted Crowmer's offer himself, but he could not bring himself to say the words.

"I did not expect this," she said. "I wanted to slap his face. Perhaps I should have." She dried her eyes and sat back. "Your father would be so ashamed."

"No! Never!" Ingvar replied quickly. "He would be proud that you are doing what needs to be done. And he would encourage you to go about it with no fear, with your head held high." Ingvar said the words but was not sure he believed them. His guilt was a burning, visceral shame.

That had been a few months ago. The wedding itself had to wait until the weather turned. The sun beamed down, stripping all the chill from the air with its bright embrace. Spring was near.

Everywhere Ingvar looked were bright colours: vivid green grass, the yellow, purple and white of early daffodils, violets and snowbells, and the rich garb of the wedding guests. Yet, Ingvar's mood was black.

He put down his cup and scanned the crowd for his mother. His capacity to feign a smile and make polite talk was running out, especially as the main topic of conversation was the gracious Earl Crowmer and his growing popularity. Ingvar knew he needed to leave before he said something he would later regret.

Sir Sighra Vaikhari turned from a conversation and looked over towards Ingvar, with a slight smile on his face as always, as if he were amused by a joke that only he had heard. His expression changed as his eyes met Ingvar's, his fading smile replaced with a strange, knowing stare. Ingvar quickly turned away.

He thought the tall, dark-skinned swordsman had given him a slight nod. Maybe he had imagined it. He strode across the lawn towards the track. His horse was hitched on the grass before the orchard.

"Leaving so soon?"

Ingvar's head swung around as a voice came from his left. It was Crowmer, striding across the lush grass.

"My Earl." He inclined his head. "Much work is needed at my estate, and I would arrive home before dusk."

Crowmer studied him silently for a moment. He was wearing a long, scarlet dress robe, trimmed all over with gleaming gold thread. His fine black boots were tooled with silver and built up at the heel. He towered over Ingvar.

"You stand at a crossroads, Ingvar," he said, voice low. "One path lets your family persist and prosper under my Earldom. The other"—he paused, raising an eyebrow meaningfully—"does not."

Ingvar opened his mouth to respond, taken aback, but Crowmer cut him off.

"Speak not. I only wished to get your attention. Someone else would talk with you before you leave." He pointed over Ingvar's left shoulder.

Ingvar turned to see a figure in a bright dress, standing at the edge of the orchard. Olya.

He turned his back on Crowmer and strode over to where Olya stood in the shadow of the trees. The stones of the track felt sharp beneath the soles of his boots. "You are beautiful today."

She did look beautiful, although she coloured at the compliment. Her fair hair and pale skin always made her stand out in a crowd.

"I have something I need to say to you." Olya spoke firmly, tucking a stray strand of golden hair behind an ear before fixing him with an unwavering stare. Her hair hung loose for a change, brushing the shoulders of her pale-blue gown. "You need to listen properly and not overreact."

Ingvar narrowed his eyes.

She took a deep breath before speaking. "You must give Crowmer your oath."

"No."

"Do not refuse without considering it first!"

"No, Olya!"

"Listen to me, Ingvar." Olya moved closer, her brow furrowed. "Do not let your stubbornness be the death of you and the end of your family!"

"You would have me kneel to a man who would kill me if he could?"

Olya sighed heavily.

"He killed Frankess, and without his uncaring ambition, my father would still live! No, Olya, I will not kneel to him."

"Fate curse you!" she swore with sadness in her voice, her face pained. "Curse you and your stiff neck! Your standing is low. You have few allies and, however proud, you are not strong!" She paused, then went on in a more level tone.

"Crowmer *is* strong. Swear to him and you will be under his protection. Swear to him and your life and lands will be safe."

"I will not."

"If you do not"—Olya took a step closer—"then one day, and maybe soon, you will find that you will have to answer at the point of a sword."

Olya was taller than Ingvar and he had to look up to meet her steely gaze. He returned her stare. The soft noise of the wedding faded into insignificance and his ears filled with the sound of his own breathing.

"And if that happens"—Olya dragged the words out reluctantly—"I cannot promise that it will not be my hands on the hilt."

There was a deeply uncomfortable silence.

"Well," said Ingvar in a low voice, after what felt like an hour. "What price friendship?"

Not waiting for an answer, he turned on his heel and strode away.

CHAPTER FIFTEEN

Ingvar brooded angrily on Olya's words as he rode home, berating himself and cursing her in equal measure for days afterwards. She must see that he could not kneel to Crowmer. Not after everything he had done.

It was the first day of Chaldeveev, the first month of spring. Ingvar dragged himself out of bed and plodded reluctantly to the fields. The time for spring ploughing and planting had come, and there was a lot of hard work to be done.

"Could do with a few more hands, sir." Hekyn leaned on his mattock, glancing around at the huge area of unploughed earth. "The spring workers must come soon."

"Aye," replied Ingvar. "They will come. Perhaps tomorrow."

It was a local custom that at spring planting and autumn harvest, labourers would arrive at the estates of local nobles. There were a few weeks of hard work to be done, and a pocketful of coin could be earned. Ingvar had opened the family's money chest earlier that day and there was enough there for some hired hands. Only just, but the alternative was unploughed fields, unplanted crops, and a very hungry winter. It would have to be enough.

But no hands came. Half of the week had passed, with Ingvar joining Hekyn and Lamaina in the fields every day and working from sunup to past sundown. His hands were blistered, his shoulders hurt like fire, and still, no workers arrived.

The next morning, he woke with the dawn. A gentle hissing on the tiles above him whispered of morning rain. The problem of the lack of spring workers had preoccupied him the previous evening, and he awoke with a new determination to find a solution.

He flung back the woollen sheets and rose. Striding to the window, he considered his options. He threw the shutters open. He could no longer look to his father to make decisions. There was only him. As he gazed out across the estate, a spring rain shower swept away towards the mountains. His estate.

New growth was everywhere, the trees just starting to burst into leaf and the green slopes in the distance almost iridescent where the morning sunshine glinted off the wet grass. The sky was a patchwork of pale cornflower blue, iron grey and the purest white, constantly shifting and changing as the clouds merged and parted.

Ingvar sighed deeply, the fragrant air of the land filling his lungs. He would ride to Locton. If workers would not come, he would go and find them himself.

He rode easily, relieved to have some time off digging and dragging the plough. As he reached the junction, a couple of people in drab workers' smocks scurried across his path, heading north. One of them glanced in his direction but quickly turned away, hurrying further along the track that led away from Locton.

Puzzled, Ingvar shrugged and turned in the opposite direction, heading south. It was only after he had ridden another hundred paces that it occurred to him that he should have stopped them and offered them work. He twisted in his saddle to look back up the track, but the pair were out of sight around a bend. He blew out a rueful breath and rode on.

Locton seemed quiet. There were few people in the streets and the inn itself was deserted. Ingvar pushed one of the doors open and stepped inside. He saw no one.

"Good day!" he called out hesitantly, approaching the bar at the rear of the room. "Gwenhild? Are you in?"

"Come through!"

The voice rang out from the back and Ingvar sagged with relief.

"I'm back in the kitchen! Come through!"

He followed the sound of her voice, ducking through a low doorway into the steamy kitchen.

She stood beside a bubbling cauldron, a long-handled spoon in one hand. Holding up a single finger, she indicated Ingvar should wait a moment, then she reached for a squat clay pot. She upended it over the cauldron, and a mass of fat, white beans slid out into the stew below with a soft splash.

"For this evening," she said, by way of explanation. "I expect all the workers will have a fierce hunger!" She returned the empty clay pot to a rough shelf and stirred the contents of the cauldron vigorously.

"That's why I'm here," said Ingvar. "I thought you might know, or have had word…Where are all the spring workers?"

Gwenhild blinked at him, her spoon motionless, and waited while he explained.

"None have come. We have started ploughing for planting, but no workers have come to us."

She stepped closer then, with her fists on her hips and an incredulous expression on her face.

"None!" she said. "I do not understand."

"None," Ingvar repeated. "And we really need them."

"That is what I don't understand." She eyed him curiously. "We've had a steady stream of workers coming through the village and heading up your way. It's the double pay, isn't it? They've come from miles around."

"Double pay!" It was Ingvar's turn to be incredulous. "What do you mean?"

"Word went out a couple of weeks ago. There would be double pay for all spring workers on the Ferras estate this year. I was surprised, but thought that maybe you'd be sharing the workers between you."

Ingvar's jaw clenched and an expression of fury grew in his face.

"Oh dear," she finished.

"No word of this came to me," spat Ingvar. His mind worked. "And not one worker has come to our estate." Which was no wonder. They had all walked past to get twice the coin on the Ferras estate. How? Why? He had to get to the bottom of this.

"I must go."

He turned on his heel and left without another word, his boots pounding an angry rhythm on the floorboards of the empty inn.

Rain squalled across the courtyard as Ingvar mounted. He ignored it, the fine drops whispering against his face as he dug his heels into his horse's flanks, urging it to a brisk trot.

He ground his teeth as he rode, trying to suppress a rising fury.

Should he assume this was deliberate? Was it an attempt to drive his estate to ruin? That was one explanation. Could there be any other? He shook his head. He needed workers, so if they were all at the Ferras estate, that was where he needed to go.

The chalky track passed swiftly beneath him as he rode north. A painful memory of his father's funeral came stabbing back as the northern mountains loomed up ahead. He gratefully looked away as he reached the junction, turning off right towards the Ferras estate.

The fields on either side of the track swarmed with labourers, their drab brown smocks smeared with the rich dark soil on which they worked. So many. And all being paid double. Ingvar gripped his reins.

Movement in an adjacent field caught his eye. Bright colours flashed against the dull surroundings as another rider urged their horse into motion, angling to meet him at the corner of the nearest field. It was Edvar.

Edvar had been obsessed with horses for as long as Ingvar could remember and had ridden ponies around the farm for almost as long as he had been able to walk. His easy grace on horseback was unmistakable.

"Brother!" he called out, leaping down from the saddle and landing like a cat. Stepping closer, it seemed he caught sight of Ingvar's lowered brows and sour expression and raised an eyebrow curiously. "What is wrong?" he asked.

Ingvar stared down for a moment, before slowly dismounting.

"I think you know full well what is wrong." He tried to keep his voice calm, despite the churning anger he felt. He pointedly turned and glared out across the bustling fields.

"So many?" Edvar's voice was also calm. "Yes, I know. I can't say why so many have come, but Olya and her parents say the coffers can afford it. It keeps me busy, supervising them all, though!"

So, Edvar did not know?

Ingvar stepped closer to his brother. "There are so many," he hissed, "because they are all being paid double."

"Double!"

Edvar was clearly surprised.

"How so?"

"Word got out that the Ferras estate was offering double pay for spring workers this year." Ingvar put his hands on his hips, watching his brother's face carefully. Edvar raised a questioning eyebrow.

"Double pay? Well, that explains the numbers. Very generous."

"Quite." Ingvar moved to stand beside his brother, looking out across the fields. "How many spring workers do you think have come to my estate this year?"

Edvar's eyes widened. "Oh! Oh, I see!" He turned to Ingvar. "I had no idea, I swear. I didn't think…"

"Come winter, we shall starve, brother." Ingvar spoke calmly, but firmly. "This was deliberate. This was intended to do me harm."

Edvar's face hardened.

"Right," he said decisively, before cupping his hands around his mouth and calling out across the nearest field. "Cirene! Come!" A thin woman with a hooked nose and the long grey aprons of a work leader strode over. "Pick out ten good workers and send them over to the Darelle estate," he instructed. "But tell them to return here for their wages afterwards. Yes, Cirene, yes. Still double pay. Go!"

Ingvar watched her bustle away and Edvar turned back to face him. He took a step closer.

"You know who is behind this." Edvar spoke urgently in a low undertone.

Ingvar nodded. *Crowmer.*

"But you have to understand what it is like for Olya."

He continued. "For years, Crowmer has kept them in his debt. He offered them something that cost him nothing. Security. And they pay for that, every day. They come whenever he calls and do whatever he tells them. I know Olya fears to gainsay him. She fears putting all of this at risk."

"I don't see what they mean to him," said Ingvar, as he tried to take it all in. "There are lots of other knights. Plenty of other noble families."

"You underestimate the Ferras's wealth," said Edvar, more urgently. "Their estate is worth more than you can imagine. Crowmer has been able to rely heavily on them because of that. These rich lands have fed his army. Their gold has armed them and paid them. And, since I have lived here, his knights and cavalry have been mounted on my horses. Crowmer has got his hands on all of that without spending one crown or one scrap of silver." He sighed, blinking slowly. "And his grip on them remains strong."

"Why them?" asked Ingvar, eyes locked on Edvar's. "Why not us?" He meant the Darelle family.

Edvar shrugged. "Our lands are poor," he said. "We have little to offer. He knew Father would always refuse him, in any case. He would never kneel to Crowmer. Nor would Frankess."

The two were quiet for a moment as they contemplated this.

Ingvar spoke next. "So, the only solution was to get them both out of the way. Frankess lost his lands, and his life. And, Father…" He paused, thoughts sliding into place like rough-hewn stones being set in a sturdy wall. "Arrested, and then dead."

"You're not saying Crowmer killed Father, are you?" Edvar spoke quietly. "Would even he go that far? He could have just left him rotting in jail. His death made no difference to Crowmer."

"Perhaps." Ingvar shrugged this time. "There is no way to know for sure. I would bring a Just War if I could prove it was true."

"No, brother!" Edvar spoke earnestly. "You should not even think of it. You cannot beat him. He is too powerful, too quick to respond, too clever. In any case, all he would do is demand a duel. He has Vaikhari to duel for him, and he is undefeated. Do you think you could beat him?"

Ingvar was silent. His brother spoke the truth.

It started raining again. Fine, misting rain swept across the fields and the sunlight was dimmed by the clouds. Ingvar opened his mouth to say more, as a hooded worker woman shuffled past. She walked with a noticeable limp. Blue eyes flashed from deep beneath her hood, locking with Ingvar's for a moment, before looking quickly away.

Even as she limped past, Ingvar was gasping and turning to follow. He caught up in a few hurried strides and dashed around to block her path. She stopped. Without thinking about what he was doing, he reached forward and gently pushed the hood away from her face.

"Ammie," he said, her name sighing from his lips like a hesitant caress. She lowered her eyes, but not before Ingvar noticed that her left eye was puffy and surrounded by a livid purple-blue bruise. "What has happened?" He looked closer. There was bruising all down that side of her face and there was a cut on her lip.

Ammie kept her eyes down, not answering and not meeting his eyes. Where her cheeks were not bruised, they coloured as she flushed with shame. Ingvar looked up towards Edvar. His brother seemed uncomfortable, fidgeting with the hem of his fine coat.

"What happened?" Ingvar repeated, his voice hard. Edvar opened his mouth as if to speak, but instead shook his head and gave a vague shrug. Ingvar knew his brother well, though, and his eyes gave him away. And Edvar's eyes left Ingvar's face and looked at a spot behind his left shoulder.

Ingvar turned to look at where Edvar had glanced. A low-roofed wooden shack stood there, a thin trickle of smoke rising from a gap in the thatch. It was the same shack Ingvar had seen Ammie go into the last time he had seen her here. Her married home. Ingvar's mind worked, and he turned back to Edvar.

"He has a temper." Edvar sounded almost apologetic. "At times…"

"Right." Ingvar steeled himself. He had found himself helpless too many times in recent months. Not today. Today he would act. Today he would right a wrong. He turned and strode towards the shack, his fists clenched.

"Ingvar, no!"

Edvar's voice rang out from behind, but Ingvar ignored it and thrust the door open. As he stepped across the threshold, he cast his eyes around the gloomy interior. A small window on the opposite wall let washed-out light shine in and across a small round table, a sleeping pallet with a straw-stuffed mattress and a well-used hearth.

As he stepped forward, a dark figure unfolded itself from a squatting position before the hearth, and turned to face him.

"What is this?"

Ammie's husband was tall, taller even than Lamaina. Vivid green eyes stared belligerently out from his angular face, his skin the colour of polished black beech-wood.

"Tell me how your wife came by her injuries," snapped Ingvar. "And tell me true, in the name of fate!"

If the elf was surprised, he gave no sign, apart from a slight raising of one dark eyebrow.

"My household is my own business"—his voice was quiet—"and none of yours. Leave my house, now. *Sir*." The last word was sneered in a tone of studied insolence, and Ingvar felt fury rise in his breast.

He swung his right fist at the elf in a wild haymaker. He needed to reach up, but it was a fast and powerful strike and would have put the elf on his back had it landed. But it did not. It got nowhere near. The tall, skinny elf servant simply leaned back and Ingvar's fist flashed past his nose.

In the same motion, the elf's left fist jabbed forward, catching Ingvar with a stinging blow to his cheek. As Ingvar's head jerked back, the elf's other fist hit him in the ribs; a powerful and rapid uppercut that Ingvar did not see coming.

He gasped, winded, but his instincts came to his aid and he quickly raised both arms to ward off any more blows. Another jabbed punch was blocked, and Ingvar followed up by stepping forward and throwing both forearms towards his opponent.

Surprised, the elf half stumbled, half dodged backwards, desperately trying to avoid colliding with any furniture or walls in the cramped space.

Ingvar seized the opportunity. With the elf unbalanced, Ingvar threw a punch with each hand, left then right in quick succession. The first landed as a glancing blow on the chin as his head jerked back. The elf recovered quickly, though, seizing Ingvar's left wrist as he threw the second punch.

With surprising strength, Ammie's husband twisted Ingvar's wrist, leaning backwards. It was impossible to resist, and Ingvar was pulled off his feet as his whole body twisted. The edge of the table thumped painfully into his ribs as he fell, and the whole table overturned and hit the ground with a clatter as Ingvar landed heavily on his back.

Desperately, Ingvar thrust his shoulders up and rolled into a kneeling position. He tensed to rise again, but before he could straighten his legs, a sudden solid impact to his head knocked him sideways. Pain bloomed where the elf had driven his knee forcefully into the side of his skull. He collapsed again, his knees giving way as he rolled over onto his back, dazed.

Before he could move again, a sharp weight dropped onto his right arm at the elbow, painfully pinning it to the ground. Rasping breath blew into his face as the elf kneeled over him, reaching to his left to take Ingvar's right arm in a vice-like grip.

"I know the law, Sir Darelle." He leaned close, hissing into Ingvar's face. "And it lets me deal with intruders to my home as I see fit." He lifted Ingvar's right hand, then pushed it down towards the nearby hearth, where the embers still glowed red-hot. "Be they a knight or no," he continued as his weight came down on Ingvar's hand. "Injury suffered is the intruder's fault...Sir Darelle!"

Ingvar felt the heat of the coals prickling against the back of his hand. He resisted with all his strength, gritting his teeth with the effort of holding his hand away from the embers. The elf was deceptively strong and was bearing down with all his weight.

Beads of sweat sprang out on Ingvar's brow and he roared with exertion, but still the heat grew against the back of his hand as it was pressed down into the merciless glowing embers. His arm quivered with the effort but he could not move his hand, and he cried out as it started to burn.

CHAPTER SIXTEEN

Pain bloomed in Ingvar's right hand. He roared through his gritted teeth as his skin was pressed into the smouldering embers. The pain was intense, raging through his hand; his skin blistered and his flesh began to cook.

He could almost smell it. His legs flailed, heels drumming against the floor, scattering the rushes as he tried to shift the elf off his chest. It was no use. He was too heavy, too strong, and his position was too stable to knock him over.

Ingvar closed his eyes tight as he heard his own voice, overly-loud, crying out through the burning pain.

There was a soft sound, and the pressure lifted. The weight of the elf fell across him heavily, but his hand was free. He jerked it away from the embers.

Lifting his right shoulder, he rolled the unconscious body of the elf away and looked up. Ammie stood over him, silhouetted in the doorway. Her chest heaved, and her fists were clenched.

Ingvar lay there for a long moment, stunned. Ammie reached down and helped him to his feet, although her face remained hard.

"Too long," she said. "He has waited far too long for that."

Ingvar did not know what to say. The back of his right hand felt as though it were thrust into a lit torch. He cradled it with the other arm, clutching it close as if that could ease the pain.

"Thank you, Ammie," he said. She looked towards him, her face softening. "I had hoped that would go better…"

Ammie smiled slightly. "You are a fool, Ingvar Darelle. A fine fool." She reached out and placed her hand on his arm. Her touch soothed him as if it were cool water. "What will happen now? Will there be trouble for you?"

Raised voices came from outside the shack. Both of their heads swung around as one. The fight must have been noisy. If Ammie had heard what was going on, then others would have too. Ingvar glanced down at the elf. He was breathing but had not stirred from where he lay. He did not know exactly what Ammie had done to him, but it seemed as if she had hit him very hard.

"May I take you home?" Ingvar could not hide the uncertainty in his voice, as well as the fragile hope. He thought he had lost her forever. She nodded, and he exhaled loudly, relief filling his being. He headed towards the door and she followed.

He could hear the gentle rumble of voices in hushed conversation before they stepped outside, where they were confronted by a gathering crowd. Ingvar stepped forward, cradling his injured hand, noticing that Edvar still stood watching the doorway. A group of workers had gathered around him, apparently drawn by the crashes and shouts from within.

"What is the meaning of this?" Olya demanded furiously, striding across from the house. "What have you done?"

Ammie shrunk away, almost trying to hide behind Ingvar's shoulder. He reached out with his unhurt left hand, touching the small of her back in what he hoped was a gesture of support and inclusion.

"I'm taking Ammie home with me."

He had ignored Olya's question. She stepped closer. Her face was twisted with a mix of anger and confusion, her mouth slightly open as she searched for words.

"Ingvar Darelle!" she snapped. "You have no right to take my servants away! She is married!"

Ingvar had been biting his lip, keeping his face turned away from his oldest friend's fury, but now he swung around.

"A marriage fouled by violence is no true marriage!" said Ingvar. "Your loyal elf has been beating her. You knew and you did nothing." He glanced at Edvar, who looked down, remorse written across his face. "Shame on you. When the village council hear, and I will tell them, they will dissolve the marriage." He continued walking, guiding Ammie to his horse.

"You would do this?" Olya was incredulous. "For her?"

Ammie hunched her shoulders uncomfortably and Ingvar did not answer.

"You would do this?" Olya went on. "And cast aside our friendship? Our families' old alliance? For her?"

"My friend would not have turned her eyes from this," said Ingvar, turning to face Olya again. "My friend would have done what was right, not what was easiest for them. My friend would have put people before ambition!"

He turned and pulled himself up into the saddle. A grunt of pain escaped his lips as he gripped the rains in his burned hand. Ammie mounted easily, swinging herself up in one movement to sit behind Ingvar.

"If you ride away with her"—Olya's voice was tight—"then our friendship is over. Our family alliance is finished."

Edvar took a step forward, opening his mouth to speak, but Olya silenced him with a glare.

"Think about what you would throw away, all for a helf servant girl," Olya said with a note of pleading in her voice.

"Farewell, Edvar." Ingvar turned his face away from Olya. "My thanks for the workers."

Edvar nodded, his lips pressed tightly together. Ingvar took a deep breath and let it out in a low, forlorn sigh, before kicking his heels to his horse's flanks and riding away.

He gripped the reins one-handed, trying to ignore the burning agony from his right hand by clutching it to his stomach. His insides churned as he left the Ferras estate behind, his horse moving at a walk, slowed by the additional weight of Ammie behind the saddle.

The argument with Olya repeated over and over in his mind as the familiar scenery slid past unseen. He did not regret his actions, or his words. He could not have stood aside and let that happen, and he could not have ridden away and left Ammie to suffer further harm. The thought of Ammie's bruises made his anger rise once more.

Yet, he was sure Olya meant what she said. Riding away with one of her servants was an affront to her honour and a great show of disrespect. It could only lead to damage to their relationship. No matter that Olya should have prevented it, and protected Ammie herself. Ingvar had intervened publicly and Olya would not, and could not, forget it.

Ammie's arm wrapped a little tighter around his waist as his horse stepped over some bumps in the track, reminding him of her presence. He was very aware of her body pressing firmly against his back, and he flushed. Grateful that she could not see his face, he asked a question that had just occurred to him.

"Ammie…what did you do to the elf? When you knocked him down?" Ingvar recalled too well the surprising strength of Olya's servant, and also how he had slumped onto the floor like a pole-axed ox. Ammie was silent. Ingvar felt her shuffle uneasily, and she sighed.

"I saw what he was doing to you," she said. Her voice was sad, wistful. "I could not let him do it. I could not let him hurt you, like he hurt me."

She had not answered his question but he let her talk.

"When I was young, my mother taught me to defend myself. She said, 'No one will touch you unless you will it.' And she said, 'If someone hurts you, you hurt them back so they will know they must not do it again.' I listened to her, in all things, and I learned."

They rode on, the crisp crunch of hooves on the gravelly track the only sound. Ingvar half turned back towards Ammie, feeling that there was more to come.

"The body," she said, "has certain places where life energy passes close to the skin. With a firm strike in the right place, even a very strong person will be knocked down."

"I wanted to strike him down," she continued, and there was heat in her voice now. "I have wanted to hurt him, for so long. But I knew I must not. If I were a bad wife, it would bring dishonour to Olya and to you, to both families. So I made a fist, but I hid it in my apron. I knew I could not, must not, fight back, no matter what he did."

"But then I saw him hurting you and I could stay my hand no longer."

"I am so very sorry." Ingvar could think of nothing better to say. Thinking of Ammie enduring such abuse, silently and stoically, all from a sense of duty, he felt crushed. How had they all let this happen?

"How is your hand?"

Her question surprised him.

"Um...er," he mumbled. "It's fine." In truth it hurt like his skin was still in the fire, but to admit that in the light of Ammie's suffering seemed too selfish.

"It is a bad burn," she said, seemingly disregarding his answer. "My mother will be able to treat it. She knows much."

They rode on. The pain from his hand stabbed him unceasingly, but the worry about what would happen next was worse. What chance did he have if he had lost Olya and her family as an ally?

Clouds scudded across the pale-blue sky, driven by a fresh, cool breeze from the west. A sudden shower followed and Ingvar held up his hand, the cool rain pattering onto his skin and easing the pain like a soothing balm.

He took a deep breath and let it out slowly. The breeze lifted and blew the clouds away, the rain easing. The moisture on his skin was cooling, and he tried to let his worries blow away too.

The house came into view as they rode silently up the track, and Ingvar remembered with a thrill like a strong gust that he was bringing Ammie home with him. Even through his worry and his pain, he could not suppress a smile.

"Great heart!" exclaimed Lamaina Cowl as she plunged Ingvar's hand into a bucket of chill water, freshly drawn from the well. "Strong spirit! Sir Ingvar Darelle, who brought our daughter back home to us!"

Hekyn and Lamaina had dashed out of the house as Ingvar and Ammie approached. They could not fail to recognise their daughter's distinctive white-blonde hair, even at a distance, and they fluttered with emotion as they helped her dismount.

Ammie had quickly told them the story of Ingvar's fight with her cruel husband, and when Lamaina had seen the reddened, injured skin of his burned right hand, she had been aghast and sent Hekyn off urgently to bring cold water.

"Bring some thorn-leaf!" she had instructed when Hekyn had returned with the bucket. "Two leaves. There is a strong plant growing in our garden. Go quickly!" She had thrust Ingvar's hand down into the bucket, and he gasped as the cold water stung his blistered, raw skin. "Do not take your hand out until I return," she said, fixing him with a hard stare, a twinkle in her dark eyes. Ingvar turned to Ammie and grinned as Lamaina strode out of the main hall and into the kitchen. She returned a small smile in his direction.

All the things that he had wanted to say to Ammie while she was not there whirled around his mind as he looked at her. That he missed her, that he wished they could be together, wished that the petty rules about marriages were different. He was about to speak but paused, worrying anew. Had anything changed?

It was still not considered acceptable for nobles to marry their servants, even if the noble had rescued the servant from abuse. Maybe the rules should be ignored? He knew all he wanted was to be with Ammie, and to have her near…

He opened his mouth to say something to her, but as he did, the front door banged open and Hekyn bustled in. His hair was wet, darkened and slicked down close to his skull by another rain shower, but he carried two long, tapering fronds of thorn-leaf. He held the thick, fleshy leaves before him and hurried through to the kitchen.

Moments later, Lamaina came back through into the main hall. She held a bowl made of turned wood and was vigorously grinding the contents with a thick-handled spoon. As she sat next to Ingvar, he could see that the bowl contained a thick, sticky paste that had a sweet but pungent scent.

"Give me your hand," she said, her manner brisk. Ingvar gratefully removed his hand from the bucket and Lamaina gently patted it dry with a piece of thick cloth.

Pulling the spoon from the bowl, she then carefully dabbed the cool, viscous mixture all over the reddened flesh of the burn. It stung, and Ingvar gritted his teeth, his inward breath hissing.

"Thorn-leaf and honey," said Lamaina by way of explanation. "It will ease the pain and help it heal quickly." Once the back of his hand was well-covered with the poultice, she bound it neatly with several layers of linen.

When she had finished, she took his hands in her own and looked at him intently. "You have a true heart," she said, "and your soul is strong. We are grateful that you brought our daughter back to us. You risked much to do this. But"—she lifted his hands shoulder-high, a half-smile on her lips—

"these are slow." She let go of his hands and grasped his upper arms firmly. "And these are weak. The path that you have chosen to walk will be hard and dangerous. You must become stronger to face the challenges to come." She leaned forward, lowering her voice. "Because they will come soon."

"Challenges?" asked Ingvar, although he knew what she meant. Crowmer was not finished with him, and Olya could no longer be counted on as an ally. All around him were those that would take everything he had, if they could. And if they sensed his weakness, they would.

He was not sure he could stand against them, but for the sake of Ammie and her family, he would try.

"They will come soon," repeated Lamaina before leaving the room.

※

That night, Ingvar dreamed of his father.

The four of them – Ammie's parents, Ammie, and him – had shared a supper around the long table in the main hall. Dusk fell outside, and they lit the lanterns and gathered closely.

Hekyn had baked some round, boulder-like loaves that he assured them were traditional fare in the far north of the country. Lamaina cooked a rich, thick stew from a leg of goat that had been hung in the cellar, with spicy peppers and broad white beans. At Hekyn's insistence, they tore the tops from the loaves and Lamaina ladled the stew inside.

Ingvar opened a flask of wine and they all drank. It felt like a feast. They felt like a family. The worry that had been ever-present like a jagged rock on Ingvar's chest evaporated as he talked and laughed that evening.

"We stand with you, Ingvar," said Lamaina when they had all eaten their fill. She had never been very enthusiastic about acknowledging his rank by calling him 'sir', and she seemed to have completely abandoned any suggestion of respect now. "We will all do everything we can to support you."

"Thank you all." Ingvar smiled. "It means the world to know that." Hekyn and Lamaina rose and began clearing the remains of the meal away to the kitchen. Ammie stood and made as though to follow. Ingvar caught her by the arm as she was halfway across the hall. An idea had taken him and he followed it impulsively.

"Ammie, wait." She swung around aggressively at his touch, but quickly relaxed. "The house is mine, now. I no longer need to seek my parent's approval for what I would do." She looked at him, unblinking and expressionless. He licked his lips, gathering his courage. "You could stay. Here." He paused again, uncertain. "With me. Tonight."

Ammie gazed at him for a few heartbeats before answering. "I cannot. Not yet."

Ingvar's disappointment must have shown clearly on his face, and she spoke again, more quickly.

"I am happy to be home, and grateful for what you did, but I feel I must be with my family." She patted him familiarly on his arm. "For now."

They embraced, and he tried to breathe her in, hold her in, and make the most of every moment with her. Then she was gone, following her parents out into the night, and he was left alone once more.

His sleep that night was fitful. The sensation of loneliness was oppressive. The empty house around him felt alive and malicious. He tossed and turned but dozed off finally in the early hours of the next morning.

"They are at the front door, son." Omar stood at the foot of his bed. "Did you bar the door?"

Ingvar sat up, gaping at the insubstantial image of his father. "You must go down and bar the door," Omar's shade continued, "or they will break in and take all we have."

"Who?" Ingvar was trying to get up, but his legs were not responding. His whole body felt weak and almost too heavy to move. "Who is there?"

"Go and bar the door, Ingvar." His father ignored his question. "Go quickly." His voice was flat and expressionless.

Ingvar struggled to rise, but still could not.

"I can't!" he wailed. "I am trying to get up, but I can't!"

Now a hammering noise began downstairs. Angry fists drummed against the door.

"You must hurry." Omar did not move from the end of the bed. "They will break through the door in moments."

Ingvar somehow knew his father's words were true. The noise intensified, growing in volume and threat. The door would soon break. He writhed and strained but could not get up. Tears of frustration sprang from his eyes.

"I'm sorry, Father! I can't move! I'm so sorry!"

With a loud crash of splintering timber, the door broke open.

"I'm sorry, Father!" Ingvar woke with his own voice ringing loudly in his ears. His breath came in ragged gasps. He immediately looked to the end of his bed. Of course, there was no one there.

Then it hit him anew. His father was gone. Dead. His soul had fled to pass through the veil to the afterlife, and his bones were left to moulder, high in the clouds.

It felt like an icy fist taking a grip on his heart. For a moment, in the dream, his father had been there, and he had felt whole again. Though, grief came crashing back, along with the realisation that his father was truly gone, forever.

Ingvar sank back into his blankets and curled into a ball as his body was wracked with sobs. Night closed in around him and he wept until he fell once more into an uneasy sleep.

CHAPTER SEVENTEEN

They said that Duchess Telivaina could see the future.

She was rarely surprised. Those who met her said it felt like her deep, dark eyes could see into their very heart. It was like she could uncover the deepest, darkest secrets with a single glance.

Her eyes scanned the battlefield now, watching keenly as her troops arrayed themselves across the narrow valley below.

"Mother." Her son, Yuvakudu, touched her arm to gain her attention. "Mother, Duchess, the enemy come. Look!"

Yuvakudu gestured ahead towards a pair of low, rounded hills that rose at the head of the valley.

Telivaina directed her far-seeing gaze in that direction and saw exactly what she expected to see. She had made her previous camp at a distance, giving her enemy a clear choice: they could come this way and face her army, or they could attempt to go around.

She smiled wryly to herself. It was the illusion of choice. She already had the measure of her enemy and had known they would not leave her army unfought. They would come, and they could come this way.

Cavalry bearing long, upright spears cantered easily over the grassy slopes in the distance, taking up positions on the left and right flanks. Her keen eyes could make out the colours and heraldry they wore, identifying many individual knights even from this far away. Infantry marched confidently into the broad cleft between the hills. They formed into a broad line, several warriors deep, and the front rank locked their tall, rectangular shields together with an audible clatter.

It was an imposing display of discipline and organisation, and it revealed the enemy's strength in numbers. Their commander had gained much support locally and his army was large and powerful. They had the numbers to sweep Duchess Telivaina's force away, and they had the high ground.

"Yuvakudu." Her voice was quiet and low, but many heads turned as she spoke. "Ride now. Lead the front line. You know what I have planned. Make it be."

Yuvakudu nodded respectfully, but Telivaina saw a flicker of fear in his dark eyes. A tiny hint of doubt.

"The battle will be fought and won as I have foretold. You must trust me."

"As I ever have, Mother," said Yuvakudu seriously. "Glory to the elders!" He recited the family motto and reached out to grasp his mother's hand. They held hands for a moment before Yuvakudu turned and rode off quickly down into the valley.

Soldiers stepped deferentially out of his way as he urged his horse through the gathering ranks at a brisk trot. He was an imposing figure, well over six and a half feet tall, and towered over the rest of the army even when not mounted on his powerful black stallion. His skin was even darker than his horse's flanks, marking him as a pure-blood elf, one of those who traced their ancestry back to those who had sailed across the southern ocean uncounted generations ago.

Yuvakudu was swallowed up by the massed ranks of the army and Telivaina turned her attention back to the hillside where her enemy's army was proudly arrayed. Without surprise, she noticed another block of cavalry assembled to the rear of the infantry. The tallest banners were here: the enemy commander and his most loyal troops.

No doubt, he thought that he had all but guaranteed victory today. He had forced a battle in a favourable location and had taken the high ground with Telivaina's troops constrained at the bottom of the valley below.

Telivaina's lips twitched. So it seemed.

"Herald." She barely raised her voice and yet all the soldiers nearby turned. One carried a long, gleaming horn.

"Sound the advance." The herald blew and held a rising note, and the army moved forward.

Telivaina kept her eyes on the skyline where the enemy army fidgeted and shuffled. Men turned to their neighbours to share hasty words. Anxious words. Why were they advancing? They were in a weak position to assail the heights before them. Was their commander a fool?

No, thought Telivaina. I am no fool. But I am playing a dangerous game. And when she played this game, she nearly always won.

She kicked her horse into a walk, following closely behind the rear rank of her infantry. They marched in step, long spears rising towards the sky like a well-planted field of wheat.

The jangle of harness and spurs sounded from all around. Her knights rode in a line beside her, their livery gleaming, swords resting loosely in scabbards. They would not be needed. Fate willing, none of them would be needed. The battle, and in reality the war, had already been fought. Unless she had been fooled, and it had never happened yet, her victory had already been won. Her enemy just did not know it.

It was a bright day and what few clouds there were sailed high, insubstantial wisps of white, like fleece caught on thorns. They did nothing to diminish the pleasant warmth of the morning sun. Telivaina gripped her reins a fraction more tightly in anticipation. The time had almost come.

Her infantry halted at a short blast from the herald. The slopes of the valley rose to either side, penning them in, forcing the ranks together. They stood like statues.

Nothing happened. Telivaina could almost feel the impatience from the enemy infantry. They were ready, eager, and soon their cavalry would sweep down the hillside, left and right, and trap her infantry in the base of the valley. Then, the enemy spearmen could strike. They would win the day. Hammer and anvil.

They took a step forward.

That was the moment. The time had come. Telivaina raised a hand, clenching her long fingers into a fist, and at the same moment the herald blew three short blasts on his horn.

In unison, the enemy cavalry on both hillsides spurred their horses into motion. They headed down the hill as if to strike the flanks of Telivaina's infantry. She smiled to herself. *Now.*

As one, the lead riders turned with the slope of the head of the valley and increased their speed. Before anyone had a chance to react, they were crashing hard into the flanks of the enemy infantry instead.

This, of course, was the culmination of the true battle. The outcome of the true war. It was not fought with spears, swords and blood but with oaths, debts and rewards. It had been won by carefully steering the enemy down a path that they believed was of their own choosing. In fact, an invisible hand had guided them to this point, where the truth would emerge. Her hand.

Finding themselves assailed from left and right, the soldiers had no idea where to turn. Panic spread. Shouts, screams and the harsh ring of clashing weapons filled the air.

The herald blew again but there was no need. Her infantry were already surging forward. Still holding their tight formation, they levelled spears and advanced mercilessly into the ranks of the terrified, disorganised enemy.

"Duchess?"

One of the knights riding close to her raised his voice in a question. She waved them on. Granting them the glory of battle was a fair reward for their loyalty. The knights she truly trusted were even now driving the enemy infantry into a bloody rout. The others had waited patiently, hoping for their own opportunity to impress her. Her favour was worth much.

The knights she had relied upon to make this plan work had done well. She had trusted them to get close to the enemy commander, trusted them to gain his ear. She had tasked them with spreading whispered rumours and they had done it well. They were rumours that the ambitious Earl had been eager to hear and desperate to believe.

She saw him now, the few knights still truly loyal forming a guard around him on the hilltop. Yet he could be easily identified by his fine white steed and the bright blue cloak he wore.

As she rode closer to the rear rank, heedless of the chaos of battle so near, she watched as the enemy infantry either threw down their weapons or turned and fled the field. Their allegiance had been cheaply won, and they knew the battle was lost. They had no intention of dying for this cause.

Telivaina had heard about this ambitious Count some time ago and had taken the time to find out all she could of him. He was perfect. He was ruthless enough to do whatever needed to be done and capable enough to succeed. A few rumours about the weakness of the old Earl Maurer had been enough to set the Count on his path, a path he believed would lead him to power.

Yet, all the time it was the knights secretly loyal to Telivaina who had fed the Count exactly what she wanted him to hear. Knights like Sir Creenan, who had seen very quickly where he should place his true allegiance, betraying both of his former lords to earn her favour. And the Count had been blind to it! Even when he had successfully stolen the Earldom from Maurer, it had all been part of her plan.

Now, by staging this uprising to try to usurp control of the Duchy, the new Earl had given Duchess Telivaina everything she needed. She could justly crush this rebellion and the Earl would face trial for the crime. She could legally take back the lands he had stolen – along with his own estates – as reparation. She would pass the Earldom to her son. His army would become hers.

She held up a closed fist, and the herald blew several short blasts. Her army responded, a great shout of triumph rising towards the sky as they closed in for the kill.

She glanced up towards the hilltop again and a slight scowl creased her brow. Anyone else would have cursed loudly. He had gone. She had been so close to capturing her enemy, but in the chaos, he had escaped. The hilltop was deserted.

No matter. He had only a handful of knights left loyal, and she could guess where he would go. He would soon face the justice he deserved. She rode easily to the hilltop, arriving just in time to see riders disappearing into some distant woods. The Earl and his pitiful retinue.

"Yuvakudu." She addressed her son as he joined her. "You fought well, my son. This was a great victory, and you will be rewarded."

Another elf stood beside her son, and she acknowledged his presence with a shallow nod. "Sir Vaikhari," she said by way of greeting. He was almost as tall as Yuvakudu. She suppressed a smirk at having lured the Earl's pet swordsman into her trust.

"Glory to the elders!" both elves responded, formally.

"Thank you, Mother," added Yuvakudu.

"But," she continued, "before you can claim the land and title you have earned, we must see that justice is served." She stood in her stirrups, the height giving her an eagle's view across the land. "Send the word out!" She raised her deep voice so that all could hear. "A traitor walks free in the land! A usurper! We must chase him down and make him pay for his crimes!"

She paused, casting her eyes over her gathered army.

"Spread the name of the criminal! Spread the name 'Rauf Crowmer'!"

CHAPTER EIGHTEEN

The moons rose and soared into the deep indigo sky like scraps of birch bark floating across the surface of a still pool. Ingvar watched their steady passage across the sky as evening turned to night.

He felt lonely. He had watched the three Cowls walk away from the house, their work done for the day. A rough track led away across the estate towards their own modest cottage, and after bidding them goodnight, he had stayed by the back door for some time as dusk approached and the sky above faded to a rich, dark blue.

Turning his back on the dusky scene, he stepped into the kitchen. Half-heartedly, he made himself a cold supper of stale, hard flatbread with goat's cheese and stepped back to the doorway. Checking that the bandage was secure around his hand, he made his way into the main hall and sat down at the table.

Lamaina had checked the wound and had been pleased. She had assured him that it was not going bad, and it would heal quickly. It still hurt, so he rested it on the table and used his other hand to eat. As he picked at the meal, he stared at the dark ceiling and thought about Ammie.

When he had managed to catch her eye over the last few days, she had responded with nothing more than a weak smile. He had returned a smile of his own but was filled with confusion about what it meant. Should he try to talk to her? Or should he leave her until she came to him?

He had been to the village and had presented his case for the dissolution of Ammie's marriage to the elders. He was optimistic that they would agree. Olya and Edvar could argue against it, but would they? Olya had been furious with him, but Edvar might be able to talk her round.

Ingvar grimaced as he gazed out into the closing night. There were so many things he did not know. Perhaps Ammie would be warmer towards him once her marriage was formally ended.

Both moons were edging across the sky now. Butchers' moons: one half, one showing as a sickle. Ingvar watched carefully and fancied that he could see their steady progress between the crystalline stars.

Some said that when souls departed this world through the shining veil, they went out among the stars. Was his father up there looking down on him? Ingvar hoped that he was not ashamed.

Movement caught his eye. Something ghostly-white and gleaming coldly in the moonlight seemed to be floating through the fields towards the house. His stomach clenched at the unearthly sight and he took a step back into the house.

The pale, shining shape drew closer, and he breathed out in relief. He wiped his sweaty palms self-consciously on his robe, feeling foolish. The floating shape had been a length of white-blonde hair approaching the house as Ammie walked towards him across the fields.

"Are you quite well?" asked Ingvar as she approached. "It is late to be out walking." The flickering orange lamplight threw her face into stark relief as she stood before the threshold and looked up. She was dressed in a simple dark tunic that left her arms bare.

"My parents went to the village," she said, "and I did not want to be alone." Her eyes shone with the reflected light. "I thought I would rather be with you." She stepped forward. The gentle breeze carried her subtle and particular scent to him, and he almost sighed aloud.

"Come in," he said, backing away and beckoning her to follow him in. "You will get cold standing out there." He reached around and pushed the door shut. It swung into the frame and he slid the lock into place with a slight click.

"Um…" He turned to face her. There was silence. She stepped towards him, a very slight smile on her lips and an expression of curious concentration on her face.

"You don't need to speak," she said, quietly. She raised her hands, fingertips upwards and palms towards him. Wordlessly, he copied and she tenderly, hesitantly pressed her hands to his. The sensation of her skin on his was like his whole body being doused with cool water. She exhaled deeply, closing her eyes tight.

They stood like that for a while. Ammie's eyes stayed shut but her mouth was slightly open as she breathed with long, shuddering sighs. Her hands squirmed against his, her long fingers moving from his fingertips down to his palms and back up again. His eyes never left her face, and he tried to hold the words in, but, at last he had to ask.

"What made you change your mind?"

She opened her eyes and stared at him quizzically.

"I wasn't sure how you felt…what you thought about me…"

"You are silly, sometimes," she said. She gave him a blank, unreadable look for a moment. "It's always been you. You should know that by now."

Ingvar blinked, surprised. Then he took her hands in his and smiled.

"I had hoped so, but I could not be sure. There would still be disapproval if we wanted to marry. After I brought you back from Olya's, though…I was not sure about anything."

"That elf they married me to hurt me, Ingvar," she replied quickly. "And I had to let it happen. I still liked you but I had to wait for the pain to go away."

Ingvar felt like an idiot. He had not thought of it that way. He had not taken the time to imagine what the last months had been like for her. He should have.

Impulsively, he let go of her hands and wrapped his arms around her. For a brief moment, she stiffened but then he felt her body relax. Her arms slid around his neck. They clung to each other as if time had stopped.

"Can we go to your bedroom?"

Ammie's voice startled him. He had no idea how long they had been standing in the kitchen. He had been completely lost in her arms.

"Er…yes…" He fumbled for words. "Yes, let's. It will be warmer." He took her hand and hurried through the main hall and up the stairs, his feet thumping on the treads as his heart hammered in his ribs.

Opening the door to his room, they stumbled over the threshold. Ingvar looked down at his bed, the blankets still lying askew where he had left them that morning. He felt awkward and uncertain. Ammie turned to him.

"Lie down," she instructed. "We should lie down together."

He kicked off his boots and stooped to roll onto his mattress. Despite being the master of the estate and the sole occupant of the house, he had not wanted to move into his parent's old bedroom.

His own bed was well-worn and narrow but familiar and comfortable. A few strands of escaping straw from inside the mattress prickled against his spine as he lay back.

He looked up at Ammie and opened his arms. His heart was racing. He had dreamed of her so often as he grew up, but had been so sure that he had lost her forever that he could barely believe he was not dreaming now.

Her face was strangely blank as she squeezed in to lie beside him. He stretched an arm around her, and as he held her tighter, a soft sigh escaped her lips. Her head rested on his shoulder and the sweet scent of her hair filled his nostrils.

Words spun through his mind. There was so much he wanted to tell her, but as each sentence formed, he felt that it would be unnecessary to say it aloud. He closed his eyes and breathed out deeply, trying to empty his mind of doubts, worries and questions, trying to enjoy the moment.

The world outside his bed, outside of the circle of his arms, seemed to evaporate, dissipating like morning mist beneath the summer sun.

There was a knock at the door. Ingvar's eyes snapped open, but before he had even moved, Ammie had leaped off the bed. As he swung his feet around and stood up, he heard the sound of the front door latch, as someone outside attempted to force it open.

He glanced across at Ammie, who had retreated to the corner of the room and was wringing her hands in obvious worry and distress.

"Ammie, Ammie," he said softly. "It will be fine. Trust me." Ingvar had not forgotten the dream where his father had chided him for leaving the door unbarred at night. He made sure of it now and kept a stout stave in the bedroom. He reached for it and found the solid length of oak reassuring as he headed towards the stairs.

Padding cautiously down the steps, he tightened his grip on the stave, before chiding himself for a fool. The door was barred, after all.

They had left a lantern lit in the kitchen in their excitement to rush upstairs, and the main hall was sparsely illuminated by its fading glow. Ingvar crept towards the door. The familiar surroundings of the hall seemed alien and threatening in the gloom. The far corners remained deep pools of shadow. His heart thudded as his mouth went dry.

A woody creak sounded behind him and he spun, staff raised. Ammie leaned away from him, halfway down the stairs. Ingvar shook his head and let his hands fall.

A hammering came from the door and Ingvar spun back towards the sound, his mouth dry. He hesitated, unsure whether to step towards the door or to back away. He felt that he needed to be decisive but did not know what to do.

"Ingvar! Ingvar Darelle!"

He sagged with relief. It was Lamaina's voice. He hurried to the door and began lifting the bar.

"Unbar the door! It is Lamaina Cowl. We must speak with you!"

He ushered them in. Lamaina strode into the room and Hekyn followed with his slouching gait. Both were soaked to the skin and water slicked their hair close to their skulls. It was pouring with rain, a sudden spring shower had swept through the night.

Hekyn was breathing hard and was flushed in the face, as if he had been running. He glanced up and Ingvar noticed his eyes widening slightly as he saw Ammie standing silently on the stairs.

"We come with urgent news," said Lamaina earnestly. She breathed evenly and if she was surprised at her daughter's presence in the house, she gave no sign.

"We were at the inn in Locton this evening," she began, "for the singing."

People from the village and surrounding farms would come together at the inn to share stories from Buren's heroic past. Tales of the formation of the Crown, of the hunter, Tureank, and his queen, Conferan, and of course the forging of the Twin Swords, those legendary blades that divided the ancient kingdoms into good and evil.

The people would gather, listen and raise their voices together to sing and chant well-known songs and rhymes. Lamaina and Hekyn had always gone when they could, but Ammie could no longer be persuaded. The last time they insisted she go with them, she had run from the inn with her hands clamped to her ears, unable to tolerate the crowd and the noise.

"We were chanting," continued Lamaina, "when we heard hoofbeats approaching. From the south they came, many and coming fast. We went out to the street and watched them come past."

She paused. She turned her eyes to Hekyn and then back to Ingvar. They were dark, intense pools, and her skin gleamed like polished wood in the dim, warm light.

"It was Crowmer, Ingvar," she said. "Crowmer and just his closest knights. They were bloodied from battle.

And…but this made no sense." She paused, her brow furrowed. "They were riding away from Crowmer's estate. They took the north road, and we feared they were coming here."

"No, we have seen no one," said Ingvar. He moved to the table and sat, pouring a cup of wine as his mind worked. "Olya!" He must be riding to the Ferras estate. But why?"

Ingvar worried for his friend and his brother. He and Olya were not on good terms but Crowmer riding through the night surrounded by armed knights could not be good news for anyone.

"There is more," said Hekyn, unexpectedly.

Lamaina nodded. "Yes, there is more." She moved to the table, drawing back a chair and sitting down opposite Ingvar. "One of the men following Crowmer stopped at the village and came in for a drink. What he told us surprised everyone."

"Go on," prompted Ingvar. Lamaina seemed uncharacteristically hesitant, as if nervous about what she had to say.

"He told us that he was finished with Crowmer. He said that the man was finished. There was a battle, Ingvar. Crowmer tried to take the Duchy but Duchess Telivaina met him on the field. She outwitted him. Many of his knights defected to her, or had been truly hers all along. I am not sure, the man's story was confusing. He was full of anger."

"But what he knew for certain was that Crowmer was defeated and his army was routed. What was left of it had been pursued hard all the way to his estate by Telivaina's cavalry. She had just chased him out of his estate, and that is when the man who spoke to us decided to desert from his army." She paused, looking carefully at Ingvar.

"They were riding on to the Ferras estate, but she will keep pursuing until he faces justice."

"As I feared," exclaimed Ingvar, slapping the table. "I hope Olya is safe."

"Ingvar," said Hekyn, in his soft, accented voice. "Olya was one of the knights who survived the battle. She was with him when he fled."

"Crowmer has her oath. All who worked on her estate knew she was in his pocket."

Everyone turned in surprise at the sound of Ammie's voice. She stared back unblinkingly. "Well, it's true," she finished, lowering herself to sit on the stairs.

Ingvar ground his teeth. It was true, however much he tried to forget it. Still, that was not the most important part of the news. Crowmer was defeated. He could hardly believe it was true. At that moment, he noticed Hekyn and Lamaina shared a guilty glance.

"What is it?" he asked. Their unease was clear. "Don't tell me there is more?"

"Yes." Lamaina nodded regretfully. "There is more. One more thing that you must know."

Ingvar waited as Lamaina paused, thinking of the right words.

"Crowmer proclaims his innocence," she said. "He claims that all his actions were righteous, legal, and for the good of Buren. He said it in a speech and is sending out messengers to tell it all over the north. He does not intend to surrender his Earldom without a fight, however few knights remain loyal."

She paused once more, unwilling to say more. Hekyn turned to her.

"He must know," he said, gently.

"Yes, you must know." Lamaina squared her shoulders and looked directly into Ingvar's eyes. Her face, so similar to Ammie's in features but so different in colouring, was grave.

"He mentioned your name, Ingvar. He claimed you were in league with one another. He wants all to think you conspired against Frankess, and then turned against your own father to take the estate for yourself."

"What?" Ingvar rose, furious. "How could he say that? Surely none will believe it. Why would I do that?"

"The story he spreads is that you wished to rid yourself of your father's debt to Frankess, so you encouraged Frankess to revolt with the promise of support, then stood aside and let Crowmer enact justice."

"That's madness…" Ingvar sat down heavily, his mind whirling.

"And then," Lamaina went on, "you did a deal with Crowmer to have Omar arrested so that you could take possession of the Darelle estate. He paints you as his right-hand man in the whole affair."

"No one will believe it," stated Ingvar.

"Most won't."

Ammie's voice surprised them all again.

"But a few will. And the more the story is repeated, the more people will think that there must be some truth in it."

"But…" Ingvar was bewildered. "Why?"

"When Crowmer is arrested," said Ammie plainly, "he would drag you down with him."

"Ammie…" said Hekyn in a weary, warning tone.

"She is right, my husband," said Lamaina. "The man is full of spite. And perhaps he thinks that if he can point the blame elsewhere, it will be shared when he is tried. Doubt in the court may work in his favour. That is what he seeks."

"And he hates you," said Ammie bluntly.

Ingvar stared.

"Servants on the Ferras estate spoke of it."

"But…why?" Ingvar knew Omar's stubborn refusal to treat Crowmer with the respect he felt he deserved had frustrated him as their Count, but he could not understand why his hatred ran this deep.

Ammie just shrugged in reply.

Ingvar thought quickly. The first thing he needed to do was to speak out against these rumours. The longer he remained silent, the more people would believe the tales were true. But to whom should he speak? Then a question occurred to him that he should have thought to ask earlier.

"The Duchess…" he asked to the room in general. "Did the man say where she was now?"

"He knew Crowmer was pursued hard by the Duchess's son, Sir Yuvakudu," replied Lamaina. "He would be at Crowmer's estate if he had halted the pursuit for the night. It may be that the Duchess follows him there."

"Crowmer's estate," muttered Ingvar, half to himself. "Then that is where I must go, at first light tomorrow. I can meet with her son, at least, and with luck the Duchess will have arrived."

Ingvar felt as though, if he did not confront this latest attack by Crowmer quickly, the weight of it would break him. He already felt that he would like to hide away somewhere, or just run for the hills.

Yet, he would not. As the last of the Darelles, he must fight. He must do everything possible to ensure the family endured. Especially now, when Crowmer was weak, defeated in battle and pursued by a stronger lord. He had to make a stand lest he dishonoured the memory of his father.

He hoped that this Duchess would hear his cause, and would listen. He could never be in league with Crowmer, and the suggestion that he had conspired against Frankess and then his own father was just ridiculous.

He imagined the elf Duchess inhabiting Crowmer's manor house; a spider in her web with him as an approaching fly. Would he be able to escape afterwards? He shuddered. He must do this. He must disregard his fears.

He pictured the approach to the house – the long, straight lane with the orchards spreading darkly to either side – and it reminded him of the last time he had been there. Crowmer had been dripping with self-satisfaction and Olya had been so adamant that Ingvar should kneel to the man. He knew in his heart that he had been right not to, although this was only a small comfort.

Then, a new thought hit him like a sword strike. His blood ran cold, prickling beneath his skin like winter's frost edging a lingering leaf.

"My mother...?" She must have been at Crowmer's manor house when the pursuit arrived. Was she still there? Was she safe? Hekyn and Lamaina were already shaking their heads. "Did anyone mention my mother?"

"It was not told," said Lamaina.

Hekyn spoke quickly. "I am sure she is fine."

"There is no reason for the Duchess to harm her." Lamaina reached out to lay a hand on Ingvar's.

"Even though she is the wife of her enemy?" Ingvar's voice was bitter, despite his worry. Thinking of Crowmer being married to his mother still left a sour taste in his mouth.

Lamaina gripped his hand more firmly. "More reason for her to keep your mother safe. She is valuable."

"Perhaps." Ingvar stood. "I will find the truth of the matter tomorrow. Now, I must rest."

He climbed the stairs and Ammie stood as he moved to pass. They paused for a moment, feeling the need to acknowledge their feelings for one another but also uncomfortably aware of the other eyes on them.

After several awkward heartbeats, Ingvar raised his right hand, palm outwards. Ammie quickly copied. They pressed their palms together for a fleeting, tingling moment before Ammie scurried away down the stairs. She did not look back as she followed her parents towards the rear of the house and out onto the path to their own cottage.

CHAPTER NINETEEN

The morning was dry and bright, a promise of a warm day on the wind despite the early chill. He had passed through Locton while the village was still mostly sleeping.

Lazy spirals of blue-grey woodsmoke drifted through thatched roofs here and there, showing where the occupants were beginning to stir. But Ingvar saw few people out in the streets as he rode through the village, as the sun's first fiery fingers spread out above the dark horizon to the east.

The familiar left turn beyond the southern outskirts of Locton took him towards Crowmer's estate. He skirted the tall temple, its timbers almost black in the crisp light. The sun crested the eastern hills, like a dazzling golden crown. He narrowed his eyes to slits at the sudden burst of bright light, but welcomed the flush of warmth to his face.

The ragged darkness of the northern mountains filled his vision as he turned from the sunrise. A solitary dark speck in the otherwise clear sky caught his eye. He raised a hand to shade his eyes as he followed its flight.

Even from this distance, the bulk of the bird and the huge span of its broad wings was clear, five long feathers splayed like fingers grasping at the empty air. A crowned eagle, the mightiest bird in the land and undisputed lord of the skies.

"Watch over me, Skyfather," Ingvar muttered to himself. He could not have said why the words of the ancient pagan invocation came to his lips at that moment, but he spoke them like a prayer. "May your far-seeing eyes see a clear path for me to follow."

Ingvar's ancestors worshipped these magnificent birds of prey as avatars of the eagle-god. The beliefs were commonly dismissed as pagan superstitions, but sometimes Ingvar found them reassuring. More so than thinking of the new gods, in any case. Sleeping, dead or alive, they brought Ingvar no comfort at all.

The eagle turned as her vast wings caught a rising thermal, and she soared away and out of sight towards the looming mountains. Ingvar continued along the path and soon saw Crowmer's manor house rising before him.

The track between the orchards was guarded by a handful of soldiers on each side, flinty-eyed men and women with an emblem of some sort of maned cat on their shields. Ingvar did not recognise the device or the creature. He assumed it was derived from a tale from the southern continent. It was an almost mythical land. It lay far away, across the ocean, and was full of strange creatures and mystical power.

The guards watched him warily as he approached, but they let him pass without a word.

Beyond the trees, the expansive grounds were thick with more soldiers, and a large banner had been hung from the upstairs windows. Once more Ingvar saw the maned cat symbol emblazoned across the banner in bright gold thread.

"Stop. Who are you?"

The guards on either side of the main doors to the house were not going to let him pass as easily. They were tough-looking men with boiled leather brigandines strapped over their mid-length robes. The one who spoke was bronze-skinned and bald-headed. He thrust his shield forward aggressively and eyed the longsword at Ingvar's hip with suspicion.

"I am Sir Ingvar Darelle. I must speak urgently with Duchess Telivaina." He tried to keep his voice even, but his heart was pounding. He had been so preoccupied with planning what to say that it had not occurred to him that gaining access to the house might not be easy.

"Sir Darelle, eh?" the guard drawled, lowering his shield and his eyes, studying the boar emblem Ingvar wore on his chest. "I've heard of you. I think the Duchess is going to want to talk to you straight away. In you go."

Ingvar was surprised, but did not ask any questions. He wondered for a moment why they did not ask him to leave his sword outside, but dismissed the thought as he stepped through the door and into the darker surroundings of the main hall.

Squinting into the gloom, he peered around. As his eyes adjusted to the change in light, he could make out a number of figures sitting around the wide central table. He stepped forward, trying to suppress his anxiety.

The closest figure rose and Ingvar saw, with some surprise, that it was one of the knights closest to the deposed Earl Maurer. Sir Creenan. The man who had arrested his father. He said nothing as he rose, but returned Ingvar's gaze with an emotionless glare.

"Sir Darelle," said a deep voice from Ingvar's left, as its owner stood. Ingvar's eyebrows rose in astonishment to see it was Sir Sighra Vaikhari, Crowmer's duellist. The tall elf dipped his head, that familiar sardonic smile spreading across his lips.

"We meet once more," he said, with wry amusement.

Ingvar nodded back, but before he could reply, he was distracted by the looming shadow caused by the third figure rising to their feet.

Ingvar craned his neck to look up. It was a second elf, who had been sitting next to Vaikhari. Like Vaikhari, he had short dark hair and pointed upswept ears, but where the swordmaster's skin was like dark, polished mahogany, this elf's skin was black like charcoal, tinged with a sheen of blue.

Yet, it was his height that was the most striking thing about him. Sir Vaikhari was extremely tall, half a foot taller than Ingvar at least, and yet the elf beside him was at least a hand taller. Ingvar reckoned he must have been the tallest person he had ever seen. Crowmer's hall was built with high ceilings and yet the beams were mere inches away from the top of his head.

He did not speak, but a voice came from the far end of the table. "Welcome, Sir Darelle," said a woman's voice, low but melodious. "We are happy to have you join us." She did not rise, and her voice carried a hint of amusement.

Ingvar stepped closer, approaching the chair where she reclined. This must be Duchess Telivaina. He bowed low, dropping his eyes to the stone floor.

"It is my honour, my Duchess," began Ingvar, formally.

"Be welcome, and be at your ease," Telivaina cut in, forestalling any further formality. "Sit, drink." She waved Ingvar into the nearest chair. "We have much to discuss."

The other men folded their frames into their chairs and Ingvar copied, sitting closest to the Duchess. As she poured him a cup of wine, he glanced around the room.

Little had changed since his last visit – the same furniture remained in the same places – but Ingvar noted that Crowmer's shrine to Kaled had been removed from the alcove. As he glanced around, he tried to avoid the others' eyes, but could feel their stares on him as Telivaina slid the cup across the table.

"I believe you have already met Sir Creenan and Sir Vaikhari?" Telivaina motioned towards the two knights. Ingvar swallowed and nodded, trying not to think about the circumstances in which he last met them, and also that they had both been apparent allies of Crowmer. "So allow me to introduce Sir Yuvakudu," she continued, and the very tall elf inclined his head in a shallow nod. "The general of my army and also my son."

"Well met." Ingvar glanced between the three knights awkwardly, feeling intimidated and out of place. "Well met, all."

"So, Sir Darelle." Telivaina pronounced his name deliberately and slowly. "You have become quite the pariah. Your tale is truly a sorry one. I know it well by now, although"—she paused, and directed a meaningful gaze in his direction—"I am very curious to find out how it will end."

She held his eyes with hers and he felt like he was bewitched, unable to look away. Her eyes were mysterious pools, with disturbing currents swirling in their depths. Her skin was very dark, darker than Lamaina's, but they had a similar bearing of nobility.

Her face was narrow and angular, but her skin was as clear and smooth as that of a young woman. Her eyes, though…they held such wisdom and knowledge, and gleamed with the force of a powerful intellect. Her eyes hinted at great age. Ingvar wondered how old she truly was.

"Sir Darelle?"

Her voice cut abruptly through his thoughts.

"You came to see me. What is it that you have to say?"

Ingvar blinked self-consciously. He did not know how long he had been transfixed by the Duchess's dark, ancient eyes.

"Yes, my Duchess." He shook his head. "I am sorry. I came to speak with you about the stories being spread by Earl Crowmer."

She made no response, her face impassive, but she motioned with a finger gesture for him to continue. The others remained silent, their grim stares like the steep face of a granite cliff.

"The Earl…" He stopped himself as the atmosphere in the room darkened, and corrected himself. "The *deposed* earl sent out messengers following his defeat. By you."

Telivaina inclined her head, as if graciously acknowledging praise. Ingvar stuttered slightly under her knowing gaze, but continued.

"The messengers told how I had conspired with him, first against Sir Frankess and then later against my own father. Crowmer would have all in the land believe I first betrayed an old friend, in Sir Frankess, and then set my own father up to be arrested for treachery."

"Indeed."

Telivaina leaned back in apparent satisfaction.

"Bold is he that would spread such rumours with his own mouth. Bold, or perhaps foolish?"

Ingvar cursed himself. That had the feel of a trap, baited and sprang by his incaution.

"No, my Duchess," said Ingvar, leaning forward earnestly. "I am neither. That is why I have come. I must be given the opportunity to defend myself. These rumours are false, entirely false. I could never be an ally of Crowmer."

The Duchess locked eyes with Ingvar once again, and he was drawn into those deep, dark wells as they examined him, judged him. She took a small sip of wine before setting the cup down gently.

"I have heard from some that you conspired together," she said, and quickly held up a hand to silence Ingvar, who had opened his mouth to protest. She went on. "And I have heard from others that you and your father had ever caused him frustration. That you held him in contempt and would never be his ally."

"I have also heard that Crowmer's messengers are saying that it was I that assailed him. That I was the aggressor and sprang an ambush to usurp him and steal his lands." She spread her hands in a gesture suggesting weighing. "So, where does the truth live?"

"Crowmer lies!" blustered Ingvar. Surely, she must know that. What game was she playing? "I have not, and would not ever conspire with that man…"

She held up a hand once more. "Please, peace. We are civilised here."

Ingvar pressed his lips together and tried to hold his patience.

"The truth is the lord," she said, with an unusual turn of phrase. "When Crowmer's messengers tell the tale that I ambushed him, and that I tried to steal his lands, what can I do? I can ask many honourable knights, such as Sir Creenan or Sir Vaikhari, or others who were there. Where is the truth? What did you see? Which one of us speaks false? And which holds the truth?" She paused, letting the message sink in. Ingvar was starting to understand.

"The truth is the lord," she repeated. "Who will speak up for your truth, Sir Darelle?"

Ingvar sat in silence. Of course, Crowmer's stories were false. Of course, most who heard them would know that. But, who could he find with the standing and authority to speak up in his name? Crowmer had won over all the local nobles, and even now he was defeated, there were few Ingvar would consider to be allies.

Olya? After their last encounter, he doubted she would be prepared to speak for him.

"You must know that Crowmer spreads falsehoods?" Ingvar heard a note of pleading creeping into his voice. "He seeks to drag me down with him. Or to have me share in his punishment. You must see that!"

Duchess Telivaina stared back in response, unreadable and unflinching.

"What I know, or what I think I know, are just horses riding through a dream. What concerns me is the truth, Sir Darelle. Truth that can be seen by all. Truth that is proven."

"Creenan? Vaikhari?" Ingvar turned to the other end of the table. "You both must know that Crowmer lies about my actions. Will you speak for me?"

Vaikhari shook his head, although he wore a broad smile.

"All now know that Duchess Telivaina has my oath," replied Creenan. "In the conflict between you and Crowmer, we must stand aside." He fixed Ingvar with a flinty gaze. "We cannot speak for either side in this matter."

Vaikhari nodded, his lips twisted as if on the edge of laughter.

Ingvar ground his teeth. This felt deeply unfair. He was entirely innocent in this matter, but it felt as though the world conspired to put obstacles before any path that might provide a defence. There must be a way.

"What if I were to offer you my oath? What if I kneeled to you, now?"

Vaikhari's smile grew broader and Telivaina raised an eyebrow.

"Accepting the oath of a knight who may be in league with a sworn enemy?" she replied, archly. "A man who I am pursuing for his crimes? Many would think that accepting such an oath would seem…imprudent."

Ingvar hung his head. He had not expected her to accept, but he had little left to offer.

"We have sympathy with your plight, Sir Ingvar."

Yuvakudu's words were slow and deliberate, delivered in a low, rumbling baritone.

"You have suffered much, yet so far you have retained your honour. Maurer always spoke well of your father and your family. By all accounts, you were considered faithful and reliable."

Honour. After Crowmer's plans had cut his family to shreds, his honour was all that he had left. Yet with his final act as Earl, the man was trying to steal that too.

Ingvar sat up straighter. He turned back towards Duchess Telivaina, who was wearing a very slight, knowing smile. Ingvar knew what must be done. He hesitated to say the words, knowing that it was a step that could not be reversed. Yet, he now knew it was his only choice.

Telivaina watched him patiently. Ingvar had the uncomfortable sensation that she knew every thought that passed through his mind. He opened his mouth hesitantly.

He spoke. "Earl Crowmer is a traitor, and I am not, and have never been in league with him. He has lied about my actions. He has sullied my honour. I will fight against his lies and prove my innocence in the only way I can."

Around the table, he sensed the other knights shifting expectantly in their seats. They did not actually lean closer as he spoke, but to Ingvar, it felt as though they did. It felt like the walls themselves closed in about him.

"I declare a Just War on Earl Crowmer," he said, the words exploding from his mouth like thunderbolts.

CHAPTER TWENTY

Sir Crowmer waited outside the tent, and seethed.

He had been looking forward to this summons, and what it might mean for his prospects, but being left waiting in this blazing heat was an affront. He deserved to be treated with more respect. He clamped his teeth together in frustration.

The tent flap remained stubbornly closed, and the muffled voices he could hear from within seemed full of mockery.

No. He tried to get a grip on himself. No, they were not voices of derision. They must not be. Perhaps they were already discussing the revelation he had made to the camp bailiff. Perhaps the wheels were already in motion.

He stood up a little straighter. One of the guards beside the tent glanced at him, but little curiosity showed in his tired, narrowed eyes. The rest of the man's face was hidden by the round helmet he wore, the plain steel cheek-guards framing his nose and mouth. A bead of sweat dripped beside his eye and ran down the side of his nose.

Abruptly, the tent flap was jerked aside and the open, blocky face of the bailiff peered through.

"Ah, you are here," he said, without surprise. "They are asking for you."

"I have been here for some time, waiting," Crowmer replied, his voice tight and clipped. The bailiff just shrugged and beckoned him inside.

Earl Maurer's command tent was spacious and airy. The shelter it provided from the relentless, blazing sunlight was a relief. But Crowmer was determined to show no discomfort and stood proudly once inside.

The other men in the room turned from where they had been examining a makeshift battlefield map, which was scraped into the bare earth of the tent's floor. Rudely carved blocks of wood represented different Bureno companies, arrayed against a set of carefully placed rocks to represent the Tayan army.

Battle plans were being drawn up. Without him.

"Sir Crowmer," said Earl Maurer, as he turned, his skin the colour and texture of creased leather. "I understand you wanted to speak to me?"

"My Earl," said Crowmer with a respectful nod. "I believe the bailiff has informed you that I would bring a crime to your attention. I hope that justice can be done."

The others simply looked at him without curiosity. He was used to their contempt, but the tide was about to turn. He eyed them dispassionately: Sir Jarren, muscular, dark and handsome; Sir Frankess, thin and tense as a blade; and Sir Darelle.

This third man was short, round-shouldered and belligerent. He had worn his mistrust openly since they had first met. Darelle often spoke against him and counselled Maurer against empowering him with more responsibility. His influence would soon be greatly reduced.

"Yes, that," said Maurer ruefully. "Well, out with it! Say your piece and be done."

Crowmer bridled at Maurer's impatient tone, but kept his face blank, his voice even and respectful.

"I must report a theft," he said, facing Maurer and ignoring the other men. "From you, my Earl."

Maurer waited, raising an eyebrow.

Crowmer went on. "I witnessed Sir Omar Darelle leaving your tent on an occasion when you were not here. He looked suspicious." He fixed Darelle with an accusing stare, which the man returned with a level gaze. He said nothing.

"I wanted to confirm the crime," continued Crowmer. "So I waited for an opportunity, then searched his tent. I found a jewelled ring that I know belongs to you, my Earl. I believe it is a valuable family heirloom."

Frankess and Jarren shook their heads. Darelle looked surprised.

Crowmer continued. "I alerted the bailiff to confirm the theft. I am sorry I must be the one to tell of such treachery, my Earl."

Maurer said nothing for a moment, instead glaring at Crowmer, his jaw jutting.

"Sir Tann!" Maurer called without turning his head. "Step forward! In your duty as camp bailiff, will you tell nought but the truth?"

The bailiff stepped forward. He was a young man with fair hair and tanned skin suggesting a farmer rather than a warrior. Nevertheless, he was an efficient and skilful fighter, and he had been nominated as bailiff due to his reputation for fairness and honesty.

"Yes, my Earl," he said, calmly. "My word is my bond, or may I be judged wanting beyond the veil."

"Can you confirm Crowmer's story, Sir Tann?"

Maurer sounded uninterested.

"He speaks true," replied Tann.

Crowmer noted with some satisfaction that Omar Darelle's eyes widened slightly at these words.

"Sir Crowmer did come to me, and told me of this crime."

"And did you go to Sir Darelle's tent?"

"Yes, I did."

"And did you find my ring there?"

"Yes, my Earl. It was there. On my word." Tann lifted his hand and passed a ring to Maurer. It was heavy, thick gold and bore a ruby the size of a man's thumbnail. "I have it here."

"Well, well," said Maurer, slipping the ring back onto one of his thick, stubby fingers. "What to do? What to do?"

"One more thing, my Earl," said Tann.

Maurer turned to him, faint amusement playing across his lips. Why? He should be considering judgement on the thief, Sir Darelle. What was there to laugh at?

"I also saw," said Tann, his face blank, "Sir Crowmer leaving this tent with that ring."

"No—" began Crowmer, but Tann raised his voice and continued speaking.

"I could think of no reason for him to be entering your tent while you were not there, so I followed him and saw as he put the ring in Sir Darelle's tent."

"This is falsehood!" spluttered Crowmer. He felt heat rising in his cheeks as he tried to stop his hands shaking with rage and frustration. Frankess and Jarren were already laughing openly.

"Oh, Crowmer," said Maurer, shaking his head. "Where do you think I place my trust more highly? In Sir Tann? Or in you?"

Crowmer could find no words. He had been certain he had not been observed while sneaking the ring into Darelle's tent. He had been certain that his plan would work to drive a wedge between this clique of knights. He desperately wanted to be part of Maurer's inner circle.

"It is the nature of untrusting men," said Maurer in fatherly tones, "to assume that all others do not know how to trust." He patted Crowmer on the shoulder. "I am sure you will rise in due time, young Crowmer," said the Earl, steering him firmly towards the tent's triangular doorway, "but it will not be in this way. Go well!"

Crowmer stumbled from the tent and stalked away across the camp, the sound of mocking laughter ringing in his ears.

Earl Crowmer clenched his fist, rage coursing through him as the flimsy parchment was crushed in his grip.

The same mocking laughter seemed to echo down the years, taunting him anew as he considered the message. Despite all the battles he had fought and all the plans he had made, it was the same name that rose to stand in his path, again and again.

Darelle.

He grimaced as his hatred raged. From that day all those years ago, he had sworn to himself that he would never be so humiliated again, and that he would have his revenge on those that had wronged him with their dismissal, their laughter.

Tann, Maurer, Jarren, and Frankess. He had outmanoeuvred most, or seen them dead and gone. The Darelle family, though, had always been the deepest and most persistent thorn in his side.

He had thought that putting an end to the old fool Omar would be the end of it, but his idiot son Ingvar was another who did not know when he was beaten.

And now this.

Crowmer opened his fist and let the ruined parchment fall to the stony floor of the Ferras family's great hall. A letter from the evil Duchess Telivaina telling of Ingvar Darelle's intentions. The boy was planning to declare a Just War. It could not be allowed to happen.

If he was to be tried, he fully intended to make sure that Darelle was tried as well. The boy could stand beside him in court and face the same accusations. He would find out which of them could be more persuasive. He might even convince them that the Darelle's had planned it all.

A Just War would ruin that. He could not risk himself or his champion being defeated. Darelle would be exonerated and the opportunity to make him share the blame, and the punishment, would be lost. Crowmer needed doubt. He needed the court to be unsure about Darelle's allegiance.

He strode across the hall, summoning his remaining troops. He had plans to make.

CHAPTER TWENTY-ONE

Ingvar hit the ground, hard.

He landed flat on his back on the dusty, compacted earth and every muscle in his body screamed at him to stay there. He felt as though, if he closed his eyes for a moment, he would fall asleep where he lay.

"Up."

A harsh, crisp voice cut through his pain. Lamaina.

"That was closer. Better."

"Have we not done enough?" he asked, climbing wearily to his feet. She faced him with a wooden practice sword in her hands, barely breathing.

"We finish when the sun touches the mountains," she said as she gestured away to the west, where the sky was tinged with pink and orange. The sun itself hung stubbornly a finger's width from the black smudge of the distant horizon. He groaned inwardly.

In the past week, Ingvar had had plenty of time to agonise over his pledge to declare Just War on Crowmer. He had not done so yet, and felt that he needed to prepare himself physically and mentally before that confrontation took place.

A Just War felt like the only way to clear his name – and to finally be free from the destructive influence of the man –

but only if he was victorious. The stakes were high. He could still lose everything.

"You have done a brave thing," Lamaina had gushed, after he had returned home. He had thrown himself down into a chair in the main hall of the house and told them the news. The evening was drawing in by the time he returned from Crowmer's estate, and his stomach growled as Lamaina set a bowl of spiced stew on the table.

"And you have done the right thing," she continued, sitting down opposite as he began to eat. "And you will triumph. Justice must be done against this vile man."

"Only if I win." Ingvar bit his lip anxiously. With the dispute being a case of his word against Crowmer's, a duel would be likely.

"Can you best him with a blade?" asked Lamaina, as if she was reading his thoughts.

"I do not know," Ingvar answered honestly. Before he had become Count, Crowmer had cultivated a reputation for skill-at-arms. Like everything surrounding the man, it was impossible to know what of the stories were true, and how much had been embroidered, exaggerated or fabricated.

"He cannot nominate Vaikhari, in any case," said Lamaina.

Ingvar smiled at that. The elf blademaster's defection from Crowmer's right hand gave him hope.

"I don't know that I would have the courage to declare, if I thought I might face Vaikhari in combat." He said the words, but he was not sure they were true.

He had to prove his innocence. He had to defend his honour. A Just War was the only choice left to him, no matter who he might have to face. He hoped it would be Crowmer himself. Surely, fate would grant him victory against the man who had caused him such pain, who had taken so much?

He had to believe it. Yet, the law permitted Crowmer to nominate another to fight in his stead, and the victor would be deemed to have proved whose cause was righteous.

Then it hit him. A sudden realisation of what would happen. Of what he had done. Icy splinters prickled across his skin as the grim reality dawned.

"Olya…"

Lamaina's eyes widened slightly. "No…"

Ingvar sank forward, pressing his face into his trembling hands.

Of course, Crowmer would nominate Olya to fight the duel in his stead. He was occupying her family home and they remained in his debt, beholden to him. He would like to think she would resist, but what choice might she have? Perhaps the way they had spoken to each other previously would make her keen to fight.

"I cannot win," he muttered. "I've never bested Olya in a duel. Not once."

Lamaina did not try to dispute this.

"I have doomed us. I'm sorry. I am a fool."

Now Lamaina responded. "You must not talk that way." She reached across the table and grasped his hands in hers. "You have done right in all your deeds. You are not defeated yet. Fate will be with you!"

Ingvar shook his head, eyes down. He could not bring any response to his lips.

"Ingvar Darelle," she said, seriously, "I will help you."

He smiled weakly, but did not appreciate the manner of help that Lamaina would provide. Would insist upon.

The very next morning, he woke by the grey light of the sky just before dawn streamed through his window. Lamaina thrust the shutters open with a clatter and strode imperiously around his room.

"Up. It is morning," she announced in brisk, clipped tones. She gathered up his robes and threw them onto the bed. "Your training begins at this moment. With hard work and practice, Crowmer will be defeated. Sir," she added as an afterthought.

She browbeat him into a forced march up to the summit of one of the many green hills that overlooked the estate. He puffed and panted his way slowly to the top while she jogged easily alongside. Her long legs covered the ground effortlessly in graceful strides.

Only after he descended to the manor house again, legs forced into an awkward run, did she allow him rest and food. He ate in silence, shocked and winded, as she explained.

"The body and the mind are children of the soul," she began. "But all three need one another. Your soul can overpower your enemy's, but to defeat him utterly requires a strong body and clear mind."

"I will help you make your body stronger and train it to work harder. Your mind must have focus and be free from doubt. Your skills can also be improved. I will help you practise your swordcraft."

Ingvar could not hide his surprise. "What do you know of swordcraft?" He blurted out the question before he could stop himself. Lamaina's only response was a small smile.

A short time later, he was out on the grass before the house as bright spring sunshine bathed the estate with welcome warmth. Lamaina faced him, a wooden practice sword held loosely before her. Her stance was relaxed, but her dark eyes were fixed on him, sharply observing every movement.

"Are you sure about this?" he asked, uncertainly.

She smiled. "I am sure that I can help you, Sir Darelle."

He chuckled doubtfully, but stepped forward and thrust out his wooden blade, aiming for her body.

Her riposte caught him completely off guard; she caught his blade on hers and turned it easily aside. In the same movement, she stepped in close and tripped him, forcing him backwards over her extended leg.

It was unconventional but unexpected, and effective. He tumbled onto his back. As he looked up, he found himself staring down the length of her blade as she stood over him. He flushed, feeling his face pink with shame.

"I did not know that you had ever held a sword before," he said, wonder in his voice.

"There are many things that you do not know," she replied.

That first sparring session set the tone for the week that followed, Lamaina indefatigably pushing Ingvar to train and practise through every hour of light each day and Ingvar desperately struggling to keep going when the strength of his body and his will were both pushed to the limit.

On the second morning, he had groaned bitterly when Lamaina had opened the shutters. As the light hit him on the third day, he had covered his face with the blanket as every muscle in his body protested. On the fourth day, he had gritted his teeth and had begun the exercises without complaint.

On the sixth day, he had risen and was dressing by the time Lamaina entered the room. She stared at his half-naked body unashamedly as he hurriedly pulled his robes over his head. By the start of the second week, he already felt lighter, stronger and faster.

They sparred every day. Ingvar had trained with a sword since he was a child, but Lamaina had her own deadly grace and natural balance that made her more than a match for him. He imagined that she would be a formidable opponent with almost any weapon. The discovery of her hidden skill had been quite a surprise.

He asked where she had learned to fight.

"I have learned many things," she said, as enigmatically as usual. "One can achieve much with time and curiosity."

It seemed she wanted to tell him nothing, but she taught him much.

Much of her teaching was about poise and balance, rather than strikes and parries. They duelled, standing on one leg, or balanced atop sawn logs. It was strange to Ingvar, but he felt his precision improving even as the strength in his body increased.

She also encouraged him to think about strategies he could use to gain an advantage against different opponents.

"Do not focus on beating their blade," she said, as they rested during a sparring session. "Focus instead on beating their self. Avoid their strengths and attack them where they are weak. Give them bad choices to make."

He nodded as he tried to understand.

Olya, he thought. How on earth could he beat Olya?

"If it is to be Olya Ferras that you must face," said Lamaina, as if reading his thoughts, "then you must think of what advantages you can find to use against her."

"I can think of none," he muttered, hopelessly. "She has always been the better swordsman."

That had always been the case, ever since they had started their very first sword lessons when they were children. He had always trailed behind her.

"Think not of your skills," said Lamaina gently. "Think of what is in your mind, your strength of will. The duel will be won and lost by clarity of thought and purity of purpose."

"I cannot find an advantage over Olya," Ingvar replied. "She knows everything about me." He kneeled on the ground, his blade lying on the grass beside him. He ran a despondent hand across his face, wiping the sweat away from his eyes.

"Aha!" said Lamaina triumphantly, leaning forward to poke him in the ribs with one long finger. "There it is! She has known you long. She has fought you many times. She thinks she knows what you will do, all that you can do, and what you will not do."

She beamed at him, a questioning eyebrow raised. Ingvar was puzzled and spread his arms in a slow shrug. Lamaina reached forward and poked him again.

"What would Olya Ferras never think to expect from you?" she asked, fixing him with an intense stare. "What strategy is so unlikely that it will catch her unawares?"

Ingvar's mouth dropped open. It sounded mad, but it was a logical sort of madness. 'Do in war all the things that your enemy will least expect,' so the old wisdom went. But what, in a duel, would possibly surprise Olya?

"Well," he began, hesitantly. Something had tickled in his memory. Something…that she would never expect. "We always used to joke about never turning your back on an enemy. How it was the first lesson for beginners to learn. But there is no way I could use that in a duel. Is there?"

Lamaina's eyes gleamed as she spoke. "There is a way."

Which had brought them to this point, just over a week later. Lamaina had been trying to teach Ingvar a new technique. They had practised it over and over again that day, before the sun set.

"The *tornaide* cut," Lamaina had said, after suggesting it to Ingvar, "is difficult. It's risky and dangerous for both duellists." She paused.

Ingvar opened his mouth to voice his concern, but she quickly went on.

"Which is why it will give you a chance to catch Olya Ferras by surprise."

She had shown him the technique, slowly at first. He had been filled with doubt. It required such boldness, such perfect timing and such precision of movement that he was not sure he would ever dare to try it.

"Again," said Lamaina softly, and he was jerked back to the present. He glanced up and climbed stiffly to his feet, noting that the sun had dropped a few miserable inches in the sky while his thoughts wandered back to when this had started.

His muscles complained as he lifted his sword; fiery stabs of deep fatigue shot through his shoulders, back and legs. He pressed his teeth together and forced himself to ignore it. The pain was insignificant.

He really felt that he was getting closer to mastering the technique. Lamaina had occasionally attacked him with the *tornaide* as they sparred, and it was this that gave him hope that maybe, just maybe, it could work against Olya.

It had to. So, he had to perfect it. He felt like it was his only chance.

The blades clacked together, the aged wood rebounding slightly as Ingvar advanced. Lamaina gave way, stepping back and to the side as Ingvar sought to take the centre line. She was fast, with quick wrists. Ingvar was the better and more practised swordsman but Lamaina consistently caused him problems; she made him think.

He aimed a cut, low to high and towards her hip. She moved to parry, but it was a feint. He rolled his wrists to turn the slash into a thrust. She dodged back, a willow leaf in the stream.

Lamaina had impressed on him that for the *tornaide* to work it had to be totally unexpected. To practise effectively, he had to attempt the strike when Lamaina was unprepared.

He cut downwards as she retreated; a vertical strike towards her head or hands. It was slow and too straight, and her riposte was fast. He fell back as she attacked towards his left side.

Now.

He took his left hand from the hilt of his sword, and in the briefest moment of opportunity after her strike, he reached out, pushing her hands away to the side. This all had to be fast, and precise.

As she tried to lift her hands, to free the hilt of her sword, he stepped forward. A long stride brought him closer, and as his body moved forward, he pivoted on his front foot.

Spinning on the ball of his foot, he reversed his blade and stabbed backwards as he turned his back towards Lamaina. This was the *tornaide*; a spinning strike where the blow landed as one's back was turned to the enemy.

Ingvar's back was jammed tightly against Lamaina's front, his hands crossed before his chest as he tried to hold her hands in place with his left, and his sword steady with his right.

He glanced down as he stopped moving. He swore. Lamaina's blade was at his throat.

"Close," whispered Lamaina, her lips close to his ear and her voice soft. He sagged dejectedly and stepped away. He shook his head.

"Did my strike hit, at least?" he asked, hopefully. She paused for a moment, then lowered her eyes. He swore again. "Fate be damned! I have no chance." His knees bent beneath him and he sat down heavily on the worn grass.

Lamaina put her practice sword down and came to stand beside him. She sank smoothly into a cross-legged sitting position and grasped one of his hands familiarly.

"You can do it," she said, earnestly. "You have come a long way in these last days. You have become stronger, faster, and your will is more firm. You will be the master of your own destiny in the duel to come."

He hoped she was right. Perhaps with another week of training.

"You never answered my question," said Ingvar, softly. "You never told me how you learned to fight. How you learned to use a sword. And why you kept it a secret…"

Lamaina looked away, apparently watching the last fiery glow of the sunset fading over the horizon. The sky was clear, but a few high and wispy clouds were painted orange and pink as the sun sank over the western mountains. The sky darkened.

Finally, she turned her face back towards him. Her eyes were deep and mysterious as she began to speak.

"I have lived a long time, Ingvar," she said, her voice hushed. "It is a blessing that we elves carry still, to live many times the span of years allotted to men. Perhaps, it is also our curse.

"In my younger days, I travelled far and did many things. I hold some of the memories like gold and jewels." She smiled wistfully. "Of other memories, I am less proud. But such is life, is it not?"

Ingvar nodded. He did not speak. He felt as though she were finally offering him a glimpse of a story she had told few other people.

"For a time, I was in Anish," she continued, her eyes flicking knowingly to meet Ingvar's. "I fought as one of the Royal Sentinels in their border wars against Kotev."

Ingvar's eyes widened. The Sentinels were the military guardians of Anish rulers; a standing army of near-mythical skill.

"But when the war was won, I had seen enough blood, so travelled west, looking for somewhere quiet to rest."

"And you ended up here?"

"In time," she replied with a swift smile. "I served on a few other estates first. But, I quickly discovered that they loved power, riches and making war more than they loved the land. Some of them you know." She gave him a meaningful look.

"Crowmer?" he asked. "You served Crowmer?"

"Not for long. I needed to work, but I quickly saw what manner of man he was. I could see where his path was leading.

"But," she continued, "soon I heard of a noble who respected the old ways and behaved with honour. Your father."

Ingvar smiled.

"And that is my story. Hekyn was also here, and I knew when I met him that I had arrived where fate wanted me."

"Fate!" snorted Ingvar. "Fate has been a cruel master."

Lamaina shook her head. "Your plight was not made by the hand of fate," she said, seriously. "Your suffering has been the will of that man. Crowmer believes that he is above fate. He is wrong."

"It matters not." Ingvar shrugged, grumpily. "The damage is done, whether by him or by fate. And if I am defeated in the duel, which is likely, then he will truly have taken everything."

"Yet, you will not be defeated," replied Lamaina, quickly. She gripped his hand more firmly, leaning forward as she spoke earnestly. "I know this. I feel it in my heart. You will triumph because you have something that Crowmer and Olya have not." She leaned back.

"What do you mean?" asked Ingvar. There was such a tone of surety and confidence in her voice that he could not help but pay attention.

"I saw it the moment I met you," she said, fixing him with a piercing stare once more. "I knew even when you were young that you would be a man of honour and a man who followed his heart.

"My Ammie saw it too. She was always yours, from the start. That made me glad." She paused again.

The sun had set now, the sky a washed-out ochre at the horizon fading to indigo darkness above their heads. A few stars gleamed already in the wide heavens.

"And that is what you have," continued Lamaina, "that the others do not. That is what will speed your blade in the duel. That is what will make you fight harder, and better. Because you have something that you would die for, and they do not."

A nightingale began to sing, a bubbling, varied song that flowed like cool water through the still evening air. Ingvar listened for a moment, waiting for Lamaina to finish.

"You have love," she said, with a smile. Ingvar smiled back and began climbing wearily to his feet. Lamaina jumped up in a single bound and extended a hand.

They strolled back to the manor house, their wooden practice swords tucked under their arms. The vaguest glow at the western horizon was all that remained of the day, and the sky above was pierced with shards of ice as the stars shone more brightly.

"Look," said Lamaina, touching his arm and gesturing back eastwards.

Both moons were rising, and both were full; twin ghostly discs against the darkening backdrop. It was a rare and unearthly sight.

"There used to be magic in this world, you know," whispered Lamaina, her voice breathy and deep. "The stories are true. There is power and energy within the earth and some were able to use it. Those who could drew forth power and wielded it in the world to build, to heal, or to destroy."

Ingvar remained silent, listening.

"The cost was great," she continued, "requiring sacrifice, focus and great strength of will. Yet, it was possible. Some say that it still is." She turned to Ingvar, her eyes shining in the moonlight like reflections in a deep well.

"Those whose need is great – who have great strength of character and are determined to succeed – some say it is possible for people like this to draw on the hidden power and bring it to their aid." She shrugged and turned back to watch the moonsrise.

He gaped at her. Was she suggesting he should try to use magic? Lamaina was often mysterious and occasionally superstitious, but it seemed unbelievable that even she would make this suggestion. He licked his lips.

"What are you saying?" he asked.

"I am saying," she replied, her voice firm, "that if you believe in yourself firmly enough, extraordinary things can happen. Some call it 'magic', some would use the word 'miracle', but the important thing is to believe." She turned and pulled him into a swift embrace. She was taller than he and her arms were strong.

She laid a soft hand against the side of his face for a moment, then turned away. He felt his face flushing.

"Goodnight," she said, stepping towards the path to her own cottage. "Sir Ingvar Darelle."

"Goodnight, Lamaina Cowl," he called after her, before opening the door of the house and going inside.

CHAPTER TWENTY-TWO

Ingvar slept uneasily that night. Ammie's presence in the bed beside him was soothing but still he tossed and turned fitfully.

His mind was busy as he tried to rest his tired body. He rolled over onto his side. Ammie's naked skin pressed comfortingly against his back as she moved over and wordlessly pressed herself against him. Her skin was soft and cool. Gradually, he drifted off.

His eyes snapped open.

It felt like he had been sleeping mere moments. The silence in the room was absolute, but something had disturbed his sleep. What?

Ammie's touch was absent, and even without moving, he could feel that her body was no longer next to him. The bed felt empty.

A disturbance in the air beside the bed made him turn his head. The room was dark but a sliver of moonlight lanced through the crack between the shutters. Ingvar's eyes widened as something metallic glinted sharply.

The blade of a knife. His heart hammered in his chest and he watched helplessly as another knife rose beside it. That was when he realised that two black-clad figures were looming at his bedside.

They were about to strike and he could not even move. The blood seemed to freeze in his veins. He opened his mouth to cry out, lifting an arm in a drowsy, futile attempt to ward off the blow.

Before the knives could lash out, there was a fleshy thump and a grunt. One of the shadowy figures dropped abruptly from sight. A blade glittered as it caught the light again for a moment. Ingvar opened his eyes wide, trying to make out what was happening.

The remaining intruder turned. They were dressed completely in black and gripping a dagger. Ingvar could now see a third figure, this one a ghostly-white shape in the gloom. The assassin moved towards it.

As the pale shape moved away, he saw a flash of colourless hair. He realised it was Ammie. She had struck down the first intruder and was now confronting the other. Her naked skin shone with a pale, blue-white glow as the thin beam of moonlight illuminated the scene.

The attacker thrust their knife towards her but she swivelled quickly to one side, and the stab missed. In the same motion, she grabbed their outstretched wrist and twisted it savagely. They were pulled forward, off balance, and Ingvar saw Ammie's knee rising as she pulled their forearm down.

There was an audible crack as the bone broke. The attacker screamed, a woman's voice, and fell with a thud. Movement closer to the bed caught Ingvar's eye; a gloved hand appeared over the side of the bed, grasping at the blankets.

Ingvar quickly shrugged off the blanket. As the first intruder's head rose over the side of the bed, shrouded in a deep hood, he kicked at it, hard. Their nose broke beneath his heel with a visceral crunch and there was sharp pain as their teeth cut into his skin. They moaned as they fell back to the floor.

Light poured in. The room lit up with stark, crisp moonlight as Ammie pushed open the shutters. Ingvar was still sitting on the bed, stunned, as Ammie strode back across the room.

The attacker with a broken arm was on her feet again. Her hood had fallen back and Ingvar recognised her face. He recalled her name, Tinos, and knew she was one of Crowmer's captains.

"Mongrel bitch," she spat in Ammie's direction. She drew another knife with her offhand and lunged viciously. She was fast, but Ammie was faster.

She palmed away the attempted thrust with the flat of her left hand and darted closer. Her own blade lashed out and

Tinos gasped as the bitter steel plunged deep into her breast. Even in the dim light, Ingvar could see a spray of blood paint Ammie's chest with crimson rain.

Tinos dropped her knife with a dull clatter as Ammie stepped past her. She drew back her blade as she moved and stabbed the assassin once more, this time burying the blade deep in the woman's back.

A harsh, rattling gasp escaped Tinos's gaping mouth as she fell. The floor shook slightly as her body thudded heavily onto the boards.

Ingvar looked up. He was still sitting on the bed as Ammie stood motionless, the curving shape of her body outlined in the hard, dark frame of the window. Her shoulders lifted and fell as she breathed deeply but otherwise, for a moment, all was still.

"Are you hurt?"

Her voice was steady and emotionless.

"No," he replied, swinging his legs off the bed and sitting on the edge. "I'm fine. What about you?"

She glanced down, her face in deep shadow. She dabbed at a splash of blood on the skin just below her collarbone.

"Not mine," she said, indifferently. She moved forward decisively and stepped over the body of the female assassin.

Grabbing the other, she hauled him roughly to his feet. He staggered groggily against her, but she gripped his robes with both hands and held him upright. Blood streamed from his ruined nose, a dark river pouring over his mouth and chin.

Heedless of her nudity, Ammie shifted her grip to the back of his neck and propelled him rapidly across the room. Towards the open window.

"Who sent you?" she demanded, harshly, as she pushed him through the window up to his waist. He groaned in wordless reply as she held him there by his belt, his face dangling towards the hard, beckoning ground.

"Ammie," said Ingvar, attempting to interject.

"Tell me who sent you, right now," she continued, hissing towards his ear, "or I'll drop you."

"Ammie!" Ingvar shouted to get her attention. "They are Crowmer's."

She turned and stared at him.

"The woman is Captain Tinos, and he is probably one of Crowmer's soldiers, too." He sighed wearily.

She paused for a few heartbeats. Then, she turned away, releasing the man's belt. He tumbled from the window, dropping instantly out of sight. There was a brief, urgent moan and then a final, snapping thump.

Ingvar stood, uncertain whether he should go over to her, or not. She raised her head to the sky, her profile outlined in silhouette against the moonlight.

"I can smell smoke. Burning." Abruptly, she marched towards the bedroom door.

"Ammie!" called Ingvar urgently. She paused in the doorway, eyebrow raised. He threw her a robe, quickly picked up from where it lay on the floor. "Put it on if you're going outside!"

She shrugged into it, wriggling the soft linen down over her hips even as she turned to set off down the corridor. Ingvar hurriedly threw his own robe on and followed.

The rear door of the house, leading outside from the kitchen, was hanging open. The intruders had clearly broken in this way, and as Ingvar followed Ammie through the doorway and into the night, he could tell that something else was wrong.

The acrid reek of smoke hit his nostrils and there was a throbbing orange glow in the night sky. Ammie broke into a run, following the track towards her parents' cottage and Ingvar struggled to keep up.

The cottage was burning fiercely. Flames were rising above the roof and climbing up into the dark sky. The heat washed over Ingvar's face as he approached.

Ammie was standing completely still, framed by the black hole of the doorway of her family home. Fire streamed from the windows to either side and the crackling, roaring voice of the blaze filled Ingvar's ears as he moved to stand at her shoulder.

That is when he saw the bodies.

CHAPTER TWENTY-THREE

"No!"

Ammie's howl of anguish was harsh and chilling.

She rushed towards the burning cottage but the terrible, roaring heat drove her back. Warding the scorching, surging air away with her hands, she screamed once more, a wordless shriek of keening loss that seemed directed at the flames themselves.

Lamaina and Hekyn lay together on the front step. A pool of blood, black and gleaming in the firelight, had spread from many stab wounds on their bodies. Their arms were wrapped around one another, clutching each other close in death as they had throughout their lives.

Ingvar's knees felt weak. He, too, felt the urge to go to them, to pull them away from the fire, to somehow make it better. It was clear, though, that it was too late. They had already gone.

It looked as if they had been rushing out of the front door to escape the fire when they had been ambushed, and murdered. A sob escaped his lips as gritty, unwelcome tears of grief and rage sprang to his eyes.

Crowmer had done this. Either it had been the same assassins who had been in the house, or others who had fled.

There could be no doubt that he had sent them. Crowmer was responsible.

Ammie's shouts continued and Ingvar realised they were not of sadness, but of pure, incandescent anger. As he watched, she stooped to grasp a large rock and hurled it ferociously at the wall of the cottage. It hit the burning wood with a dull, sullen thump.

"You ruined it!" she was shouting, over and over. "You ruined it! You ruined everything!" She dropped to her knees, groping in the soil in the dim light, apparently searching for more rocks to throw. She let out a guttural roar of rage as her hands found only dirt, before balling her hands into fists and punching the very ground.

Ingvar stood in helpless horror as she drove her fists down and tore at the earth, her anger palpable and uncontrolled. He had to do something, before she hurt herself.

The flames flickered as he strode over to where she knelt. She whirled, and her eyes flashed in the dread firelight. There was a wild, wounded animal in those dark, haunted eyes.

She glared up at him, then leaped to her feet. Her hands were clenched into fists, the muscles of her arms and shoulders tense.

"Ruined!" Her mouth twisted into a snarl. Then she hit him. It was a blow of impotent rage, the side of her fist to the top of his chest. He knew she could have hit him much harder.

Another blow followed, thumping uselessly against his chest. Her face was contorted, furious and desperate. His shoulders rocked back as she pounded at them again with her fists.

He shook his head. She needed him now. He reached out and grasped her wrist as her arm moved, holding it tight. He repeated this as she tried to hit him again with her other hand.

Her eyes locked on his as she struggled against his strength. Her lips pressed together. He could see the rage burning within her, an inferno of fury, but as he held her more tightly, her movements became less frantic. The roar of the fire behind her faded to a dull background noise as he focused only on her wild eyes.

She resisted him with all her strength, pulling against his grip. And then, like a candle flame suddenly extinguished, she stopped.

Her arms went limp and her whole body sagged. For a moment, he felt like his grip was the only thing holding her upright. The intense rage faded from her eyes and was replaced with…nothing. Her face became blank, her eyes staring right through him.

"Ammie…" he said, searching deeply for the right words. "Ammie, I am so sorry. I will find who did this. They will pay for what they have done."

She remained motionless, expressionless, and gave no reply.

"Can you hear me?" he asked urgently as she continued to stare blankly past him. "Your parents will be avenged."

His lip trembled as he spoke, tears of grief and frustration rolling across his cheeks. His words felt hollow and useless, the flames still licking around the house as if in mockery of his helplessness.

Standing out here for the rest of the night would not provide any solutions. Ammie's grief and shock were obvious. He needed to be strong and decisive, for her sake.

"Come inside," he whispered, heedless of her lack of response. "We need to go into the house now. We will be safe there."

He set off towards the manor house, taking hold of one of Ammie's hands as he went. She resisted slightly but a firmer tug got her moving, and she followed listlessly behind.

He tried to stifle his sobs as he led her through the dark house. His mind worked furiously as he thought about what to do next. He had to make sure Ammie was safe, he knew that much.

Step by step, he climbed the stairs and he could feel Ammie following after him. She did not trip or stumble, but her eyes still stared as if unseeing, and she did not speak a word.

"You should sleep," he said as they walked along the upstairs corridor. "Sleep now and the morning will be a new day." This saying from his mother sprang to his lips, and he said the words without thinking, grateful of something to fill the silence.

At the doorway to his room he paused. Ammie collided softly with his back as he stopped moving. There was a dead assassin in his room, who had bled out on the floor. An assassin who had possibly murdered her parents. He could not take Ammie back in there.

After a moment's consideration, he led her along to Edvar's room. She let herself be guided to the bed, and at his gentle suggestion, she sat down on it silently.

"You are safe here," he said, as much to himself as to her. He pulled the blanket up over her knees, tucking it in around her. "Just wait here. I'll be back soon."

He turned to leave the room, but stopped for a moment and glanced back at the bed. Ammie had not moved a muscle.

Her shoulders were slumped and her eyes were unfocused, unseeing. It pained him to leave her, but he could do no more for her now.

Returning to his own room, he stopped and gazed dumbly down at the scene. The slumped corpse of Tinos lay beside the bed. Even in the chalky moonlight, he could see the slick darker patch where her blood had spread across the floorboards.

His stomach lurched. He had to move the body. It could not stay there, on the floor of his bedroom. Was he strong enough to carry it down the stairs?

He stepped forward, bending to thrust his hands between her armpits. The lifeless reaction of her body was chilling. Straightening, he lifted her up. More blood dripped from where it had soaked into the front of her robes. It would go all over the house if he tried to carry her downstairs to the front door.

Glancing up, he caught a glimpse of the night sky, scattered with white stars, through the open window. The window. Ammie had dropped one of the intruders through the window already. Two assassins going through the window was not worse than one, surely?

He dragged her limp body across the room, the heels of her boots scraping on the floorboards. His hands felt wet. He swallowed, forcing down his revulsion. This had to be done.

Dropping his shoulder, he tipped her upper half through the window. The body slumped awkwardly over the sill, half in the room and half dangling out. He stepped back, drawing in a deep, calming breath.

Hurriedly, he bent and grabbed her ankles. He shut his eyes as he lifted them up to shoulder height. The body slipped from the windowsill and out, and he heard it hit the ground below an instant later. The sound was awful.

He turned away, ignoring the black smears of blood that were everywhere he looked. He was not finished yet. He had more work to do.

He strode out into the corridor, but his knees felt weak. He sagged against the wall as the image of the blades glinting wickedly in the moonlight flashed through his memory once more.

His breath came in shallow gasps. He had been mere heartbeats from a brutal and bloody death. He could not have defended himself. The blades would have plunged into his flesh and he would have bled out into his blankets.

All but for Ammie. Without her, he would be dead. He did not know how she had done it. He could only assume she had heard the kitchen door being forced open and had leaped out of bed while he remained asleep. She had then been able to surprise the assassins, who had been expecting him to be there alone.

They had not bargained for Ammie. Her response had been nerveless and brutal. Thinking about it again, Ingvar felt uneasy about how easily she had defeated two trained killers, and how calm she had been.

He had never seen that side of her before, and even though her actions had saved his life, recalling them brought a cold chill deep in the pit of his stomach. He had thought he knew her well.

Standing upright again, he forced himself on down the corridor. Ammie was a problem for tomorrow. He had other, more immediate concerns.

Taking the steep stairs two at a time, he hurried through the main hall and out through the kitchen door. He steeled himself for what he knew he would see as he followed the track to the Cowls' cottage once more.

The fire was dying down, the blazing flames giving way to glowing, orange embers. As he got closer, he could see that part of the roof had fallen in, giving the house a drunken, unbalanced appearance.

As he had moved through his own house, he held onto a faint, foolish hope that his eyes had deceived him. That he had not seen the bodies. That perhaps, they were merely hurt and would have risen from the flames.

It was a pointless, painful hope.

There they were, lovers in life and locked in an embrace in death. Lamaina and Hekyn Cowl, cruelly murdered on the orders of Rauf Crowmer.

He made himself look at their hunched, singed bodies, even though the sight was almost too much to bear. A childish howl escaped his lips and he pressed the heels of his hands into his eyes. With his father dead and his mother taken, the Cowls had felt like all the family he had. Now they, too, were gone.

Tears gushed from his sightless eyes as he collapsed to his knees on the hard, cool ground. It was a long time before he moved again.

CHAPTER TWENTY-FOUR

The sound of something hammering on the front door echoed through the house. Ingvar opened one eye, blearily trying to understand what the noise could mean.

It came again, a woody, insistent sound that forced him from sleep and demanded his attention. They were coming for his father. No, they were coming to tell him that his father was dead. No, they were coming to take his mother away. They were coming to kill him.

Another round of urgent knocking broke through his sleepy confusion. He sat upright in bed, breathing hard. The knocking was real.

Then the events of the last couple of days came back to him and he slumped back onto the bed.

By the time his grief had subsided and he had been able to rise, the fire that had engulfed the Cowl's cottage had died down. What was left behind broke his heart anew.

The cottage was all but gone, reduced to charred, blackened timber and grey ash, and still there, huddled together on the doorstep, lay Lamaina and Hekyn. He could barely believe that these bloodied scraps of flesh were the two people he had known and loved. He could not make it seem real in his mind.

He knew they could not stay where they lay, so he moved them. One at a time, he carried them away from the cottage, cradling them in his arms as he staggered across the fields.

A small copse of trees lay to the south of the house. Within was a clearing where there was a patch of rough, scrubby grass. Beneath, generations of Darelle servants lay, their bodies resting in the long sleep while their souls fled through the shining veil.

Once the two bodies lay side by side on the dewy grass, Ingvar returned to the house. Hindered and made clumsy by the darkness, Ingvar felt the night slip by as he lit a lantern and found a broad-bladed shovel.

With his limbs weighed down by a growing fatigue, he trudged back to the dark grove. The stars swirled above him as he began to dig.

By the time he returned the last shovelful of dark dirt to the grave, the cruel, uncaring light of dawn was filtering through the trees. The grove was striated with the narrow shadows of the overhanging branches as Ingvar gratefully dropped the shovel. His exhaustion was absolute.

He laid Lamaina and Hekyn in the same grave. He did not have the strength in his body to dig two, nor the heart to separate them. He wept freely as he cast the soil over their faces.

He could barely believe that he would never see them again. He made himself remember that their souls had already departed. They were now free of the world and together in the eternity that they deserved.

As the morning light grew, he staggered back to the manor house. The vivid, fertile green of the surrounding fields and the bright, joyous song of birds seemed to mock his steps. All he saw was grey. All he heard were his own ragged sobs.

He did not manage to climb the stairs. He sat heavily in a chair at the table in the main hall and quickly fell into a restless, uncomfortable slumber, his head resting on the unyielding boards.

He woke abruptly, worrying about Ammie. The brightness shining through the narrow windows from outside suggested that the day was already full. Muscles in his back, shoulders and legs screamed at him as he rose stiffly. He shook his head. The pain was not important.

Ammie was still exactly where he had left her, sitting unmoving in Edvar's bed. As he set a jug of water and a flatbread from the griddle beside her, he could not tell if she had slept. Maybe she had stared blankly at the wall all through the night. The thought pained him.

"Good morning, Ammie," he said, speaking softly to her. "It is a new day. The sun shines." She did not react, and soon he left her with a promise to return.

He stepped out into the daylight and blinked. It must be past noon. He picked up the shovel from where he had carelessly discarded it the night before and trudged wearily to the front of the house. He had two more bodies to bury.

The two dead assassins could not be left where they had fallen, near the front door of the house. Yet, Ingvar could not tolerate the thought of them resting in eternity on his estate. He quickly decided what to do.

There was an old tradition that burying bodies near roads or streams was a bad omen. It would make it more difficult for the souls to pass through the veil and to receive their judgement beyond. Demons deep in the earth would trouble their long sleep. A burial like this brought shame and dishonour to their families. These killers deserved no better.

He saddled his horse and led another from the stables. Gathering his strength, he lifted the two stiff, grey corpses, one by one, and laid them over the back of the spare mount. Their hands dangled grotesquely towards the ground. He looked away.

A short walk took him to the junction where his estate track met the gravelly, hard-packed road to Locton. He moved to the grassy verge and began to dig.

Digging the grave was quicker work this time. Daylight helped, and the ground was soft. He did not attempt to dig so deep. They did not deserve it.

A couple of hours passed as he sweated in the spring sunshine, but before long, it was done. The dirt was piled over and he hoped that the assassins' souls would be troubled in eternity by the passing of many feet and thudding hooves.

"May you fail to find your way through the veil," he muttered, as he leaned on the shovel. "May your rest be disturbed and troubled by demons."

He passed a weary hand across his face, wiping away a sheen of sweat, and glanced up towards the sun. It was a good way through its daily arc, shining down on the northern mountains as it made its journey towards the western horizon. The day wore on.

Ingvar gathered what was left of his strength and courage and drew a deep breath. He had one more task to complete. A task he was already dreading.

"Ammie," he said, gently. "Will you come outside?"

He had returned to her after rinsing the dirt off his hands in the water butt beside the stables. Hours had passed, but it did not seem as though she had moved, although she had eaten the food he had left for her.

"We must have a funeral for your parents," he continued in a low voice. "Will you come and send them off with me?"

She did not move, or give any sign that she had heard. Ingvar sighed, the worry for her a solid, physical pain in his guts, before heading outside alone.

The funeral would be simple and short, and yet Ingvar could not let it go unmarked. He made his way to the family shrine, the polished white stone of the memorials of his ancestors like spectres gathering silently around him.

Near the edge of the plot, he drove two staves of white oak into the dark soil. He had shaved the bark away from the top half of each stave so the heartwood stood out, pale and severe. After cutting four shorter sticks, thumb-thick, he stripped away the bark in the same way and tied them diagonally across the staves about halfway up.

Stepping back, he looked closely at the two memorial icons. The crossed sticks and the upper part of the stave, with the heartwood exposed, formed a five-pointed star. The *pentang* represented the five gods, each point a bright, white shaft to represent mourning. This symbol had been used in memorials since the new gods had arrived in the world.

"May you pass safely through the veil," he said out loud, squinting as tears rolled down his face once more. "May your judgement be fair, and made with the kindness you showed others in life. May your souls find the peace they deserve in eternity."

He paused then, a chill wind twitching his robes while the sunshine warmed his back. "Goodbye, Hekyn and Lamaina." His voice was thick with emotion. "I shall miss you." Wiping his eyes, he turned and strode back to the house.

At a loss for what to do next, he stumbled upstairs to his own bedroom. The blood had spread and dried into a dark stain across the floorboards. The room smelled unpleasant, but he was too tired to care.

Even though it was the middle of the afternoon, he crawled into his bed, the blankets spread haphazardly across his legs. As he laid his head down, he shut his eyes and tried to forget the events of the last days. But death haunted his dreams.

It was almost a relief when the persistent hammering at the door summoned him to wakefulness and away from his dark and bloody nightmares.

With sudden, but reluctant urgency, he climbed out of bed and rushed downstairs. Throwing open the door, he was confronted by a familiar scene that stirred painful memories.

A host of soldiers were arrayed before his threshold. They were all mounted as if for war. Their leader, a solidly built man with a hard face, spurred his horse forward a few steps. Sir Creenan.

"It is time," he said. The scales of his armour were dull and grey in the flat morning light. Heavy clouds blanketed the sky from horizon to horizon.

Ingvar blinked in surprise. The events of the last couple of days had left him feeling drained. Everything else had been forgotten.

"Did you hear me?" demanded Creenan. "We cannot wait. You must be ready."

"Now?" replied Ingvar, weakly.

Creenan said nothing for a moment, fixing Ingvar with a blank, level stare. Then he dismounted briskly and strode over to stand before the doorstep.

"My Duchess grows impatient," he hissed, leaning in close. "She has graciously offered you this chance to prove your innocence. She will wait no longer. Her army waits beyond Locton, and at dawn tomorrow they will march to arrest the traitor Crowmer. It would be a trivial matter to arrest you, too, as his accomplice."

Creenan stepped back, straightening. "Come now," he said in a louder voice, pitched to be heard by his troops. "Come and declare Just War, with me as witness, and prove yourself." He fixed Ingvar with a flinty stare. "Or," he continued, "do not. It is of no import to me."

Ingvar closed his eyes for a moment. Perhaps he should just accept Telivaina's justice? It was tempting. It would be a much easier path. Yet, he knew he could not sully his father's memory with such a surrender.

"I will come now," he announced, his voice heavy.

※

The ride to the Ferras estate made him feel as if he were already on trial. He rode at the front of a procession, with Creenan and his household guard following at a distance behind.

Ingvar could not overhear their talk, if there was any. He imagined them discussing the duel and his chances. The thought caused his guts to clench with anxiety, and he breathed deeply in an attempt to dispel it.

He had glanced south as they joined the main road, gazing towards where Locton huddled at the base of a shallow valley, but had seen no sign of Duchess Telivaina's army. But he believed they were there, probably camped to the south. She had nothing to lose, and much to gain.

If Ingvar lost the duel, he would be arrested immediately as a traitor; a willing conspirator in Crowmer's plots. His lands would be seized and would, likely as not, be granted to Telivaina along with Crowmer's estates, as reparations for their crimes against her.

He sighed heavily, the dull grey clouds that hung oppressively over his head matching his dark mood. Even if he was victorious, and was proved innocent, he would be beholden to the Duchess for her leniency. She had granted him the opportunity of the Just War, after all. She had no obligation to allow him this.

Would she let him ever forget that? He doubted it.

He was still worried about Ammie. She had not said a word for the last two days, and had not moved from Edvar's old bed. She had eaten and drunk a little, but otherwise, she had been completely unresponsive. It was like she was not there. As if she had gone somewhere else.

His quiet words had gone unheeded, and it gnawed at him that he could not seem to give her any comfort. Perhaps she blamed him for her parents' death? It would be fair. He had caused most of this mess.

All he could do to help her now was to win the duel. If he could prove his innocence, he could secure his lands and live on in safety. He had to.

"Darelle!"

Creenan's voice rang out from behind. Ingvar looked up with a start, to realise that he had almost ridden past the track to the Ferras estate. So soon. The ride had seemed to take no time.

He did not feel ready. He felt less ready than he had been a few days ago. His sleep had not refreshed him; he had barely eaten and the loss of the Cowls weighed on him heavily.

Yet, he knew who to blame. He could not let this defeat him. He had to use it to channel his anger and overcome his fatigue, his weakness. He set his jaw resolutely and steered his horse down the track.

Darker clouds rolled over, spreading down to the feet of the northern mountains, their higher flanks fading into the gloom. As the daylight was shrouded, the wind rose. A chill gust blew, whispering that despite springs's arrival, winter could not be forgotten.

A delicate sprinkling of pure white fragments fluttered across Ingvar's vision and delicately brushed against his face. For a moment, he thought it was unseasonal snowfall, blown down from the lofty peaks of the Derufin Mountains. Then, he looked again and realised they were petals of blossom.

Dreadthorn hedges lined the track, and their spiked branches were laden with frills of white blossom. As the harsh wind blew, the tiny petals streamed out across the path, spinning lightly to the ground in a dizzy dance.

As his horse crushed the fragile carpet of pale flowers beneath its hooves, Ingvar could not help thinking of mourning. He should be clad in white this day, in memory of Ammie's parents. Instead, the land clad itself in mourning colours. He had lost so much.

The track opened out onto the yard before the manor house. A rank of troops stood shoulder to shoulder on the opposite side. Their shields and tabards bore Crowmer's stylised eagle's talon, emblazoned in white. These were his only remaining troops.

As Ingvar scanned the row of men and women, all hardened, experienced soldiers, a flash of blonde hair caught his eye. A chill breeze scoured his very heart. Olya.

She caught his gaze and held it, her blue eyes stern and unflinching. He read enmity in that stare. He mourned anew for a friendship lost.

Beside her stood Crowmer himself. His emotions were writ in plain language across his face: contempt, hatred and fury. His blue cloak billowed in the cold breeze, and both he and Olya had their hands at the hilts of their longswords.

Ingvar looked back over his shoulder. Creenan had brought his troops to a halt at the end of the track. They remained there, close enough to see and hear all that happened, but not near enough to become involved in the duel. This was his fight, alone.

He swayed in the saddle as he curbed his mount in the open space before the house. Fear and isolation pressed down on him like heavy grey clouds clustering around the peak of a lonely mountain.

Every eye was upon him. Their stares raked over him, piercing him like so many spears. In that moment, all he wanted to do was to turn and go, galloping away and never returning to this place.

The faces of his father, of Lamaina and Hekyn, and of Ammie flashed before his mind's eye. He set his jaw and forced himself to stare directly at Crowmer. He knew what he was about to do was his duty, his noble responsibility.

He breathed in deeply, then opened his mouth and spoke the words.

※

The Darelle house was mercifully quiet. As she sat on the bed, Ammie had heard Ingvar's voice as he spoke with someone downstairs. It sounded like they were at the front door.

He had spoken to her, too, but she had not been ready or able to talk back. Not yet. That must have been obvious. He would understand.

He had tried to be kind, as he so often was. There were no words she could use to respond to him yet, though. He had to see that.

The front door slammed with an air of finality, and Ammie listened closely. No footsteps sounded inside the house. Ingvar had gone, and she knew where.

Her eyes changed from vague and unfocused to dagger-sharp, and she rose smoothly from the bed and strode to the door.

CHAPTER TWENTY-FIVE

"Say that again."

Crowmer's voice was cold as winter.

"If you would seal your fate."

Even defeated, and backed into a corner like a hunted animal, Ingvar found his enemy's voice threatening.

"Or choose the path of good sense," Crowmer continued, "and turn around. Ride away."

Ingvar took a deep breath to steel himself. A sudden gust caused the thorny bushes to wave their laden boughs, blowing snow-white petals haphazardly across his vision to settle softly on the ground.

Lamaina, Hekyn, Father, he thought. *Send me the courage I need. Let fate be with me.*

"I declare a Just War against Rauf Crowmer," Ingvar proclaimed loudly. He managed to keep his voice calm and even and deliberately omitted any of Crowmer's titles. "He has spread lies about me and defiled my honour. May fate speed my blade and prove that I speak true."

Crowmer grimaced but stayed silent. The wind spoke instead, whispering a hushed, insistent song.

Creenan's voice rang out instead. "Do you accept the challenge of the Just War, Earl Crowmer?" he asked. "To refuse is to concede to the challenger—"

"Yes, yes!" Crowmer blurted out. "I accept, as I must! And I will nominate a champion to fight the duel on my behalf."

Ingvar's heart stopped beating. Or so it seemed, as he waited for the announcement that he had expected, and dreaded, for weeks.

"I nominate," continued Crowmer, "Sir Olya Ferras."

In that instant, Ingvar looked towards Olya. Their eyes locked. Time seemed to stop moving; all else ceased existing outside the frozen tableau of the two of them beneath the blizzard of blossom petals.

Then Olya was turning, moving, brushing past Crowmer to stride into the open space, and the spell was broken. Ingvar shook his head and tried to concentrate on what he needed to do.

Where were Olya's parents? Where was his mother? And Edvar? He had seen no sign of them since he had arrived. The questions sprang into his mind, and he tried to brush the concern away. He could not find answers now. All else apart from the duel must wait.

Olya had drawn her sword and was waiting for him, standing with her feet shoulder-width apart, and her back straight. Proud. Stern. Confident. Beneath her tabard, she was unarmoured apart from a thick, padded gambeson.

Duels were not fought to kill and a thick arming jacket provided a good level of protection from most strikes that would be deemed a winning hit. Additional armour beyond padded gauntlets was considered unnecessary and prevented the duellists from moving freely.

Ingvar dismounted and stepped forward, trying to suppress his nerves, trying to recall Lamaina's teachings. She had made him feel confident and able, and he had to rediscover that feeling, and quickly.

Turning away from Olya, he tried to put her from his mind to concentrate on the little things he had to do to be ready.

He dipped his fingers into a pouch near the neck of his scabbard, then withdrew them covered in black ash. He shut his eyes as he daubed the black stripe across his face, from temple to temple. Now he was ready for battle.

He could not resist a glance towards Olya, and he saw she had done likewise. The thick, dark streak of ash jarred against the paleness of her skin. Her eyes shone out, a piercing, icy blue.

The wind was still chilling, but a bead of sweat trickled down his brow. He tucked his gloves under one arm as he unbuckled his sword belt, drew the long blade, and laid the scabbard carefully on the ground. His longsword would not be sheathed again until the duel was over.

Shutting his eyes, he sucked in a deep breath. It was time. Snugging his thick, padded leather gloves over hands that trembled slightly, he hefted his sword and strode forward.

"The Just War will now be prosecuted by duel," announced Sir Creenan. His voice rang out loud and strong so all that were gathered could hear.

Ingvar kept his eyes fixed on Olya.

"Do you both swear to be bound by the outcome?"

Ingvar leaned in close to Olya and spoke in a low voice so that only she could hear. "You do not need to do this." He tried to stay calm. "Crowmer is finished. His power over you will soon be nothing. You must know that he lies."

Olya's face was hard and as forbidding as an iron-bound door. She looked exhausted, though, her face lined and her eyes deep with grey shadow. There was something else in her expression, too…fear?

"There is so much you do not know," she spat, mouth twisting with displeasure. "You have set your own path, and this is where it ends."

Ingvar blinked, surprised and disappointed. If Olya was still his friend, then there was no reason for her to fight for Crowmer. She had clearly chosen her true allegiance. His friend had gone.

"I swear that I will honour the outcome of the duel," he proclaimed. "And I will be judged on my actions when I pass through the veil." *And I will win,* he thought, holding Olya's stare.

"As will I," she announced.

Olya's eyes flicked in Crowmer's direction as she spoke. His face was impassive.

"I stand as witness and judge," continued Creenan, "and enforcer of Duchess Telivaina's peace, until she arrives herself."

The wind howled once more, its voice a moan of keening sadness.

"The duellists may begin when they are ready. Fate must now play its part."

Despite the shivering trepidation coursing through his body, Ingvar offered up his blade and extended the point towards Olya. She paused for several heartbeats, before reaching out with her own sword and tapping his swiftly. The blades rang together; a harsh, foreboding sound.

They began.

Ingvar raised his arms and took a high, hanging guard. With his sword's hilt above his right brow, he attacked immediately, thrusting his point down towards Olya's neck.

For a moment, she was surprised and could only twist away. Ingvar stepped forward to follow and his blade move rapidly, swinging high cuts that Olya had to parry.

As he moved, he could hear Lamaina's voice in his head, telling him how he should fight and correcting him on his form. There was concern in Olya's eyes as he backed away and took another high guard.

"At the start," Lamaina had said, "do things differently to usual. You are not trying to win the duel so soon but to make her think. Make her wonder. She will worry about what other tricks you have learned."

So, he attacked once more. Olya had often been the aggressor when they sparred in the past, but today would be different. Ingvar moved smoothly, weight transferring between his feet as his sword flashed down from high and forced his old friend to retreat.

Olya glanced towards the manor house again. It was not the first time her attention had wavered in that direction, and it made him think. He lunged forward, trying to capitalise.

She may have been momentarily distracted, but she was still very skilled, very fast. His cut was slightly over-extended and she beat his blade aside before counter-attacking rapidly.

He swayed, managing to get his sword in the way. They rang together. She circled the point of her sword expertly, her wrists supple, binding up his blade. He backed away desperately and flinched as he felt a tug on his arming jacket.

The tip of her blade had sliced a shallow cut across his middle, but had only hit cloth. He looked up at her quickly, a question in his eyes.

Was that a winning blow?

She shook her head.

No.

They continued.

Ingvar felt a bead of sweat run down his brow as he spread his legs and took a very low, wide stance. Another suggestion from Lamaina.

"We will train in many ways," she had said, as they practised something else new. "Then in the duel you can fight in many different ways. You can ask Sir Ferras many different questions."

He attacked again, less directly this time. He took big strides, side to side, and his sword whirled as his strikes came at her from different directions.

She backed away a couple of steps, her eyes darting as she tried to read his attacks. Then she stepped closer, block and halting his sword for a heartbeat. She had taken one hand off the hilt of her sword and used it to guide his blade away before thrusting hers at his legs, one-handed.

He bent double, pulling his legs back to avoid the point and then quickly whipping his head out of range as he backed away. That was the Olya he knew. He smiled, grimly. Even tired and distracted, she was as skilled as any swordsman he had faced.

Lamaina spoke to him again, her words echoing in his memory.

"After a time, return to your normal style."

The conversation could have taken place out on the grass, or over a meal in the house, or while running in the hills. It was hard to recall clearly. These past weeks, they had talked of little else.

"She will think you have used all your new tricks, or that you grow tired," Lamaina had reasoned. "Or both. Either way, she will think that she now knows exactly what to expect from you. She will be confident, maybe too confident. And that is nearly the time to strike."

Besides, Ingvar could feel his fatigue growing. A dull ache was building in his arms, and he was already breathing hard.

Olya watched him carefully as he moved back, then she glanced furtively in the direction of the manor house once more. What was in there that preoccupied her thoughts? he wondered.

Her next attack was savage. A thrust to the centre, and a cut that raked towards Ingvar's neck, followed by a downward stab. Desperately, Ingvar jumped back, parried, and swayed aside.

Another rapid cut that he barely avoided left a gash across the front of his arming jacket. That was too close, but he shook his head. Not a hit. She had not beaten him yet.

Ingvar took several steps back and risked a glance in Crowmer's direction. His brow was heavily furrowed, as he glared hard towards his champion, Olya. He looked anxious. Perhaps this duel was not going as he had hoped. That gave Ingvar heart. He knew what he had to do.

With a shuffle of his feet, he lunged, and as Olya moved defensively, he pressed on, using the momentum of her parry to flick his blade around hers, threatening her face and chest. The harsh, tinny sound of blade clashing on blade filled the air as Olya parried.

He gathered his resolve. One lapse in concentration, one moment of weakness, would be all that it would take for Olya to land a winning strike. He could not ignore what that would mean.

The duel would be lost. By the laws of a Just War, his case would be lost too. His guilt and complicity in Crowmer's rebellion would be proved, in the eyes of all that would matter. He would be imprisoned, his home taken by the Duchess and his lands forfeited.

Worse, he would lose Ammie. And she would lose him. She would have few rights as the servant of a disgraced, dispossessed knight. Either she would be retained at the estate, under the shadow of the place where her parents were murdered, or she would be moved elsewhere. Traded uncaringly to another household.

Would they care for her as his family had? Could they ever understand her?

His whole self was filled with despair at the thought. He could not let it happen. Even Olya would not stand in his way.

They circled each other warily. Olya raised her sword high, forearms crossed and the hilt above her head, with the point aimed down at Ingvar's heart. Ingvar shuffled his feet, finding balance, knees bent.

Olya stepped forward and he moved to block, but it was a feint and she quickly uncrossed her arms and turned the thrust into a powerful low cut. Desperately, Ingvar dropped the point of his sword to parry and danced back. The strike missed, but only just.

His heart thudded rapidly in his chest. That had been much too close. A finger's width of air was the difference between losing everything and surviving to fight on. He must make his move soon, before she broke through his defence.

It was now or never.

The speed with which he made the decision, and then acted, startled even him. But the moment that he stepped forward instead of backwards, he was committed. He had made the first step of the *tornaide*.

As he moved closer to Olya, he saw her sharp blue eyes widen, just slightly. Surprise. His left hand came off the hilt of his sword and reached out towards her hands.

She tried to pull them away, but as she pulled them back, they were already moving in the direction that Ingvar wanted. The momentum of his own hands pushing hers moved them quickly upwards. With her hands and sword being pushed up and to the side, her body was twisted, open and vulnerable.

He thrust his right leg forward, his own body twisting to follow his hand. Time slowed. The rapid hammering of his racing heart became the steady throb of a war drum. Something…changed.

As he planted his foot close to Olya and continued his turn, he felt a strange sensation. Beginning where his foot touched the ground, a lifting, rushing feeling rose through his body. Even as his body spun, pivoting on his right foot, this new feeling filled his being. He felt light, but strong. Fast and tense with barely suppressed power.

The longsword held in his right hand only felt flimsy and insubstantial, like a springy hazel rod. He spun it backwards with ease, feeling the cold length of the blade press firmly against the side of his body as he completed the turn.

With a surge of energy, he completed the *tornaide*. His arms were crossed before his chest, his left hand gripping Olya's sword hilt and his right hand on his own. The sensation rushing through him built to a crescendo as his back pressed firmly into Olya's chest.

Everything accelerated, the wind stirring his hair as time seemed to return to normal. Olya made a soft expression of surprise, barely more than an exhalation. A quiet 'Oh' escaped her lips, close enough for the wind of it to brush Ingvar's ear.

He paused, curiously. The strange rising sensation had gone as if it had never been there. Had he imagined it?

Olya sighed again, her breath a soft caress against his neck. The gravity of the situation returned to him with a jolt. It was not done yet.

He pushed at Olya's hands and spun away, reversing the *tornaide* and dancing back into a defensive stance. Lamaina's voice came back to him once more.

"It will not be over," she had said. "Even if you hit. She may be able to hit you back. You must remain alert."

He looked at Olya while his legs bent in a defensive stance. She stepped backwards. Her eyes still held surprise as she tried to raise her sword. Instead, the point dropped towards the ground as she pressed her left hand to her side.

Ingvar glanced down. His eyes widened in alarm. His sword was painted red for over half of its length; a vivid, angry-red tongue.

A dark patch was spreading through Olya's arming jacket, beneath and around where she was pressing with her hand. Her splayed fingers were already stained with bright, crimson blood.

He had struck with the *tornaide*. He had cut her deeply. His heart froze.

Olya stumbled to one knee, a look of bald incomprehension spreading across her face. He could sense everyone looking on, holding their breath, trying to contain their shock.

The duel was won.

Olya dropped her sword. It hit the hard dirt with a clattering thud.

"Sir Ferras cannot continue," Sir Creenan's voice rang out.

Ingvar barely heard. He was staring at Olya as she collapsed painfully to the ground, doubled up over the deep wound in her side. She had not said a word.

"Sir Darelle is the victor!"

Ingvar felt numb. None of this seemed real. He knew he should go over to where she sprawled on the ground but his feet felt fused with the very earth. What had really happened when he did the *tornaide*? His sword was very red.

"No!"

Crowmer's roar of fury was bestial. Ingvar's head snapped around to face him.

"This cannot stand!"

As Ingvar watched, Crowmer surged in his direction. With a smooth, practised motion, his sword was in his hands, as he marched furiously across the open ground.

At that moment, many things happened at once.

CHAPTER TWENTY-SIX

Sudden noises of fighting rang out from within the manor house.

Blades clashed, voices shouted. The shrieks of pain and fear were loud and intense; Crowmer halted his charge. He turned his head towards the house, an unusual expression of concern and curiosity on his face.

As he paused, the patter of feet and the clatter of weapons being readied came from the opposite direction. Creenan's men scurried past him, moving to surround Crowmer's troops. Weapon hafts were gripped tightly as the two groups glared uneasily at each other.

Ingvar turned to look at Creenan. He was standing back, his arms folded. It seemed as though all he had been instructed to do was to control Crowmer's troops and witness the duel. He did not appear prepared to intervene further.

Then, the manor house door exploded outwards. Ingvar turned, eyes widening in utter surprise.

Ammie stood there, a pale figure outlined in the dark mouth of the doorway. Her whole bearing had changed since the last time Ingvar saw her, huddled in the bed in Edvar's room. She was full of vigour and purpose, and she carried a long, ornate dagger in each hand. Both daggers were dark with blood.

He had no idea how she had got there, but she moved with efficient determination as she threw open both doors and stood to one side.

Edvar burst through the doorway, with Olya's parents following closely behind. They looked pale, drawn and anxious. Edvar quickly spotted Olya's slumped form and his cry of anguish turned Ingvar's bones to ice.

The three of them hurried over to where she lay, stumbling at times and leaning on one another. Another figure came timidly through the doorway. His mother. She shaded her eyes against the bright light and moved to follow the others.

He had a moment to feel relief at seeing her alive and well, but just a moment. Movement closer by drew Ingvar's attention, and he turned to see Crowmer advancing once more, his longsword bared.

"This has gone on too long," he hissed. "Whatever else happens, you will not walk away from this place. Not this time."

He advanced rapidly as Ingvar dumbly attempted to bring his own sword up to defend himself. It was like he had forgotten how.

The rain came then. A sharp gust swept a brisk shower across the scene. Heavy, cold drops spattered on Ingvar's face and ran down like bitter tears.

Crowmer's blade slashed down. Ingvar had a heartbeat to watch it arcing towards his neck. He was moving his own blade to parry but too slowly. He blinked.

He opened them again at the sharp sound of clashing blades. Crowmer's longsword was next to his face, held back from his neck by a long dagger. Ammie stood beside him, where she had rushed to divert Crowmer's strike.

"This fight is mine," she growled.

Crowmer looked surprised and confused, before recognition finally spread across his face. He scowled. Then Ammie attacked.

Her twin blades licked out and Crowmer found himself on the defensive. As Ammie danced around his sword, moving close and threatening him with rapid cuts, all Ingvar could do was watch.

A hand landed on his shoulder. He spun. It was Creenan.

"It is over," he said. "You are victorious. There is no need for this, now. Crowmer will be subject to Duchess Telivaina's justice."

Crowmer cried out in pain and rage as one of Ammie's blades slashed across his upper arm.

"Tell her to stop," insisted Creenan. "Tell your helf girl to stop!"

Ingvar watched as Ammie pressed her advantage. He thought about how Crowmer had orchestrated Ammie's troubled, forced marriage. As fear darkened Crowmer's face, Ingvar remembered anew the assassins in his room and Lamaina's lifeless body.

"I will not," he replied firmly. He could not deny her this.

Creenan turned and glared at him, half in surprise and half in annoyance. His hand went to the hilt of his sword and he took half a step forward, as if to intervene.

Ingvar moved in front of him, his bared longsword still in his hand, gleaming red. He said one word. "No." Then he turned away.

Ammie was advancing on Crowmer, step by step. Her knees were bent and she crouched low as she held the daggers wide, points inward.

Crowmer clearly knew the danger that the short, fast blades posed and was circling, arms outstretched, his point in constant motion, keeping her at a distance. He handled the sword as one with a lot of practice; in this case his self-made reputation did not seem exaggerated.

But Ammie was fast, limber, and more skilled than Ingvar had realised. He could see Lamaina's influence in her smooth movement.

Crowmer attacked. He feinted a cut, then quickly thrust his blade forward. The point of his sword was aimed at Ammie's chest, surging through her defences.

She was too fast. One dagger moved to guide his sword away as she twisted sideways. Her other hand lashed out, the point dangerously close to Crowmer's neck. He swayed back and launched an underhand cut as a riposte.

Ammie dodged back, out of range, and dropped into her ready crouch once more.

A commotion to Ingvar's left caught his attention for a moment; raised voices from a small crowd gathered around something on the ground. His eyes flicked in that direction then quickly returned to Ammie and Crowmer. It would have to wait.

Ammie was circling her opponent again, stepping smoothly sideways, her daggers held at the ready. Her eyes never left Crowmer's face. Crowmer himself was impassive. Whether he recognised Ammie and understood the reason for her hatred, or whether he was surprised, he gave no sign.

He attacked quickly, longsword lashing out high, then low. Ammie's blades flashed as her body arced away gracefully. She avoided the blows easily. Crowmer's expression was cold.

There was a moment of stillness. Crowmer kept the point of his longsword extended, moving to keep Ammie at the end of it. Ammie leaned back as if retreating, moving her weight over her back foot. Her arms drew inward and her knees straightened, as though she was tiring.

Ingvar drew a breath. He knew what was coming.

Lamaina's voice came to him again, as if she whispered in his ear.

"Lie to your opponent," she had said, a prelude to a lecture. "When you are strong, appear to be weak, and if you feel weak, pretend to be strong. Make them worry about your attacks when you wish to defend, and when you are about to attack, convince them that you will only defend. Always make them walk a path of your choosing."

Ammie's attack was sudden and devastating. She launched off her back foot and surged at Crowmer, daggers arcing through the air.

Her left and right hands moved rapidly as she cut at him, seeking an opening. Crowmer retreated, stepping backward and trying desperately to bring his own sword to bear. Now, his eyes were wide with fear.

She pushed his sword aside as she moved into close range. Lashing out with daggers, elbows and knees, each movement flowed into the next like tumbling water. A rapid lunge, a man's voice grunting with sharp pain, and Ammie was thrust backwards by Crowmer's outstretched arm.

Crowmer slapped a hand to his upper abdomen. Blood oozed between his fingers. She had cut him deeply and his face was twisted in a grimace of pain. His longsword hung awkwardly from his other hand. Ammie regarded him carefully, daggers raised. Crowmer opened his mouth to speak.

Ammie did not let him. At that moment, she dashed forward. It was unexpected and bewilderingly fast. Crowmer barely had time to raise his sword.

She struck. The lethal points of the blades punched into Crowmer's body. Once, twice, three times. The keen edges slashed across his ribcage, his shoulder and his arm as he raised it in a futile attempt to ward away the blows. A wordless, despairing groan escaped his lips as blood flowed freely from the wounds.

Ammie dropped back into her defensive crouch once more, but the fight was over. Crowmer's blade thudded to the ground as his fingers faltered, losing their grip. His knees buckled and he collapsed onto his back.

Ammie moved forward and stood over him, her teeth bared in a grimace of triumph. Ingvar moved to stand beside her as the sound of Crowmer's ragged breathing filled the stunned silence. His legs were shaking, heels drumming on the packed earth as he desperately tried to fill his punctured lungs with air.

"Not…yet…" Crowmer gasped, his eyes rolling in his head. He lifted himself up, gathering his strength to utter one final word.

"Fate!"

His exclamation rang out, and then his body was still, slumping back onto the ground. Rauf Crowmer was dead.

Ingvar reached out tentatively to touch Ammie's shoulder. He could feel the quiet tremors that coursed through her body. She shook his hand away and kneeled beside Crowmer. She still held her daggers and glared down as if daring him to move again.

"Ingvar!"

An anguished shout came from behind him, and he spun. It was Edvar, and he was kneeling on the ground. His face was ashen and lined with worry.

He kneeled where Olya had fallen. Olya. Ingvar's mouth went dry. The duel and the winning strike had been driven from his mind by the chaos that had followed.

As he hurried over, he glanced down at his sword. The blade was still painted red, darkening towards black as the blood dried. He shuddered.

He froze as he took in the scene before him. Olya's parents kneeled on the ground around her. Etsel hovered nearby, wringing her hands. A dark pool of gleaming wetness had spread around them, darkening their robes where they brushed the earth.

Olya…his heart lurched as he looked down on her. She was breathing, but in shallow, rasping gasps. Her eyes were sunken in her face, which was drained of colour. Her lips were grey.

"Do something!" urged Edvar. His hands were pressed to Olya's arming jacket, trying desperately to staunch the wound. They were drenched in blood.

"It is too late."

Olya's voice was a bare whisper, but her words were clear. Ingvar sank to his knees beside his brother.

"I am sorry," Ingvar said. "I never meant for this. I would rather have lost." He bowed his head.

"No," croaked Olya. "This was justice. This was the law."

"There is much I regret," said Ingvar. He meant how his relationship with Olya had soured, but in truth he had plenty to feel shame for besides. "I wish it had never come to this."

Olya coughed, a raking, spluttering sound. Blood bubbled at her lips. Her mother and father moaned.

"I go..." she gasped, "to meet my judgement."

Her chest fell for the last time, her eyes becoming slack and unfocused. She was dead.

Her parents clutched at her, as if they could drag her back to life. Edvar whimpered his grief, tears moistening his cheeks. Etsel came to stand beside her two sons, but spoke no words.

The rain squalled, then stopped, a brisk gust whipping the raindrops over them as a fine mist. Fragments of blossom were blown onto Olya's face, the pure white petals standing out starkly on her fading skin.

That familiar face, present in his life for as long as he could remember. When he had first held a wooden sword, it was Olya he faced. When he had been given his first longsword, Olya was at the same ceremony as she received hers.

They trained together, faced battle together, and spent countless hours riding to and fro across Buren together. His guts twisted as he remembered the times they spent under dusky light in the fields of wheat, lying together, their naked skin slick with sweat as they taught each other about the ways of love. It seemed so long ago.

"Why did you do this?" said Edvar, his voice thick and filled with bitterness. "Why?"

"I had no choice," said Ingvar, but his words were as the wind; insubstantial and fleeting. Footsteps at his shoulder made him turn. He looked up into Sir Creenan's hard face.

"This tragedy is regrettable," he said, his voice low and pitched for Ingvar's ears only. "But the outcome of the duel clears you of the accusations. You are innocent of any wrongdoing, under Bureno law. The defeated knight was in league with the criminal Crowmer. There are no reparations to pay. You are absolved, and your lands and garrison are yours to keep."

Ingvar nodded dumbly. It did not matter to him now. Nothing did.

"But," continued Creenan, more firmly, "the killing of Crowmer was not lawful. He was to be subject to the justice of Duchess Telivaina. Your helf servant girl must answer for the crime."

Creenan turned and strode purposefully towards Ammie. Ingvar was still too numb and shocked to move. Ammie was motionless, staring down at the body of her enemy. Ingvar watched helplessly as Creenan reached out towards her.

"No," said Ingvar, trying to force his legs into urgent motion. Then, he said more loudly, "Wait. Stop!"

Too late.

Creenan laid a firm hand on Ammie's shoulder. She jumped to her feet, a blur of furious movement. Her hand still clutched her bloody dagger and she swung it viciously.

CHAPTER TWENTY-SEVEN

Ingvar had known what would happen.

Ammie was still quivering with the thrill of battle, tense like a drawn bow. Creenan had spoken loudly of his intention to arrest her, and then had touched her roughly and without warning.

It was too much for her. Too much for her to take without lashing out.

The point of the dagger whistled through the air, quicker than thought. Ingvar could not look away. Creenan's head jerked back as the cruel blade slashed through his throat without slowing.

Blood sprayed from the wound. Crimson rain arced into the air as Sir Creenan clutched at his throat with despairing hands.

He died without uttering a word. His final breath gurgled in his throat as his lifeblood poured out onto the soil.

The troops standing guard over Crowmer's disarmed forces went very still. Many of them glanced at each other, and then, without a word, a handful advanced on Ammie.

They had seen what she could do with a blade. They would surround her and overwhelm her. She would be killed or taken.

Ingvar lunged forward and grabbed her arm. Her head swivelled but her arms stayed down. They shared a look. There was understanding in her eyes. He pulled her behind him and turned to face the oncoming soldiers, raising his sword once more.

"There is no need for this, Sir Darelle," said one of Creenan's men. "This was not your doing." He had a curve-bladed axe in his hand, but it was lowered as he paused his approach.

"Just surrender the girl," said another, a ruddy-faced woman wielding a slender sword. "She has committed two murders here. All saw it." She gestured expansively to the rest of the troops behind. The gesture also took in Crowmer's former soldiers, who seemed to have surrendered all remaining loyalty after seeing him die.

Ingvar said nothing, but stood his ground in front of Ammie. They were right, of course. Ammie had just killed two people. Nobles. Not in battle, not in a Just War or duel, but in cold blood.

She was a murderer.

No more a murderer than the assassins that Crowmer had sent, the ones who had taken her parents' lives, but they had already faced justice. What hope did Ammie have if they took her away?

They would lock her up, that was certain. She would be badly treated. As a servant, a commoner, and a criminal, she would have few rights and none would care what became of her.

If she made it to trial? There was a hanging pole outside the walls of Seyntlowe for those found guilty of such crimes. Such was the law.

"Ingvar, be sensible."

A reedy voice beside him made him turn his head. It was Tasivus Ferras. His eyes were red-rimmed and he looked very old, but his face was calm.

"It is over," he said, moving to stand in front of Ingvar. "You did what you had to do in the eyes of the law. You are proved innocent. You can return to your estate and live on! There need be no more fighting."

Ingvar looked at him, then glanced back towards Olya's body.

Tasivus sighed heavily.

"Yes, we are devastated to lose our daughter," he said. "But we cannot blame you. You were merely doing your duty to your family honour. The blame lies at the door of that awful man." He pointed towards where Crowmer lay.

"He threatened us, daily. Held us at knifepoint and told Olya that he would kill us before her if she did not comply.

And at the same time, he whispered in her ear. Poison and lies. By the end, she was convinced that all our misfortune was the sole doing of you and your family. Her mind was twisted. We had already lost our daughter."

Ingvar looked at Olya's father in horror. He had no idea it had been this bad. The old man's eyes were wet with tears again.

"But now it is over," he went on, smiling weakly.

Watery sun broke through the swirling clouds. The rain had eased, leaving a fresh, damp scent in the air.

"He is gone. We are free, subject to the Duchess's justice. Ferras and Darelle can renew their alliances and reclaim our ancestral lands."

His gaze hardened and he turned to glare towards Ammie.

"We cannot harbour criminals, though. We must hand her over and let justice be done."

Ingvar shook his head. He had been so close to happiness, after all that he had endured.

"Ingvar, please!"

Tasivus raised a claw-like hand to grip his arming jacket.

"It is such a small price to pay." He paused, then leaned in close and lowered his voice. "After all, she is but a servant. And half-blood at that."

They gripped each other's hands tightly. Their fingers were interlaced like twisted branches that had grown together, now entwined and inseparable.

Ingvar led the way, Ammie following as they walked briskly along the uneven mountain path. The ground sloped upwards before them, soft green slopes giving way to sparse, rocky heights.

The brisk, gusting wind whipped broken clouds across the pale sky. One moment they walked in bright sunshine, the next moment the landscape was shrouded in shade.

The indecision of the weather matched Ingvar's conflicting emotions. He did not know whether to be happy about what he had gained, or to weep over everything he had lost.

Yet, he hoped there were brighter lands ahead. Over this mountain pass and down into the wide lands beyond, where the sun would be shining. There must be somewhere ahead they could be safe and happy.

The decision had been no decision. He had known immediately what he needed to do. Thinking of doing it had frozen him with fear.

He had been shaking as he turned away from Olya's father, whose thin, droning voice went on like a chill winter breeze, reasoning, persuading and cajoling. Ingvar ignored him.

He focused instead on the only person who truly matter to him at that moment. As he faced her, he could read the tension and uncertainty in her body, the way her fingers fidgeted and the way her eyes flickered over his face. She was probably trying to guess what was in his mind, and what he was going to do.

Behind him, he could sense Creenan's troops' hesitation and could hear the soft metallic sounds of weapons shifting in clammy hands. He was a legitimate, land-holding knight again now, and they were reluctant to move against him.

Ammie's fate was in his hands, along with his own.

She was a murderer. She was his saviour, twice over. She was depending on him utterly in this moment.

He studied her open face with its unreadable, mysterious expression. He stood still, while inside he wrestled with his feelings. He felt like he was being torn in two.

All he had ever wanted was to be at home. The thought that had sustained him through all the danger and horror of battle, and the hardship of his journeys, was the warm pleasure of returning to his family home.

The blocky, square-built house with its pale stone, red tiles and dark wood was where he felt his soul truly resided. Living there at peace once more had sustained him through these difficult last years. That place was where he had always hoped his path would lead.

And now, it was within reach.

He closed his eyes and imagined himself as an older man, lord of the manor. He could take a noble wife and there would be children. Heirs. His family name would endure and prosper, and he could live out his days in comfort, safety and honour.

He would be able to bring his mother back home and look after her as she aged. She looked tired and careworn, and she deserved kindness. Then, he looked to his brother, still weeping at the side of his beloved wife. He did not raise his eyes, but Ingvar hoped a reconciliation might be possible, in time.

The sun emerged from the clouds. He raised his eyes to meet Ammie's once more, and his heart broke anew. He mourned again for all that he had lost, and all that he would lose.

They were bound to one another. Life without Ammie was not a life he could bear. A life where she was taken and locked away, or worse. It was unthinkable.

From that point, things had moved quickly. He knew they must, lest he lost the strength to act at all. Lest Telivaina arrived and detained him. Gathering his authority, he approached Creenan's troops.

"You will stand down," he ordered, "and wait. No move will be made against any of my family or household without my direct order."

They looked perturbed, but obeyed without a word.

"And look to your dead," added Ingvar, motioning towards Crowmer and Creenan's lifeless shapes.

He returned to where the Ferras family were gathered, to find Ammie carrying a large and bulging cloth bag, as if ready for a long journey.

"Did you know?" he asked in surprise.

"I hoped," she replied, with a slight smile. "I have blankets, food and water. Enough for a few days' travelling."

Next, he went to his mother. Their embrace was lingering and tearful. He had not realised how much he had missed her, and now he would be leaving her again.

"Maybe you can return," she whispered into his ear. "This will all be forgotten, in time."

"Yes, I will try," he replied, and the lie was like an ember on his tongue.

"She saved our lives, you know," Etsel added, her eyes on Ammie. "Crowmer had his worst thugs guarding us, blades at our necks, to make sure that Olya fought to win. Then Ammie came in through the back door. She was like a hurricane. They had no idea what to do, and she didn't hesitate."

Ingvar's eyes widened slightly. That explained the noises of fighting and Ammie's bloodied blades.

"I've never seen the like."

His mother tailed off, the look in her eyes somewhere between awe and horror. Ingvar turned away.

"You blame me." He moved to stand over Edvar.

"How can I not?" Edvar replied, his voice bitter. His hands and robes were dark and dirty with Olya's blood. Ingvar nodded.

"I understand," he said, and he truly did. "But I hope that in time you will see that I had no choice."

Edvar looked at the ground.

"Both estates will now fall to you, Ferras and Darelle. You will have to swear to the Duchess, but she is wise and powerful. You will all be safe if you can make her an ally."

Edvar nodded dumbly. Ingvar hoped he would do what needed to be done.

They could not travel south. Telivaina's army was marching from that direction and would not let them pass.

Besides, there was nowhere in Buren where justice for these crimes would not pursue them.

Northward there was hope. North, over the mountains and down into the wide expanse of the valley of the Great River. Those lands were sparse and lawless. They would not be hunted so far. They could be safe.

Their departure was hasty. They needed to be gone before Creenan's troops realised they were escaping, and before the Duchess arrived.

An old and little-used path led from the back of the manor house and up into the hills. Ammie knew of it and led the way.

They passed the Ferras family shrine, the memorials sombre and gleaming white in the sunshine, then climbed blocky steps steeply upwards. An undulating roar filled their ears, and around a sharp bend they were confronted by the impressive sight of a foaming, churning waterfall.

They glanced at each other and hurried on without speaking. This was a sacred place.

Above the falls, the path wound through damp, quiet woodland before ushering them onto the wide green expanse of the upper hillsides. Not another soul could be seen as they trod quickly across the short, springy grass where sheep grazed.

Ingvar reached out a hand and Ammie took it in hers. The touch of her skin was both soothing and reassuring.

It was only at that point that he realised he was still clutching the hilt of his longsword, held awkwardly in his other hand. The point had been dragging along the ground, scoring a line in the soft earth.

He recoiled. It was still red, a vivid reminder of the violence and death that he wanted to leave behind. Olya's face, ash-grey and full of pain, came to his mind as he looked down at the blade.

Opening his fingers, he let it fall. The bloody weapon fell to the ground with barely a sound. He would not hold a sword again.

The blade lay on the path where Ingvar had dropped it.

Ingvar and Ammie hurried away, hand in hand, across the landscape dappled with fleeting sun and looming shade.

They did not look back. They were leaving their old life behind. Ingvar Darelle would no longer walk a path of blades.

THE END

Ingvar and Ammie return in Tann's Last Stand; an adventure novella by the same author.

Available on Amazon.

THANK YOU

Thank you very much to my test readers; Claire Sutton, Rich Patterson, Francesco Desideri, Rhydian Murphy and Morgan Christensen. Without your feedback and encouragement I doubt I would have completed this book.

Thanks also to Claire Cronshaw, my editor, for going the extra mile and boosting my confidence.

I'd also like to mention Tea Spangsberg, S.R. Morton, Lynn How and Eryn McConnell for offering advice, support and solidarity in writing. You have been very kind.

A special mention is needed for Paul Bennett for sharing his vision of the Lands of the Twin Swords, and taking time out to hit me with actual swords.

Lastly, thank you to my wife Claire and my son Jim for providing patience and tolerance (Claire), and endless inspiration (Jim).

Printed in Great Britain
by Amazon